THE HELPER

A NOVEL

M. N. SNow

This book is a work of fiction. The characters, incidents, and dialogue are drawn from the author's imagination and are not to be construed as real. Any resemblance to actual events or persons, living or dead, is entirely coincidental.

First Edition

ISBN-13: 978-1539630661
ISBN-10: 1539630668

Lyrics from the song *Helen Keller Man* printed with permission.

Lyrics from the song *He Said, He Said* printed with permission.

To the memory of my mother and father:
Jean Craik Snow and Donald McLean Snow, Sr.
Thank you both for everything.

Prologue

Coyote peered through the bushes and watched the scene unfold. The four legged Trickster knew the humans needed his help. He just didn't know if he wanted to give it. They could certainly use it, but would it be the best for all concerned? *And,* would helping them provide him with the most satisfaction? He would just have to watch and wait, as they would. Helping, hurting, hot and cold, part god, part animal. The Trickster.

The Ojibwe, or Chippewa, of northern Wisconsin, Minnesota, and Canada didn't have a Trickster that walked on all fours. Nope, theirs stood upright on two legs. Part god, part human. Many of the tribe thought this a better figure, more appropriate given the Trickster's nature. Especially the *human* part. Prone to fits of anger, jealousy and resentment. Able to alter events in a way that only a god could, but given to episodes of what can only be described as Trickster-ness. That could only be described as, well, *human.*

His name is *Nana'b'oozoo.* A child of the heavens and of the earth, growing up parent-less. Some of the Ojibwe People went so far as to describe him as Jesus-like. After they had found out who Jesus *was,* that is. Before that time he was only, as he still is, Nana'b'oozoo. God and man, together as one, walking the earth. With god-like talents and human traits. Said not without a certain amount of pride, especially when compared to the four legged Legend of southwestern and western tribes. Not an animal like theirs, but a *man*. Upright, on two legs, just like us. Pride not an emotion limited to gods. But a Trickster is as a Trickster does, and so they shall. And so shall we.

People fail and people fall. Often noticed, quite often unnoticed. A story as old as time. A story as old as *stories*. As likely to happen today as it was in the time before time. And if you think tragic surrenders and mythic tribulations happened only in the past, you are truly mistaken. One need only look at tonight's network news or read today's newspaper. There are people plummeting from sight every second, often taking others with them. Heck, you only need cast your glance as far as the cubicle next to yours, or peer across the factory floor to see the possibilities. How much do you really *know* about those people? Do you think that it is not going on around you even at this moment? When a county worker in Florida goes on a rampage and takes three people down with him, do you think that is fiction? When a postal worker or a high school student or even that traffic-jammed driver ahead of you snaps and takes it out on those surrounding him, do you think that is fiction? Let me clear something up right now. That tree philosophers talk about, you know, the one falling in the woods? I'm here to tell you that just because you're not there to hear it, it still makes a sound. Quite often the sickening sound of that very same tree squashing an innocent passerby. Do not doubt that for a moment.

And yet, sometimes that falling tree, for seemingly no reason at all, does not hit the ground. Sometimes it is brought back upright, before it hits. Before the destruction occurs, it finds itself standing straight, and taller than before, having been helped by a force or forces unseen. Again, do not doubt me for a moment, it happens.

This *last* reality makes up hope for the eyes peering through the bushes. We know they are there, we have seen both sides of the outcome far too many times to doubt it. The eyes are there and they can help us. The question is, the *hope* is, will they help us?

Many, many times people fall and fall hard. And sometimes they are Helped.

...Cast me not away from thy presence,
and take not thy holy Spirit
from me.
Restore me to the joy of thy salva-
tion,
and uphold me with a willing
spirit.

Psalm 51, verses 11 and 12.

I'm the Helen Keller man, staring at the sky.
Helen Keller man, don't know how or why.
Am I who I think I am, or am I just a lie?
Helen...Keller...Man

lyrics from *"Helen Keller Man"*
by Velva Scourge

Hi, I'm Greg and I'm back from Honduras.
I was down there teachin' little kids to kill.

lyrics from *"He Said, He Said"*
by Mortal Engines

1

Trickster tells his tale…

The first time John Sloan Helped someone was in 1971. He was four years old. He already had a sense that he was different but was too young to know anything more.

John's mother Roberta had dragged him, along with his five-year-old brother James, to James's kindergarten class. Roberta was always dragging extra kids along—always a bit behind, as is the case with mothers of children who have husbands who earn their wages over the road. Darn good wages both Roberta and her husband Hugo would agree, but nonetheless things like kindergarten fell upon Roberta's shoulders much more squarely than Hugo's. At that time they numbered five children, from ages two to nine, with one more to come in another year or so.

Tall Roberta, five-feet, seven-inches of dark flowing hair, red lipstick, and flashing brown eyes, lugging John along with James to school on that gray, northern Wisconsin, December day. They were late for the four-hour, afternoon class and Roberta went over to Mrs. Hinkley, James's teacher, to explain how Theresa, the nine year old, had spilled Campbell's tomato soup on Tracey the two year old and a chain of events had started. Theresa was home sick from school, and should have been in bed, but she wanted to help her mom and it had all gotten out of control so very quickly, as Mrs. Hinkley knew so well. She had twenty-six little potential soup spillers that could quickly bring schedules to a halt.

While Roberta was laughingly commiserating with Mrs. Hinkley, John had wandered over to the brightly decorated Christmas tree that a few of the other children were admiring. He stood back a bit from the others and he smiled. And he felt it. What he was to come to feel quite often during his life. His "extra-ness", his "*special*-ness," stood up a bit inside of him and said, "watch and wait." Goose bumps broke out on John's arms and back. So John did as he was told. He watched and waited... and he glowed.

Three little girls and one little boy were carefully stepping around the twinkling Christmas tree. They were playing a guessing game. They were guessing which of their classmates had brought in which decorations. They would point and touch an ornament and say, "oh, that's from Terry Archambault. And that star is from Ruby Cerdich."

One of the girls was being extra careful. She had straight, jet black hair that spilled all the way down to her lower back and a smile that was all the more beautiful for its missing front teeth. Her name was Lorraine, but Lorraine wasn't smiling much these days. No, life was not a big barrel of grinning monkeys for little Lainie as of late. Lorraine, or Lainie as her dad *used* to call her, had a secret. And she couldn't tell anybody about that secret. Nope, she couldn't tell a soul, and if she could have put it into words she would have said that the secret was killing her.

Lainie had brought in a beautiful stained glass angel that hung from a silver string. Lainie's mother had made that angel for last year's Christmas tree. That turned out to be the last piece of stained glass that Lainie's mother Evelyn was ever to make. Evelyn was diagnosed by the middle of January and had lasted until spring. This was Lainie's first Christmas without her mother, and Lainie shouldn't have brought

the stained glass decoration to class. It belonged in the basement.
Lainie's father Douglas had been *very* firm about that. Lainie was not
to touch any of her mother's things. They *stayed* in the basement! The
very back of the basement. Crouched, dusty, hidden.

Douglas had been so devastated by Evelyn's death that he had
taken everything connected with her, boxed it up and trundled it all
down to the basement where it was now stacked in the darkest recesses
of the musty, dimly lit cellar. Every article of clothing, every brush
and comb, every picture that included Evelyn was grimly boxed up
and taped shut. *Especially* the pictures. Douglas had sent Lainie to
her aunt Agnes's house one Sunday shortly after the funeral and
finished the chore in an afternoon. Anything that included death's
hollow scent was now shut away down-cellar. These boxes included
all of the stained glass pieces that Evelyn had so lovingly crafted. And
the boxes were not to be touched or spoken of. Lainie's father was
very clear on that fact. He had sat Lainie down that Sunday evening
and told her not to touch the boxes and not to speak of the boxes.

"Mommy is dead", her dad had choked out. Lainie could still see
her father's empty eyes staring out the window and hear his haunted
voice, so unlike the voice she knew, tell her in no uncertain terms that
"*she wasn't to touch anything in the back of the cellar. Ever!*" That
was the last time Lainie and her father had spoken of her mother. Her
dad had changed.

From that point on her dad had started fading away. Not only was
Lainie losing memories of her mother, but it also seemed that her
father was disappearing, bit by bit and day by day, right before her
eyes. What did she do wrong, she thought? Why did God do this? I
miss my mommy and why can't I crawl up into my daddy's lap
anymore? Lainie thought that *she* might be disappearing too, and this
really scared her. When she held out her arm and looked at her hand
she could still see her fingers but she wasn't sure that they weren't
fading a bit. She would stand in front of the full length mirror on the
back of her bedroom door and stare at herself and sometimes see that
she was not all there. No, she was not all there, *at all*. She thought

that she might be turning into a ghost and that scared her so badly that one day she almost peed in her pants. Frozen white and swaying in front of the mirror she had seen nothing. Lainie didn't look in that mirror anymore, but she remembered.

This was the secret that Lainie carried hidden inside her that day in the classroom. This and more. Lainie had snuck down-cellar, found the boxes that contained her mother's stained glass pieces and found the angel. Her mom had made it 'specially for her and she just had to bring it to class for the tree. She *had* to bring it or she would disappear completely and no one would ever be able to see her again. She would still be alive and walking around, but she knew that no one would be able to see her.

As Lainie and the other children circled the tree looking at the pretty ornaments, "ormaments" Jimmy Tong called them, John watched. He felt the *something* swell up and glow inside of himself. He intuitively knew that he was there to Help, whatever that meant. He didn't know who he was there to Help, but he understood that *something* was coming on none the less. Lainie caught his eye, and in spite of the fact that she looked so sad, he felt good. No, not just good, or even great. John felt perfect.

Lainie spied her mom's angel hanging from the branch where she had placed it with Mrs. Hinkley's help. She stood still and looked at it, mesmerized by the light dancing out from the different colored pieces of glass inside of it. The light seemed to dance out to her and twirl around her. The shards of light that were coming out of the angel's eyes shot out and stopped right in front of Lainie's face and seemed to be *looking* at her. The other kids had moved on to the other side of the tree and Lainie was alone, frozen in her spot, surrounded by light from the stained glass angel. Lainie was petrified. She didn't think this was any angel anymore. Gosh no. She saw her mom's eyes and maybe something darker and horrible behind that. Bad eyes.

John watched all of this, and saw and felt it too. He now knew that Lainie was falling. She was falling into a dark pit in horrified slow motion. John was only four years old and didn't know this in words, but he knew it just the same. He saw it in pictures that appeared in his mind. In spite of it all he felt perfect. He felt a power plant swell through him, humming away and powering up.

John watched as the hypnotized Lainie swayed and started inching toward the tree. Lainie wanted to touch the angel. She was being drawn to the angel against her will. Her arm was outstretched and her pointed finger was moving toward the angel to touch it. It was right at this time that the children on the other side of the tree started goosing each other and when Jimmy Tong started tickling Rosemary Banks, Rosemary let out a shriek. A loud shriek. A fingernails down the blackboard shriek that shatters glass, and causes fillings to vibrate, kind of shriek. This shriek caused Lainie's feet to get tangled up and she tripped in her trance-like walk toward her mother's shining angel. The trip was turning into a fall as Lainie stretched out both hands toward the tree, toward the angel. One hand grabbed a branch and stopped Lainie's slow motion fall. But Lainie's other hand, her offending hand, had grabbed her mother's angel. Horrified, Lainie looked and saw that she was squeezing the angel with her other hand. She was squeezing it so hard that she was going to break it, and so because this was her *mother's* angel, Lainie's only link to her lost mom, she let go of it.

Things slowed down and John was able to see through Lainie's eyes. The stained glass angel came loose from the tree and was starting its fall to the floor. John was helpless to stop its flight and knew that this wasn't his job to do. John and Lainie watched as the twirling angel head-over-heeled its way to the brown tile floor. Just before its slow-motion descent reached the floor it was facing up and there were beams of colored light shooting out of its angel eyes looking directly into Lainie's. Nothing had stopped, the angel didn't hover and look into Lainie's eyes, but there was one split second, one nano-second, one *moment* where its eyes glowed beseechingly into Lainie's eyes. "Help," they said. And then the angel hit the tile floor and shattered.

A kindergarten classroom has a certain level of noise to it. A buzzing murmur at the best of times, much louder at other times, but breaking glass has a tendency to get everyone's attention even if they are preoccupied five-year-olds. Then, quickly as you can say "Jimmy Tong said Patricia Barnes was full of crap", the room was silent. All eyes intuitively sought out Lainie, and as quickly as that, the buzz returned. It returned for all except Lainie. Inside Lainie all was silent. Lainie had shattered too.

Mrs. Hinkley was quick to rush to Lainie's side, somehow knowing that it wasn't Lainie's fault but also *not* knowing how important the angel had been to Lainie. John's mom Roberta also came quickly over and helped get Lainie seated in one of those small kid's chairs that we wonder how we ever fit in, and helped Mrs. Hinkley start the process of cleaning up the shattered stained glass pieces.

John found himself sitting in the chair next to Lainie. He saw her big brown eyes fill with tears and knew that she had lost. Not that she *was* lost, suggesting a situation from which one could be found. No, no, no. Lainie was only five years old and she *had* lost. Never to win again. Shit, never to lose again. Lainie was five years old, it was Christmas, her mother had died, her father was disappearing, and she had broken her mother's last present to her, that she wasn't supposed to touch. Ever! Lainie had lost. It was OVER and John knew it. Lainie had reached a pivot point and been catapulted in a direction from which there was no return. Five years old and already over. And if you think it doesn't happen, think again.

John sat in the chair next to Lainie and John's newly realized *extraness* sat down in it with him. He was only four years old, not five like Lainie which is huge to kids, but he knew what to do. He took his left hand and grabbed Lainie's right hand and said, "Hi Lainie. My name is John." He hadn't known what to say until that moment, hadn't known to clasp her hand until that instant, and yet that is what he did. That is when John felt it happen. In an amount of time that knew no time, John had the whole story—Cancer, death, a disappearing father,

her fading mirror image, and now this. This is when the "little bit of extra", that was really a whole lot, did what it did.

Lainie looked into John's green eyes and it happened. John felt the flow pour out of him. A rushing, gushing, flow of good and of light and of *Perfect* that splashed back and forth over them. It felt like pure love and a lot more. It felt like crawling in bed with his mother and father times nine gajillion and John didn't even know his multiplication tables yet. Shoot, he was still learning his adds.

No other words were spoken. John held Lainie's hand while Mrs. Hinkley and Roberta finished the sweeping up and the rest of the children got back to the business of being, well, children.

As John grew older there were often more words spoken and more time involved but when he was young the Helping rarely involved more than a greeting and two names. His and theirs. John realized he wasn't really doing anything. There just seemed to be a pipeline that poured out of him. It was good, and it washed, and it turned losers into winners. Or more accurately the Lost into the Found.

And Lainie knew. She knew that she was washed. And clean and loved and they both accepted in that instant that Lainie would not remember much of that instant and John would. That's just how it worked. Lainie had been *Helped,* with a capitol H, and for the first time, John Sloan was a Helper. John felt warm and good and older and perfect. He somehow grasped that no one would ever realize what had just happened. He also knew that because of this Helping, Lainie would go home and talk with her father and he would cry and she would cry, and that Lainie's dad would stop disappearing and Lainie could look in a mirror again, and that they would go on together as father and daughter.

It was good. That had been a long time ago, thirty-plus years, but John could still remember how very good it had been from that very first time on. Yes, being a Helper was good. The ability to Help was good. And now it was gone.

2

 John was thirty-eight years old and afraid in a way that was totally foreign to him. He had known fear before of course. He was like other folks in every way. He *was* different but not *that* different. Actually, he was just like other people in every way, with one exception. He was a Helper and now his ability to Help was gone, and with it his identity. He was beginning to realize that his talent was not just a tool to help others, his extra-ness was tied in completely with who he was. Maybe that was good, maybe that was bad. Either way it didn't matter much 'cause it was *gone*.

 Shit, John *had* known fear before. Little ones, like the apprehension of going from grade school to junior high school, boy that seemed like a laugh now, to big ones like taking a midnight bus ride across the levee to Parris Island and Marine Corps boot camp. Hell, he'd come under hostile fire on numerous occasions in the time he'd spent in the Marine Corps. That was fear, but without the time to roll around in it. Just fear and adrenaline and action. No, the fear he had now also included the time factor. It stayed. Twenty-four/seven it stayed, with no time off for good behavior. He not only had the fear but also the time to think about it and how it would never leave and how he was stuck with it and how at 3 o'clock in the morning you could think two separate thoughts at the same time. One, how fucking scared you were and two, the watcher part of his mind could think how this was not just a situation but the rest of his life. Oh shit, this wasn't fear. This was terror.

The closest thing to this was when he had awakened from a dream, at about eleven years old, horrified that he might one day lose his ability to Help. Rather appropriate, he thought now. But he had known immediately, God he had KNOWN, that it would never leave him. He had always had it and he always would. At eleven years old he had crossed that chasm of fear with no more than a skip to the other side. Well so much for skipping. He had lost his "special extra" and there was no getting it back.

John tripped back over the years to all the people he had Helped and especially to little Lainie and her lost mother and her lost angel and he knew something else. He was Lost. Not lost like being separated from your parents in Value Village. Not lost like being separated from your company and leading your three-man squad of forward observers through a mother-"f"-ing rain forest in Panama. No, he wasn't lost like it was a temporary condition. He WAS lost. As in "John, I know thy true name and it is Lost." This wasn't a condition, it was a way of being. An understanding that that is how and what you are. "Hi, my name is John and I'm left-handed, with green eyes, and oh yea, I'm fucking lost!"

John now knew exactly when the pivot point into loss had come. He hadn't been aware of it at the time but he could see now the point of departure. The moment when the tip of his vaulter's pole had touched ground and lifted him into the air, but instead of just going up and over, he had gone up and over and continued falling. Only to find himself still falling, and much much lower now than his initial point of departure.

The pivot point, the pit for his vaulter's pole, had come when Deena had said thank you and goodbye. And in a *note*! Without even so much as a by-your-leave or a fuck you in person, no it had been in a *note* left on that most intimate of places, his pillow. I love you and goodbye. And Deena had been one of him, or he had been one of her. They were both similar in that one peculiar and glorious way. She had had the extra. She had been a Helper too. They had met and fallen in love. She had also needed *help* and he had Helped her, been amazed that he could *help* a Helper he was in love with. And then she had said goodbye.

Deena hadn't been in the state he was now in. She had still been extra while being lost herself. John's position was now hers and more. He was lost AND no longer extra. Shit!. "You're in it up to your neck now, Johnnie boy."

John had always understood how his Help-ees felt. That was part of the deal, part of the process, part of the fucking *exchange*. He sensed a person's state and truly empathized and then the sharing happened as it happened. Sometimes, in rare cases, it even took a week to develop and during that time he would not only get to the point where he would share their lost-ness during the exchange but also feel it during the period leading up to that.

But now, oh Lord, now it was different. No, not different, but more. Infinitely more. He had fallen and couldn't get up. "Quick, someone get me a beeper. Call the nurse! Code fucking red! Get the paddles greased up and shock me back to *me*!" Well, still got the old sense of humor John thought. It's of no fucking use, but at least it's still there to fuck with me.

John had loved Deena and he had Helped Deena and now Deena and his "sweet spot" were gone. Let the trudging begin.

3

John was five-feet, eleven-inches tall, with thick, curly dark brown hair and olive green eyes. He took a quiet pride in his physicality. He had always been athletic, always running somewhere, or chasing a ball, or pushing an up, and for this he was thankful.

The Sloans were an active family and his stint in the Marine Corps had only cemented his love of physical activity. He would always engage in active sports because of this. The Corps had taught him that you didn't have to feel good to work out. Heck, if feeling good and wanting to be where you were was a prerequisite for fitness then most Marines would never get in shape at all if you were to listen to all of their bitching. A good Marine could wake up deathly hung-over, with two hours of sleep, gripe about the intricacies of a life governed by Uncle Sam, put out a cigarette, perform a perfect right face, and still run five miles. Shit, even a not so good Marine could do this! It just came with the territory. Although the bitching had never really been a large part of John's vocabulary. Oh, he had the words and knew how to string them together but he just never really got the hang of it until lately. He would just tell himself, in words he had first learned in boot camp, "small price to pay to be one of the world's finest" and get on with it.

This had been confirmed as a good way to set your mind on Okinawa. John had made the mistake of partying in the village of Kitimai the night before PT, that's physical training for you scuzzy ass civilians. John had bumped into a friend from boot camp in the enlisted-men's club. The friend had suggested Kitimai after winning a sweet little bundle of cash on the quarter slot machines and they had been off on their drunk. John had stumbled back up the hill to his barracks just as the wake-up lights flickered on at 4:30am. It being July in Okinawa, and already eighty-six degrees and possibly one hundred and *ten* percent humidity, John knew he was poked. Poked right in the pooper as his bud PFC Dunleavy would say—but this time not by the Big Green Wienie, but by his own actions.

Three miles into the eventual six mile run John knew he was shot. Damn, a run drop. How embarrassing is that?! John hadn't even dropped out of a run his first month on the island and that was seven months ago. Just as his platoon was running up a deadly steep and crunchingly long stretch of road Drill Instructor Cracker's voice boomed in John's mind. "Small price to pay to be one of the world's finest, pigs." And John had smiled. Smiled through the boozy sweat and the nausea and the cramps and right then he realized something that would stick with him for some time. He found that when he kept that smile on his face, even if it was forced, that it was somehow connected to his ass. Which caused him to smile even more. Anyone knows that if both your face and your ass are smiling you can get through just about anything. That was John's trick anyway and it was to serve him well both in the Marine Corps and out. Sometimes, "fuck it, small price to pay to be one of the world's finest" was the best advice.

And knowing he was a Helper. Those two, seemingly opposite, thoughts kept John flowing though life with the secret knowledge that from time to time, he would get that inner warmth, that inner glow, and know that an opportunity to help someone with his gift had arisen.

His experiences Helping had shown him that there was a "good" in him that could and should be used. His responsibility was to make use of it whenever and wherever possible. John found as years passed and he met other Helpers such as himself, that he made use of his extra-ness about as much as the others. He was just an average Helper, if there even was such a person. He met other Helpers occasionally and found that there was a rhythm to their lives that he shared. He may have been a *bit* more likely to be guided to situations where he could use his talent yet he knew that he broke no records. He wasn't a saint, or even saintly, even though he considered his talent God given or, better yet, God connected.

John met others like himself roughly once or twice a year. They enjoyed comparing notes as much as he did. Their radar would connect and they would be drawn to each other. Almost always in twos. Occasionally in threes. Rarely in mores. There was just so much going on when Helpers met that more than two was simply impractical. What with conversations, and mind flows, and general cosmic "to and fro-ings" shooting back and forth between them there was only so much room at the trough. And a convention was out of the question! That would open a world of misunderstanding as well as possibly fry their brain-housing-groups.

The chance encounters lasted longer depending on whether or not the two Helpers liked each other or not. Not so silly when you think about it. They were pretty much like other folks and human nature ran through their veins same as the next. John was more likely to share these exchanges with females. This was not by a large margin but was still the case more often than not. He also had Helped a few more women than men. This was not a valuable piece of information. It was only something John acknowledged to be true, like the color of his hair or his left-handedness. It was something that just was, that was all.

John met another Helper for the first time when he was eight years old. Mrs. Abbott. Mrs. Abbott had been his third grade teacher and he had changed her life. Their encounter had also sent a boomerang of fate arching out into the future, quietly whirring and sizzling its way around until decades later it would swizz back toward John and home in on his neck.

4

John's parents had moved early in the fall of his eighth year. This was 1975. The move was precipitated by a merger of trucking companies which required a Sloan family relocation from northern to southern Wisconsin, if John's dad Hugo was to keep his job. So Hugo packed up the family and they headed south, a move more figurative than literal for most people since Wisconsin was rarely thought of as having a south by anyone outside of the wintry state.

But south they moved, the whole tribe.

"Down by all those Germans," Hugo said. "They're different, you know. Clannish. Don't care for outsiders." Which was laughable since Hugo was all of those things and more. He secretly appreciated it in others because it cemented in him his own feelings on these matters. "A Swede is a Swede and all others must be satisfied with second place at best," he would often roar to his giggling children through his great red beard. "And Germans! Germans," he would shout. "The ones down here only marry from inside their own clan. And you know what that leads to don't you? Inbreeding! That's why they're all so damn bullheaded and just plain goofy." Then he would pick his laughing children up, tossing them wildly in the air, bellowing that they were, by God, Swedes dammit. A gift straight from all Norse Gods. Swedes! God's "Frozen Chosen."

Then, if Roberta was in the room, he would amend his bellowing. "A Swede is a Swede and all others must line up in due course." But, he would wickedly admit, the Irish were entitled to sole possession of second place, but only because they had produced Roberta his loving and lovely wife. He would then wink at his dark-Irish bride and pronounce that all others must scramble for the leavings and since Germans weren't such good scramblers they were probably somewhere near the bottom of the barrel. Since his children were only half Swedish, but *were* descended from HIS Swedishness, they were all entitled to sit at the head of the table as well. This was allowed by him and him alone, in spite of the fact that an Irishman had let a Swede sneak into the hen-house.

The children weren't all aware of the meaning of hen-houses and what that had to do with their being granted this head of the table status but it thrilled them to no end. Even as John's brothers and sisters were growing into puberty, with its inherent distancing from one's parents, they couldn't hide their joy at Hugo's good-natured rantings.

Theresa, the oldest, would occasionally toss out,"Dad, I've never heard of a Swede with the last name Sloan. Maybe you're Irish too!"

Hugo's eyes would darken playfully as he mumbled an expletive, "bastards at Ellis Island" being his favorite, and then he would rise up to his full six feet one inch, and declare that it was a blessing after all that they had been given the name Sloan when his grandparents came ashore in New York harbor.

"The clerk asked my grandfather his name and when he said Aronsohn the silly son of a sea cook thought he said Aaron Sloan. And because of that putrid pencil pusher's mistake we became Sloans instead of Aronsohns. Had I been Hugo Aronsohn instead of Hugo Sloan I would've taken over this entire country and had to declare it as a territory for the King of Sweden which, in hindsight, even I Hugo Sloan," he would shout," can see would have been the one mistake of my life." Hugo being a true blue American *and* a veteran. "So you see kids," he would continue,"it was God's own hand preventing me from living a less than perfect life!" When Hugo got on a roll he often didn't make sense even to himself.

These genial rantings were always greeted by a chorus of "Oh dads" and Hugo would gather his lovingly offbeat children into his lovingly offbeat arms and whisper, "plus you grandpa Mulcahy would *never* have let an Aronsohn date his beautiful daughter Roberta. Ahhhhhhh now, but a Sloan he could stomach," said Hugo affecting a terrible Irish brogue. "Even if the Sloan was one as big and ugly as me! So I just figured, why spoil the man's dreams." With that statement uttered the ritual would be complete and the jumbled, cacophonic life that was the Sloan's would trickle back to normalcy. Or what passed for it in their family. With Hugo's final shouts of "a Swede is a Swede" trailing them to their corners of the house, they would resume their hectic, filled to the brim with love, lives.

Because of a merger of two trucking companies, and because of a harried Ellis Island clerk, and maybe because we turned right in the fifth grade instead of left, the Sloan family found themselves in southern Wisconsin in 1967. And John found himself entering a new school for third grade.

5

John was eight years old that October day he came to Mrs. Abbott's third grade classroom. Late again, this time thanks to spilled oatmeal and a lost lunch bag, neither his fault. Mrs. Abbott was kept waiting for John's appearance that day, although she didn't know it, and now we must keep her appearance from you for just a bit longer. We're going to take a bit of a detour. A side road, a sidebar, a wee bit of a trip in the sidecar. Life is one big detour and if you miss *them*, well then, you've missed your life.

Where would you be right now if you *had* turned left instead of right in the fifth grade? On any day. Not a figurative left or right turn. A literal left turn instead of a right turn on the way, to say, gym class one day. C'mon, really think about it. Certainly not where you are now and certainly not reading this book. You might be in American Samoa repairing fishing nets or broadcasting soccer scores on the local radio station. Unless of course you *are* in American Samoa right now, in which case you might be in Superior, Wisconsin cooking eggs to order overnights in the Embers Restaurant on Highway Two. To misquote John Lennon, "life is the detour you are taking while you are waiting to get to what you think is your life over there on the main highway." And sometimes detours are not as pretty as the thruway but they are truly more interesting and they *still* get you to where you were going all along. Which is right here, right now.

At eight years old John had been experiencing his special ability to Help others for four years. He had Helped six people starting with Lainie and the broken Christmas angel. His extra-ness had altered two children, one teenager, and three adults. It had all just flowed out, and altered, and changed, and amended people and he was starting to come into his own with his abilities.

He was especially thankful for the adult man he had Helped. A man who definitely needed a detour off the highway of life that he was currently heading down. It had taken place in the basement bathroom of the Palace movie theater in downtown Superior. The Palace was old even then, all gargoylee Gothic, with shabby, misshapen velvet curtains inside the theater, and the requisite dark and dingy downstairs bathroom.

John was at the aforementioned dank restroom when it had happened.

John was standing at the urinal, which was huge to a little boy of seven. Its discolored, cracked porcelain wrapped around him as if it wanted to grab him, swallow him, and take him whole. And it wasn't just the creature double-feature that brought this thought on. Nope, something was starting to happen and at that moment John's pipeline of Helping opened up. "Whoa, this is different", thought John. It had never happened before when he was alone. John was leaning his head back, looking at the forty-watt ceiling bulb, finally doing his business, when the man entered the bathroom. Or rather the man came through the door, let it close slowly, and then just stood there, frozen, staring at John as if he knew he would be there. Furtive, possessive eyes, and tongue-tip licking lips.

Oh, thought John, here comes my reason for opening up, in all his seven-year-old innocence. John's extra-ness was opened with a brilliance and a completeness that he had *never* experienced before.

Holy crap, thought John, it's more whole than ever. It was beautiful and at the same time a bit scary.

John's oldest sister Theresa had just started teaching him fractions, or trying to teach him fractions since his seven going on eight-year-old mind could not quite fully grasp the concept. John suddenly understood fractions while leaning back at a dirty (shitty Theresa would've whispered) movie theater urinal while a man balancing precariously on the edge of a meltdown slowly walked over and stood at the urinal next to him. "Holy crap, John thought, "I'm more whole than ever. I'm seven-fifths."

John sensed that the man's name was Alfred and that he was thirty-four years old, that he hated the name that he shared with his father, Alfred senior, and that something had happened to Alfred Jr. in this very bathroom that he had struggled with his entire life.

Alfred Jr. had snapped earlier that evening and broken down. He had found himself being dragged zombie-like to the Palace theater ticket counter to purchase one adult ticket for the creature double-feature. The pieces of Alfred's pathetic puzzle began sweeping together and forming in John's mind.

Alfred had watched himself falling into nothing as he had descended the sticky, dirt encrusted stairs to the men's bathroom after having been able to hold out against the torment for only thirty minutes of the first movie. The part of him that watched himself knew that he was powerless to control the thing he was becoming and the things that he must do. He also knew that the last little *good* part of himself that watched this new creature he would become, would soon be completely gone. The last little flame of himself as he hoped to be would be gone. He had descended into Hell and Alfred knew that there would be no "and He rose again on the third day" for him. He had fought this his entire life and now the will to fight was gone. He had given in and as sure as he knew there was a Devil in Hell, he knew there would be a little seven going on eight-year-old year old boy waiting for him at the urinals. He knew that he would approach this boy just as he had been approached in this very same bathroom.

Alfred knew that he would coax this little boy into the farthest corner stall, would lock the door, some unzipping and fumbling and crying would occur, and then the two of them would emerge forever changed. No going back and you can forget about that passing go and collecting two-hundred dollar shit.

John saw all of this and more as Alfred took his spot in the urinal next to John's. Viewing the movie of Alfred inside his head he understood it as much as his seven-year-old year old innocence, and the Light, would allow for. He understood but without having his innocence shattered. He was just incredibly saddened by it all. John's abilities unfolded in a way they never had before. And he helped them unfold as well. For the first time in a Helping John exerted effort. He added his effort to the effortless unveiling of the "what was to come." He just knew that he had to. He *had* to. This one required it all. And for the first time John truly felt the Source of his pipeline. He had always kind of known where it came from but this time he was *there* too. And here too. And in-between as well. John was experiencing transcendence completely.

A glowing, transcendent, seven-year-old John turned to Alfred just as Alfred was unzipping his bulging trousers in the next urinal.

"Hello, Alfred", he said, "my name is John.

Then John said something that he didn't completely understand. He said "I am Light." Not I am the light or there is a light, or how bout a fucking Bud Lite, if they even had light beer back then, but "I am Light."

"Don't be afraid, Alfred."

"*I* am Light." This last "I am Light" was not even in John's voice, which made John's skin shimmer with goose bumps and pure joy. It was the voice of All, of the Light. It was the voice *of* Light.

"There is a Light and you are in it too." This was back in John's voice again and now it was all happening so quickly as to be beyond time itself. In the snap of a finger that was also an eternity.

Jeez, the boy in John thought, this sounds like the bible. John thought this even as he was unfolding and enveloping Alfred in the

Grace. And there *was* a light. A light so bright and so white that it was without color. It was everything and it was everywhere and it *was*, make no mistake about that. It *was*!

And in that eternal instant Alfred was altered. The tears of despair that had been pinching out of the corners of his eyes dripped slowly onto his shirt as time stopped. Alfred was bathed in the brilliant searchlight that made all, good and bad, visible to him. The Light that poured out of John, but was not John. A light that John was a part of and a conduit for. *The* Light. In that instant, in that snap, Alfred knew that there was a light and that he was part of it too.

"You can zip up your pants, Alfred," John said to the openly weeping man. "Go home and be you. Go home and live your life," John said in words that came from beyond himself. Words that he didn't know to say. "Go home and remember the Light. Go home and *be* the Light that is in you."

With that John stepped back from the urinal and turned to wash his hands. As he started soaping up he was aware that his mind was humming the song "You Are My Sunshine. My only sunshine, you make me happy when skies are gray. You'll never know dear, how much I love you. Please don't take my sunshine away." John loved this song. He and his sister Theresa would sit cross-legged and sing this song together, with their faces almost touching, and laugh till Theresa said she might have an accident. It was a good song John thought. Maybe the best song there ever was. "Please don't take my sunshine away," John thought.

Alfred? Alfred was changed completely and forever. You see, what we're talking about here is the *shit*. The real thing. Not some band-aid, not some "oh, I got a little help so I can limp along OK now, I guess." What we are talking about here is the real fucking McCoy. Alfred did zip up his pants and walk away from that bathroom as the man he would become. He went to trade school and became a plumber and even worked on this very bathroom's urinal without an itch or a worry or a trace of who and what he had almost become. A breath away from being lost for good and forever and Alfred had been

Found. He had been Found with the help of a little boy named John. Unlike most others Alfred did remember part of what happened. He remembered the Light and his favorite song from that day until the day he died many years later was "You Are My Sunshine."

"Please don't take my sunshine away," John had sung that day. "My lips to God's ears," John would think years later. Years later when John's sunshine was taken away. Completely.

6

See what I mean about those detours? Not very pretty are they? They get rough, and the road is patchy and winding, but they do get you where you're going. And where we are going right now, and finally—you may be thinking, is the third grade. Remember Mrs. Abbott? Let's see if we can't meet her...

John walked to the front of Mrs. Abbott's classroom and handed her the folded white slip of paper he had been given in the office. He was late, remember? The aforementioned spilled oatmeal, that thanks to youngest brother Henry, and lost lunch bag belonging to little sister Tracey. John liked Mrs. Abbott as soon as he had turned from shutting the door and quietly entering her classroom. He had seen her before she had seen him. She had glanced briefly toward the door as he entered, but turned back quickly to shush the murmuring class that had noted his late entrance. He had a chance to look at her then. Bright orange hair frizzily flowed out from Mrs. Abbott's head like water spraying from a garden hose that had been dropped on its nozzle whilst washing the car and couldn't be stopped until you fought your way back through the jet of water and bent down through the shower to turn it on its side so the handle of the nozzle would unclick and stop.

Not the thick dark red that John's father Hugo had. No, this was cartoon orange. Hair that was barely contained by the ponytail rubber band that Mrs. Abbott knotted around the bottom of her carrot mane, somewhere near her shapely backside.

She wore thick, rimless granny glasses, "hippie glasses", his sister Theresa whispered in his mind, and John knew then that she was twenty-six years old and that this was the first school she had taught at, following student teaching of course. John didn't usually know people's ages and other details like that unless he was going to Help them. Sometimes it happened, though. He would catch bits of information on someone in the brief exchange of glances during a first meeting. They just registered in his mind and were filed away for further use if needed.

John *really* liked Mrs. Abbott when she turned back to him and said, "Well hello, young man. Would you be the dashing young John Sloan, our new student?"

That's how she talks to kids, John thought. The class didn't even giggle at him when she referred to him that way. No, they smiled at her like they were in on the *inside* part of an inside joke, and then swiveled their young heads back to him, tennis-match fashion.

"Well yes, ma'am, I guess I am," John stumbled out.

This did get the classroom laughing a bit. Mrs. Abbott had a gleam in her eye as well.

"Let's see what this note says then, and after that we will find you a suitable throne for matriculating the wheres and why-fores of this most honorable of grades, the third," Mrs. Abbott replied.

Cool. John really liked Mrs. Abbot now. Thank goodness too. This new school thing was making John kind of nervous. He walked up the side of the classroom and stopped along the side of her desk. John looked up into her robin's shell eyes and *knew* that she had a daughter with those exact same eyes. At exactly the same time as John realized this, a slight cloud crossed Mrs. Abbott's brow. Not a storm cloud, or a tornado, or a black cloud. Just a wisp of a slight, blocked from view, can't see through, cloud. Then her bright, orange-haired smile was back.

As he handed her the note he understood that she had known *his* name as soon as he had entered the room. *Before* she read any note from the office with his name on it. "Hey, what's this?" he thought. And while they stood connected, with his hand on one side of the folded slip of paper and her hand lightly pinching the other, John knew that she was like him. She was a Helper. Could they have been smiling any broader?

John let go of the note from school secretary Bea Wyland and thought that this was going to be a very fun year. Yes, he really *was* going to enjoy matric-u-latin' in Mrs. Abbott's most honorable of classes, the third. "Gosh, she's got me thinkin like her already," thought John. She *is* a good teacher. He was looking forward to finding out what matric-u-latin' meant, along with wheres and why-fores. Third grade was good! Not bad for a new kid in a new school on his very first day is it? Why don't we just see where this leads...

7

John and Mrs. Abbott formed a special bond from that first day on. He felt right at home in his new school. It was nice that the class had welcomed him without any of that crappy stuff that could sometimes happen to the new kid in class; all the challenges from the tough boys that came with being new, or the popular girls snotty looks that could try to put a new kid in his place. No, Mrs. Abbott's third grade class was a safe place to be, and safe places to be are *good* places to be. You could learn there. You could learn math and language and science. You could learn to laugh with others unselfconsciously. You could also learn, maybe for the first time, to laugh with and at yourself. "This is a good place", thought John as he hopscotched home from school after that first day.

John stayed after on his second day of class to clean the chalkboard for Mrs. Abbott. She had asked him to stay late, if that wouldn't cause a problem with his mother, and they both knew why. So they could spend some time together. As Helpers. Exchanging the flow. There would be some talking but they also knew that just being alone with each other would be a treat.

Mrs. Abbott asked John if he liked his new school and at the same time her mind reached out and wondered as to how long he had known about his gift.

"I like it just as much as can be," John replied, while his mind answered "just about forever I think."

Their exchanges continued on like this for twenty minutes or so, as their voices responded to one set of questions and their minds another.

"Wow," thought John as he bathed in the comforting waters of their presence, "this is so cool."

"It is, isn't it?" Mrs. Abbott thought back. "Doesn't it feel lovely young John?"

"Oh yes, ma'am, it does," his thoughts replied.

Mrs. Abbott let him know that she had met others like themselves from time to time and that he could look forward to this kind of thing happening in his life too. John knew then that that little bit of loneliness inside himself was being taken care of. He had felt just a little bit separate because he was a Helper and, as cool as that was, he *was* different from other people. Now he didn't even have to worry about that. Neat!

Anyone looking through the classroom door window would have seen a gifted young teacher spending time with a contented and happy student. They would have been absolutely correct in that observation. Someone with the *gift*, another Helper, would have seen that and more. They would have seen the bright flow of colors passing between teacher and student. They would see the flow of energy that washed back and forth simultaneously, encompassing the entire front half of the room. They would have felt the Peace, which did pass all understanding, and they would also have most likely stayed an observer. These things could sometimes get tricky in threes or especially fours. They would have observed and perhaps just sent out a quick little lick of their own flow in passing. Just a quick acknowledgment that they too were passing, and hello, but carry on and maybe we too can spend some time together one day. Yes, these things were usually best in twos. And Oh, what a beautiful two it was.

Almost a three. John, Mrs. Abbott, and their Source. Shit, if you wanted to get nuts about the whole thing, call it a five with each of their Sources being separate and part of a greater Source at the same time. The most apt description however was One. All had joined into a one. And One, when it was made up of more than one, was beyond words beautiful. It was the "where we all hope to go." It was peace and it was indeed a beautiful thing. Cool, huh? No shit, cool!

8

The same month, October, 1975, that John entered Mrs. Abbott's class another eight-year-old boy, Toivo "Dusty" Hakkila, was entering a third grade classroom as the new kid in school in Superior Wisconsin, the town John's family had just left. Dusty had missed bumping into John by three weeks. Dusty was even entering John's old school. Not the same classroom as John, however. Toivo "Dusty" Hakkila was entering a new class that had been created for Indian children. The correct name now I suppose would be Native American or Indigenous or First Nation. Back then, and still today for many, it was Indian. Toivo "Dusty" Hakkila, pronounced TOY-voh and HACK-i-lah, was three-quarters Chippewa which to the knowledgeable and/or politically correct and groovy is Ojibwe, or even better Anishinaabe.

Dusty was born on the Bad River Indian Reservation about eighty miles east of Superior, in the dense north-woods on the south shore of Lake Superior, near the border with Michigan's upper peninsula. His father Earl was half Ojibway (now am I'm knowledgeable or politically correct?) and half Finnish. Earl's drunken Finlander half was definitely in charge after Dusty's birth when Earl had staggered into the nurses station and shouted "We're naming the kid after my God-dammed grandfather Toivo or I'll tear this fucking house down!" Earl could be quite a persuasive man when present, which he wasn't much then, and hadn't been at all since John's sixth birthday. Earl had then lit a cheap cigar, inhaled, exhaled, vomited, and passed out on the hard, cold, and now quite digestively decorated tile floor of the reservation clinic. Dusty's mom Jeanie was a full blooded Chippewa. Oh, and did I mention? Dusty was a Helper. Not that it fucking helped him all that much, but he was a Helper.

Dusty was now living in Duluth, Minnesota, just across the bridge from Superior, Wisconsin. His mom Jeannie, although a former beauty queen and pride of the reservation, had lost her spirit after Earl took off, and had given Dusty up to a succession of downwardly spiraling friends and relatives, and now spent most of her days drinking grain alcohol mixed lightly with the area's prized apple cider, and mixed with hard cider when she could get it. Not quite enough kick in the old grain alcohol, gotta add some hard cider to really give it some punch! Fuck.

Duluth is the much larger and more prosperous of the Twin Ports of Duluth, Minnesota and Superior, Wisconsin, at that time roughly ninety-thousand population to thirty-seven thousand for Superior. Superior being the hard luck, red-headed step child of the family. Think San Francisco versus Oakland and you get the general idea. Duluth, situated on great rocky hills overlooking St. Louis Bay and Lake Superior, and connected to the topographically, and economically, flat Superior by two vast bridges. Not that Duluth wasn't without crime. Quite often it was worse than Superior but Superior was just poorer and generally more run down *and* filled with drunken Minnesotans half the time, thanks to looser liquor laws and later bar times. Filled with people that didn't have to wait for Saturday night to get drunk and thrown in jail. No, Tuesday fucking morning would do just fine. You can get a certain sense of a place when it's downtown is filled with "bar-fly" type bars sporting home made signs saying "no kids in the bar after 5pm." Which, when you think of it, is pretty liberal when the bar opens at 7am. Hard luck, hard drinking, and pray for a job from the shrinking pool of union work still left in the area.

Dusty found himself living in one of Duluth's neighborhoods that gave it's ugly step-sister across the bay a run for their money. He was shuffled from the homes of drunken relatives to drunken foster homes in Duluth's west end. Recently he had been living with a second cousin named Eunice and her flavor of the night boyfriend Catch, who was "Jesus Christ, anything but" as Dusty had been muttering to himself since the mean, greasy-haired blonde, merchant sailor had moved in. They had a room at the end of a fifth-floor hallway in the august Seaway Hotel. Bathroom at the end of the hall if you please. Home to drunken merchant mariners, skid row whites, and Indians. Eunice managed to be part of all three; drunken, skid row, and Indian. Just a fine place to raise a boy.

Dusty had been Helping people since he was five, not that it mattered much to him. The way he already figured it, most of them had it better off than him *before* he even Helped them. *And* since he couldn't even Help the people closest to him, his mother and father, what in the hell good was it? But he still Helped all five times the opportunity had presented itself. He couldn't help it, pun intended.

His first time had been memorable though. He had helped a teenaged girl on the reservation. She had been heading home to slit her wrists, smear her body with the blood, and fall asleep for good when Dusty had crossed paths with her. She had been changed and Dusty had broken his Helping cherry. She was now in the social work program at the University of Wisconsin, way down in Madison, and would go on to lead peaceful protests against a variety of issues, especially war, marry a vet, and help change the lives of many kids back home on the Rez. Dusty had been so charged up after that that the let down when he had tried to Help his parents had been that much greater. Dusty could've used the break that meeting John, another Helper, would've provided. Instead he waited seven more years before he met another Helper, but that, he would come to believe, had definitely been worth the wait.

At eight-years-old he swore, smoked cigarettes, had a wicked little sense of humor, and knew more than most kids twice his age. You could say Dusty had a bad attitude. Deservedly so, perhaps, but bad nonetheless.

We'll visit with Dusty once more before he meets John in boot camp at Parris Island. By then Dusty will have found out what is worse than being a Helper with a dismally shitty life. He'll know what it is to have had the opportunity to *save* someone from Hell, from the Abyss, and to turn his back on that opportunity. Dusty's a fuckin' trip, man. Oh, now it's on to Chapter nine.

9

The bond between John and Mrs. Abbott was fully developed from the moment their hands simultaneously touched the slip of paper John had brought in from the principal's office introducing him as a new student. Fully formed. Now, over the remainder of the school year, all they had to do was enjoy it, and enjoy it they did. They bathed in it. Mrs. Abbott knew that this was John's first experience with another Helper and she remembered how sweet that had been for her. What she knew, and John didn't, was that these meetings didn't usually last as long as theirs did so she enjoyed the situation as much or more than John.

The class accepted the bond between them without hesitation or recrimination toward either. John was never called teacher's pet for the amount of time he spent with Mrs. Abbott. It really wasn't that much more than what the other students spent with her. Mrs. Abbott had a way of making each student feel special and wanted and needed. Being a Helper didn't *necessarily* make someone a good teacher, being a good *teacher* did. And Mrs. Abbott was going to be a great teacher.

The pair would usually just spend a little time together after class was over. They soon stopped the double communication of saying one thing out loud and another with their minds. It wasn't necessary. They still did both occasionally but that was only because they almost always seemed to have their "quiet" exchange going on and sometimes this would overlap with real conversation. Their minds had just locked in with each other. Their connection was a pilot light that was always on, burning low, only needing a reaching out by one or the other to bring it to full flame.

One month after John had entered the class he realized something. He was straightening desks and his mind asked Mrs. Abbott, "We're together longer than most aren't we, Mrs. Abbott?" Even as his mind sent this question he knew the answer. This happened often, as if the asking of any particular question was important and that by simply asking it he was being provided with the answer. The question was an important part of the process and yet, because it had been asked, no response was needed.

"Yes, we are together longer than most John," Mrs. Abbott replied.

Mrs. Abbott then opened a drawer in her mind and John was able to meet all of the other Helpers that Mrs. Abbott had met in her twenty-six years of being extra. John saw that Mrs. Abbott had met her first Helper when she was eight-years-old too.

"Oh, that was fun wasn't it?" John thought.

"I will never forget it, John," thought Mrs. Abbott his way.

"Do you think we were meant to meet?"

"Of course, dear, all things *can* have a purpose whether we realize them "up top" or "down below."

What she actually sent was consciously or unconsciously but this was received in John's mind as "up top" or "down below" and they both knew this. John also now knew the meaning of consciously and unconsciously.

"I guess you're right about everything being able to be put to use, huh, Mrs. Abbott?" John's mind had answered and they had both dissolved into laughter. Both out loud and in their minds.

"Oh you *are* a little something, aren't you my Master John?" smiled Mrs. Abbott.

"You know John, you still have to study your vocabulary book. I can't give you extra credit for this", thought Mrs. Abbott as she lightly pinched the giggling boy.

After they had settled down and gotten back to their respective chores John wondered, "We were both eight-years-old when we first met other Helpers. Is everyone eight when they first have a meeting?"

"No, John, it quite often happens then, but it can happen either before or after too," she responded.

"But if eight is when a lot of us meet other Helpers maybe that's why you're a third grade teacher, huh, Mrs. Abbott?", said John's mind.

The kaleidoscopic aura around them intensified as they both came to this realization. Mrs. Abbott knew then that she was meant to teach third grade. She hadn't known this before. She had just been drawn to it for no apparent reason, as so many of us are drawn to things which later reveal the hand of Providence.

"You're like a way station, Mrs. Abbott", John thought to her, "like in the pony express days. You are the first stop on each riders' long journey. Just like in cowboy days! And maybe not just for other Helpers but for all kids in your class. And maybe it's even more than that," John said, pausing as a new idea flooded in, "Wow, it's like you're like a great big mom!"

Tears formed in Mrs. Abbott's eyes as this blessing sunk in. John got a little choked up too and the part of him that was eight had turned away for a second until Mrs. Abbott wrapped him in her arms and rocked him back and forth.

Mrs. Abbott knew there were many reasons why she was teaching the third grade. She loved teaching. She loved children. She loved how their eyes would light up when they understood something for the first time. She *was* needed and because she was a teacher the world benefited in some small way.

Mrs. Abbott realized once again that there are many purposes in life and they can happen simultaneously. Infinite purposes quite often happening at the same time, gently overlapping like multiple currents in the ocean. Everywhere at once thought John and Mrs. Abbott, at the same time. Everywhere at once.

10

It was May, near the end of their year together, and John and Mrs. Abbott were together after class having their usual dialog. "One part talk, ten parts thought," smiled John. "Like a recipe."

Mrs. Abbott had been sensing for a few days that John had something to ask her but he wasn't sure if he should or not. She hadn't known what the question was. John's mind had automatically shut that off from her because of his hesitancy. She could feel his mind ruminating over something, mulling it this way and that, but she hadn't sensed any great urgency and figured it best to let whatever he was chewing on percolate itself to the top on its own.

John *did* have a question to ask Mrs. Abbott but he wasn't sure just how to go about it or if he should even ask it or not. It didn't seem like a tough question but an intuition told him that there might be more going on that he couldn't see, and it might be none of his beeswax. It *really* might be none of his beeswax. They were both Helpers but John was still a young boy and Mrs. Abbott was still an adult and the Sloan household was strong on respect for others. There was quite a lot of good-natured ribbing among themselves but all of the Sloan children were taught, and shown by example, the need for respect. Especially respect for their elders. This was only proven more necessary when the reverse was show. And John had seen the reverse and remembered.

Finally John's mind had sent out a query," I think I should ask you a question, Mrs. Abbott, but I don't know if I should or not."

"Why don't you think you should ask me?"

"Cuz I guess maybe I'm not sure if it'll hurt or not, or something like that. It doesn't seem wrong but I don't want to be disrespectful. It's really not good to be disrespectful."

Mrs. Abbott realized that there might be something more going on here than just asking a question. "Who would get hurt, John? Me or you?"

"I think you would, Mrs. Abbott, and I don't want to hurt you. Especially you. It would be wrong to hurt you and you're a grownup and my friend and I don't want to be bad to you."

As curious as she was about the question Mrs. Abbott wanted to probe a little deeper into John's mind about this sudden fear and she did. And John could feel her in there and he was on guard and Mrs. Abbott could feel that. He was hiding something. Maybe more than something, maybe a couple of things.

"Why are you afraid to ask me, honey?" asked Mrs. Abbott.

"Cuz it could be none of my business and it's really bad to not respect your elders", said John. "Sometimes really bad."

Normally Mrs. Abbott would have corrected John's "cuz" to "because" even in their thought talk, but this was not the time for that. Something *was* going on here but John was keeping it from her and though she wasn't trying to overwhelm his mind with hers, the probes into his mind she was making were being parried easily away.

"Well we're here together, John, and it's safe, so if it's OK with you why don't we try it? Just a little bit at a time. Now before you ask the question you want to ask me, should we talk about something else? Does it have anything to do with respect?" asked Mrs. Abbott.

"Uh, huh," said John and with that, the first level of defense that John's mind had set up slowly started to fade. "It does."

Mrs. Abbott's mind yawned open a bit further and joined John's at his fading first line of defense.

"Do you know my older brother Don?" John asked.

Mrs. Abbott did recall the mischievous, dark-haired, front-tooth spaced boy, just a couple of years older than John—a little taller than average, and whip-thin, but strong looking and always running somewhere.

As Mrs. Abbott started to reply, "well yes, honey, she did know him by name from the hallways and from the lunch room and from recess," the story started to unfold. Not all at once but with an old newsreel quality in her mind. John sent it piece by piece and her mind watched it roll by.

"You see, Mrs. Abbott, one day my brother Donnie climbed McNamara's tree..."

It had been in Superior, before the move and Don had been climbing Mr. McNamara's pear tree. Don knew that this was against the rules. One, because it was Mr. McNamara's tree and he hadn't been given permission and two, because Mr. McNamara was mean as an old snake, and big too, and wouldn't give Don permission to climb that gnarled old pear tree if the universe was crumbling and there was no food left anywhere on earth. And of course that's why Don had done it. He had been dared by Timmy Rostopich from across the alley.

"C'mon, Donaldi, climb old Gutbuckets' tree why don'cha! Are you chicken?" Timmy taunted. "Shit, he ain't even home anyway I don't think."

Now Sloan children were very bright but they could also be quite mischievous too. And chicken they were not. They were Sloans, and Swedes too! At least part-way.

Don was halfway down the tree with a load of pears in his pockets when old Gutbuckets, who was in fact home, had stormed out of his house and across his front yard to the tree. This was enough to send Timmy, who was no chicken himself, and a Bohunk to boot, which he thought was even better than a Swede, flying down the street to the safety of his own house. Don could see the fury building as Mr.

"Gutbuckets" McNamara marched toward him and he scrambled to get out of the tree. Just as Don had fallen down the last four feet of tree, McNamara arrived.

John had seen this all happen from down the street. John had been walking down to the bus stop to wait for their father Hugo. Hugo had been out on an extended truck driving run for the past three weeks and he loved to be met by his kids at the bus stop when he returned home. When he left on his trips for Twin Ports Trucking he always had Roberta drop him off in the family car and he would say, "Now don't you worry about picking me up, my love, I'll call from the terminal when I get home and take the city bus home or hitch a ride if it's too late for the bus." Then after one long hug and two deep kisses, one in the car and the other through the open window because he couldn't *not* kiss her again, he would be off. It was a game they always played and it was also true. Hugo missed his family more and more the longer he was gone and his return from these trips was like Christmas and a family reunion all rolled into one.

All of these variables were coming into play on that August afternoon as this little drama acted itself out. While the whole neighborhood knew that Hugo Sloan was a large, even-tempered man, they also knew that he was indeed a man to be reckoned with. His temper, rarely shown, was legendary. So much so that if ever he was pushed to the point of true anger he would bite the right side of his lip to remind himself of his anger and to help stop himself.

Hugo had had to teach himself this trick as a teenager. He had worked bailing hay "out in the county" for a poverty stricken family with a drunken abusive father. If he could remember to bite his lip he was less likely to use his over sized fists as battering rams which he had eventually done on the abusive farmer after he caught him whipping his daughter's back bloody and then pouring vinegar on the open wounds to increase the pain and humiliation. Hugo knew that he had beaten the farmer far too thoroughly but had been unable to stop himself. Hugo had snatched the vinegar bottle from the man's hand, beaten him to the ground with it, and when he found himself kicking the man senseless he had finally stopped. With a sudden, innocent touch, he had lifted the sobbing daughter and brought her to the ramshackle house and into the arms of her defeated mother. He then had returned to the barn and, lifting the bloody farmer up with one arm, told him that that would NEVER happen again. "EVER", he had shouted in the farmer's swelling face.

Hugo then took a long walk through the hay field and realized that it was only by some act of Grace that he hadn't continued stomping the man to death. It struck him then to bite down hard on his lip to control the rage that could boil up out of himself. From that day on Hugo used that technique to much success. On the few occasions when he had gone over the edge all had agreed that the person on the receiving end had truly deserved it, and that they had just had the simple misfortune of receiving their just desserts at the hand of one so powerful and capable as Hugo Sloan.

Hugo had stayed and worked the rest of the summer for the family and, even after he recovered from his injuries, the farmer never laid a hand on any of his family again. To the relief of all he had drunk himself to death less than a year later. A huge sigh of relief could be heard throughout the farmer's valley on the occasion of his death and the biggest had come from his family. And everyone had known that while Hugo may have been a bit too savage, in the end justice had been served swiftly and deservedly.

Now while Mrs. Abbott was coming to understand all of this, courtesy of John's mind, Gutbuckets McNamara hadn't a clue as the little one-act tragedy was unfolding beneath the fruit-laden pear tree. He was new to the neighborhood and kept to himself. All of the actors were finding their places as Gutbuckets grabbed the crumpled and penitent Don and held him up against the tree by handfuls of young Don's t-shirt. John was coming up the sidewalk from one side and finally the fourth character had turned his corner from the bus stop and entered the play from the other direction. Hugo.

Hugo's good-natured ways were a bit off that day. His company had kept him out seven days longer than promised so it had been a full twenty-one days since he had seen his family. He had had a loud argument with his dispatcher over this, a man new to the company, and the topper was when he had dropped his last load he had been blamed for damage done to the load by the crew that was unloading it. He and the surly foreman had stood toe to toe and eye to eye which was as rare for Hugo as it was for the foreman. The foreman had finally come to his senses just as Hugo had started to bite the right side of his lip. The foreman intuitively knew that he was about to cross a line that he might not return from. So he had turned his wrath back upon the crew who were secretly delighted at seeing their boss back down from a scrap.

Hugo missed his family and as he turned the corner he saw John first. Hugo's heart melted as he got his first glance at family in three long weeks. The next thing he noticed was the scared look on John's face and he followed John's eyes to the source of his fear. They both saw that Gutbuckets had taken his belt off and was smacking the bare legs below Donnie's cutoff jeans. Gutbuckets had pulled Don's t-shirt up over his head and it tangled his boyishly muscular arms so that he couldn't protect himself.

"MOTHERFUCK", Hugo bellowed.

John had never seen ground covered so fast as his father now covered it. One second he was two front yards away from McNamara and the next he was five feet away from the beating. Jeez, thought John, he was there and then he was way over *there*!

"You stop NOW, COCKSUCKER," Hugo roared. "NOW!"

John had never heard his father use language like this before.

Gutbuckets did stop, but his own fury prevented him from thinking clearly. Don dropped and lay quietly hiccuping and sobbing in a heap at the foot of the tree. As Hugo bent down to pick Don up, McNamara swung his thick leather belt down toward Hugo and caught him full on the face. The large buckle whipped into Hugo's nose, breaking it. This was McNamara's latest mistake. His next was to stop and admire his handiwork. He stood gloating while Hugo slowly stood upright with blood trickling out of his broken nose.

"Fuck YOU, you dumb Swede", sweated McNamara with a half laugh. "Fuck you and those ash-trash kidsa' yours."

McNamara now saw that not only was blood shooting out of Hugo's crumpled nose, it was also pouring out of a hole that Hugo had bitten along the right side of his own lip.

"You keep those little white niggers of yours off my property or I'll beat you down too!"

Years later even Don would wearily laugh that this had been one big mistake too many on Mr. Gutbuckets McNamara's part. One big mistake. And bigger mistakes were still to be made.

McNamara once again swung his belt toward Hugo's face.

"NO", John cried. He shouted it even more for his dad's sake than for McNamara's.

"NO, please don't," John cried out.

Too late to do any good, you may well surmise, as objects in motion tend to stay in motion. We now see that *emotions* in motion tend to stay that way as well.

There is an "almost grace" that can happen during violence. It is not pretty and it should not be welcomed but it can often be observed. Instinctual movements by the participants witnessed in a type of hurried, slow motion. A violent ballet, and this dance was just beginning.

McNamara was big and he was strong and he was expert in the optional uses of the belt. He was also about two steps behind in this little drama. McNamara had swung his belt and buckle toward Hugo's face and Hugo stood straight and still and let it come. He stared directly into McNamara's eyes even as the buckle tore a gash deep in his left eyebrow. Hugo had blood pouring from his misshapen nose, the hole in his lip, and now from the three-inch raw furrow that had been plowed through his forehead. McNamara was about to be brought quickly up to speed in this little one act-er. He was stunned that the abuse he had meted out was so stoically taken. He felt the first whisper of fear in the pit of his stomach and his legs quivered slightly. McNamara, a man of infinite mistakes, was about to make another.

"No, please don't do it, dad", John cried, now at the foot of the tree holding his silent brother, knowing what was coming. Reading his father's mind and comprehending the violent pictures there. "No, dad, don't! You'll kill him."

"Aw, let him do it, Johnnie", Don resigned. "Let him do it."

Something registered in the dim recesses of McNamara's mind. "He's saying don't do it *dad*, not don't do it Gutbuckets. What the fuck!" This thought, while true, was acknowledged in a totally incorrect way by McNamara and he swung the belt a final time. This was a critical mistake. Critical.

"No, dad, don't!" screamed John again.

Hugo simply reached out with one huge paw and caught the belt buckle in his fist. He then quickly, and almost poetically, reeled Gutbuckets in. With the belt now wrapped in his hand Hugo moved this same hand to McNamara's throat and pinned him against the tree. McNamara was now revisiting fear he had not known since his own abused childhood. Hugo held him pinned to the tree and with his free hand now punched McNamara savagely in the face. Since the back of McNamara's head was pressed against the tree, and Hugo's fist hammered from the opposite side, a double effect was felt. Quite vicious. Hugo quickly and methodically set about administering the beating. First he punched Gutbuckets full in the face while the back of Gutbucket's head was against the prickly pear trunk. He then turned the stunned man's head sideways and punched his right ear which, of course, also brought damage to the left when it bounced of the rough tree bark. Hugo then spun him completely around and punched the left ear which brought more tree damage to the right. There was only one direction left unpunished and Hugo now expertly lined Gutbuckets up for the final blow.

"No dad, please don't", yelped John one last time. A message unheard and unheeded by Hugo.

No cars passed on the street. No insects hummed and no chipmunks chipped. John's attention was distracted by an enormous black crow which had squawked and flapped its way onto the telephone line in front of the tree. Licking the last bits of road-kill squirrel meat off its right leg and claw as if dipping into a box of popcorn, settling into a balcony seat at the Palace Theater just as the opening theme swelled, on a shoot-em-up western. One last squawk and then no sound at all. Just heat. Nothing for anyone to do now but watch.

Hugo held Gutbuckets by the back of his neck, lined him up, and pushed his face into the tree. And then this man of family and love and respect brought a thunderous fist into the back of McNamara's head splitting his face in two against the ragged, bloody, trunk of the pear tree. McNamara crumpled, unconscious, in a pulpy heap at the foot of the tree.

Silence, punctuated only by Hugo's ragged panting. A pause, while this small part of the world caught its breath. A count of three, and then of five. Two beats more and still the world had not exhaled. Finally time could stand still no more and the spell was broken. This little corner of the world breathed again. The crow took off and a corpulent honey-bee lazily buzzed past John's line of sight.

"You boys run home to your mother now, and tell her to phone the ambulance", Hugo told his sons. "You get a move on or I do believe this piece of shit will die."

Hugo remained at the tree while his boys ran home to fetch the ambulance. He used his Army first-aid on Gutbuckets. He laid Gutbuckets out and made sure he was breathing. His took off his shirt and put it underneath Gutbuckets misshapen head. He cleared Gutbucket's mouth of teeth and skin to provide an airway and, when he had done all that he could think of to do, he sat next to him and waited for the ambulance.

The police eventually came, as well. Hugo's defense was aided by two observant widows, nosy actually, who both told the same story to the officers. Hugo had seen his son being beaten and had then been attacked himself and had thrown only four punches. Hugo explained this himself to the edgy detective at the precinct house.

"I don't need to see you ever again, do I Mr. Sloan?" said the detective keeping his distance from the hulking, flushed, and bleeding red head.

"No you don't, and no you won't, detective", Hugo said. "I just let him get the best of me."

Detective Ronstad thought Hugo had gotten that a bit backward, but he knew what Hugo meant.

"You're free to go but watch that temper of yours Sloan", finished Ronstad. "You kill a man with those fists, even human garbage like McNamara, and you'll spend a long time wishing you could see your family."

Mr. McNamara was never seen again. A for-sale sign had appeared on his front yard and a smiling family of four, the Jacobsons, had moved in and invited all the kids in the neighborhood to pick pears from the tree.

"We really don't like them anyway", the jolly, sawed-off father, Jake Jacobson had laughed. "They give us gas! So help yourselves anytime."

Everyone did except the Sloans. They never ate another pear from that tree.

McNamara was rumored to have taken his broken face and broken spirit to Rice Lake to live with a sister. And indeed he did live there, a broken man, until his death some years later.

When he returned from the police station Hugo gathered his family together and spoke to them. He told them that while Mr. McNamara's actions had been severely out of line, he had been wrong too.

"There was enough blame to go around", Hugo said. "And yes Don, you shouldn't have climbed the tree. Especially *that* tree, in *that* yard. You must respect that, but while you were wrong, you were also doing what boys do and I was much more in the wrong."

"Don't you see how when you are even a little disrespectful of other people and their property how things can get out of hand?" Hugo went on. "Now, it was my fault and I accept that, but please kids, you must always try to treat others with honor. Promise me that."

The children all nodded their assent, barely able to look at their father whom they had never seen in such a state.

Hugo had tears in his eyes as he looked at each member of his family and told them that he would never raise his fists in anger again and he never did. From that day on Roberta meted out all of the spankings in the Sloan household, which were few anyway. And he never did fight another person for the rest of his long life.

"Oh, John", said Mrs. Abbott "you know that wasn't your fault, don't you?"

"But I couldn't *Help*, Mrs. Abbott, I didn't even think to use my Helping to keep things from getting so bad", whispered John's mind. "It was so quick and I was so scared but I didn't even *try.*"

"John, you *couldn't* have Helped," replied Mrs. Abbott, who now saw in John's mind how he had cried himself to sleep for a week after the fight. How John had vowed to use his gift whenever possible from that day on.

"Honey, *It* decides when we Help, like it or not", thought Mrs. Abbott to her forlorn little friend. "Did you feel any of the feelings *that* day that you felt those times when you *did* Help people?"

"No, Mrs. Abbot, I didn't. I didn't feel any of the power or any of the knowing or any of the openness."

"So you see", continued Mrs. Abbott, "for some reason you weren't supposed to Help that time. It just wasn't meant to be. I can't just decide to Help someone either. I only know that when the power comes on, that is when I Help. Don't you think there have been times when I wished I could use my Helping to change a situation?"

"I guess so", sniffled John's mind.

"Well there have been," she said. "Sometimes I wished it with all my might, but it just doesn't work that way. Or we do get the chance but not in the way we would have liked to. Not in the way we would like it to work out. But we still have to use it every chance we get, OK? It's part of who we are and what we do."

"Yes, Mrs. Abbott, I know," concluded John. "I know and I will."

But with all her special abilities and all her fine qualities as a human being Mrs. Abbott couldn't see into the future. Not this time anyway and she had no way of knowing, that while John *would* always use his special talent whenever given the chance, that many years later he would *lose* that power and it would bring so many things circling back in toward the drain for both of them.

11

Sometimes things just get out hand, don't they?

Have you ever wondered just *how* you're supposed to act? I mean should you do everything that you can, hoping that if you do everything right then the Gods or God will smile down on you and give you what you want, or at least keep things from getting worse? Or should I just do whatever the hell I want cuz things are gonna happen as they happen anyway? That's a toughie, isn't it? Oh yea, baby, that's an E-Ticket question. By the way I know the answer to that question. The God or Gods question, I mean. Well come to think of it, I know the answer to the other questions as well. Sucks, doesn't it? But I gotta tell you this, even at this early stage of the game, stick with it. I'll be here with you. I will, and it will be good and it can be fine. Trust me, I'm here for you.

Oh, and we're still not done with this little two-parter. You know the one I mean right? The why and the what. We haven't left the classroom yet. We've gotten the why part out of the way. *Why* John was hesitant to ask, but now we should take a peek at the what. The *what* he was gonna ask. I hope you've fastened your seat-belt already, cuz this could get bumpy. Shit, it should get bumpy if I'm doing my job in any kind of fashion. And I promise you I am or my name isn't......ha, thought you had me there didn't you?

Now where were we? Oh yes, it's May and we're staying after school with John and Peachy...

12

John and Mrs. Abbott quietly resumed their after-school chores. John was feeling somewhat better but still felt shy about where this was going. He walked up to the chalkboard and began clapping the long, floppy rubber erasers together. He felt good enough to snort playfully at the chalk dust cloud he was raising. He thought maybe it would help clear the air. Ha, in more ways than one he thought.

Their minds had drawn back into themselves after their last exchange concerning the fight and respect and such, but now the glow opened up again. Their minds couldn't help but reach out to each other. Water seeking its way back in to where it should flow.

John was the first to reach out.

"Can I call you Peach, Mrs. Abbott?"

John sensed a hesitation in Mrs. Abbott which had never been there before. It wasn't as if their minds were *completely* open to one another, as John had just proved earlier when he had kept things blocked from Mrs. Abbott. But when they were "mind-talking", as John called it, there was usually never a lag. At least not coming from Mrs. Abbott. Quite often they seemed to be ahead of each other.

"For some reason I just thought I should ask", John added. "Oh, sorry Mrs. Abbott, you're not Peach are you? You're Peachy, right? I mean, your *real* name is Dianna, but they *call* you Peachy, right?"

Mrs. Abbott's face and mind darkened at the name Peach. She felt a firewall go up inside her. Or maybe it hadn't gone up at all, maybe it had come down a bit. As if it had been so thoroughly set in place that only by coming down a bit could it even be remembered as being there.

John sensed this too. This was new, he thought. It's like a big picture window that's very dirty. You can see that there is something on the other side of it, but you can only make out the shapes, not their meaning. Everything is all smeary and blurry behind it.

Their minds were running on high-test now and John could feel the struggle going on within Mrs. Abbott. He could feel the tension and sense that she was trying to come to terms with some sort of dilemma. Mrs. Abbott knew he felt it too and then she felt the flow, first from John toward her and then the even back and forth of their minds locking in together. In their minds' eyes John could see Mrs. Abbott grab a spray bottle and some newspaper and begin to wash the window clear.

Mrs. Abbott suddenly felt overwhelmed by emotion, as if she was falling back into a well that she had fallen into before. She was the one to hesitate this time and then she answered John's question.

"Yes, John, you can call me Peachy on the inside, with your mind, anytime you want, honey."

"Your mom called you that didn't she?" replied John.

"Oh yes, sweetie, she did."

John could see behind the picture-window at the exact moment that Mrs. Abbott had said Peachy. He could see a younger Mrs. Abbott rocking a little baby girl in her arms. They were together in some sort of a hospital room, in a wooden rocking chair draped with a brightly crocheted blanket, facing a dingy, chicken-wired window. Just like my mom knits, John thought. John knew that this was a place of nuns, and of help, and of pain too. The realizations were coming slower than was usual for him. One at a time, bit by bit, instead of the "all at once" he was used to.

"Peach is the little girl isn't she, Mrs. Abbott", John asked and knew.

"Yes she is, John."

"She's yours isn't she, she's your little girl, huh?"

"Yes my love, she's my little angel Peach."

John could see the baby's wispy red hair and feel the connection between mother and daughter. John also felt the sadness in the mother's heart. Then two nuns came into the room and told Mrs. Abbott that it was time and that this was for the best. John saw silent tears roll down Mrs. Abbott's face and he also saw the bright eyes of the child go from Mrs. Abbott's face to the face of the closer of the two nuns.

He saw something else, too. He saw the telltale, kaleidoscopic colors of a Helping begin to appear. John knew that Mrs. Abbott had then opened her mind fully and Helped her baby girl. He could see the loving Help flow from Mrs. Abbott into her child. The nun, Sister Mary John Ignatius, gently lifted the baby out of Mrs. Abbott's arms while Sister Angela Robert knelt down next to Mrs. Abbott and wrapped her in cloistered arms. John also saw something that he wasn't sure Mrs. Abbott could see. Little Peach was glowing. The little girl was pulsing a sweet white light as the nun took her from the room and her mother's arms.

"She's gone isn't she, Mrs. Abbott?" John asked.

"Not gone, honey, just gone from me," she answered. "Just gone from me."

"Does she have the gift, Mrs. Abbott?" asked John. "I think I saw the gift."

And then stars struck and scales were lifted and the blind saw. Mrs. Abbott did too. John hadn't even noticed the Helping he was now passing to Mrs. Abbott but she was blinded by it and then saw, and was amazed. It had snuck up on them both. A great big, Beverly Hillbillies, heapin', helpin' Helpin.

"My God, John, I think she does. She does have it," choked Mrs. Abbott. "She *is* one of us! Thank you, John, thank you so much!"

"You're welcome Mrs. Abbott,... Peachy," blushed John. "Remember I am Light and so are you," sent John, completing the mystical and spiritual transaction. "There is Light."

"The gift must have gotten passed along while I was Helping her," realized Mrs. Abbott. "*That* was the Helping! And I was so mad at God for letting this all happen. And then for not being able to Help Peach the way I thought it should be done. Why couldn't she stay with me, I wondered? But the Helping was called for, and happened. I knew it would help her future, at least, but I was still so mad at God."

"Uh-huh," said John, just to keep her going, and frankly because he didn't know what else to say. He was a kid.

"I feel so much lighter, John. I didn't even know how much of that load I was carrying. It feels so beautiful to be Helped. So beautiful."

John was then struck with the knowledge that this was only the beginning. He saw the circles and layers of life overlapping and knew that Mrs. Abbott and Peach were to overlap again. Mrs. Abbott saw this too. Not how, or when, or under what circumstances, but that it would be.

What Mrs. Abbott now knew, and John didn't, was that she wasn't the only one who would overlap with Peach. No, the layers of life often touched all involved in many different ways. Mrs. Abbott then saw a bit of John's future troubles and vague images of how paths would cross and a little of how all involved would be laid open to pain and possibilities. She also knew that John did not, and *should* not see this now.

"There's stuff here I can't see, Mrs. Abbott?" frowned John, a bit crestfallen. "Should I be seeing some stuff now?"

John looked sad and hopeful at the same time and Mrs. Abbott felt the Universe smiling yet again. Sometimes the old Universe piled it on just when it was needed and she felt the Light and the Peace and she did what was only right and true to do. She Helped John back.

"Thank you, John, for opening me up," she said and with that Mrs. Abbott opened all her Helping valves and pushed toward John's mind. "Thank you so much, my dear. Thanks to you I now know that my daughter is alive and well and someday our paths will cross in love. For that I am eternally grateful, John," thought Mrs. Abbott into the deepest recesses of John's mind. "I am Light, John. There is a Light and you are in it too," finished Mrs. Abbott. "You are Light too."

John then experienced what it was like to be on the receiving end of the flow. He felt the glow and the completeness of being the Helped instead of the Helper. He knew that Mrs. Abbott was happy and that he had Helped her and that now she had Helped him. He also sensed that he wasn't seeing the whole story but that that was OK and perfect as well. He watched himself glowingly vibrate and then watched as his memory of some of what had just happened was erased. "Just like what happens to them," he smiled. "Wow, this is so neat."

"You Helped *me*, Mrs. Abbott," John laughed. "Holy batshit, Robin! Oops, I mean holy cow, that was so cool."

"Yes I did, honey, and you Helped me too," smiled Mrs. Abbott. "And holy batshit is right!" she laughed.

With that the Helping was complete. Mrs. Abbott now knew about her daughter's place in the world and John now knew what was necessary and didn't know what wasn't. The circle was complete for the time being.

"If it's all the same to you, Mrs. Abbott, I'm not gonna call you Peachy," John said. "I like Mrs. Abbott just fine."

"Oh my, John," said Mrs. Abbott hugging John close, "you can call me anything but late for class," she choked, sharing her classes' private joke. "I like Mrs. Abbot just fine," she thought both to John and to herself. "I like Mrs. Abbott just fine now."

Here endeth the third grade.

13

No, I don't think we're going to have a Chapter thirteen. Let's pretend we're in an elevator and go right on to fourteen. Waddaya say?! Why? Why not. I'm not superstitious but you can never be too careful! Kind of like saying, "I've got confidence don't I?" So here we go, straight into Chapter fourteen... maybe.

Intermission

On second thought. Did you ever notice that smoke rises? Unless you're blind you must have. It may not have registered but I'm sure you get the general idea. Smoke becomes smoke in whatever process it's involved in to make it smoke and then it rises. Just like steam. Pure white, harmless, never hurt anybody in its freakin' life except maybe an unlucky pipe fitter, steam. Smoke however is dirty, noxious, harmful and generally a pain in the ass unless it's 1820 and you're sending smoke signals to your uncle One Less Toe over in the next village, but even that might be bad news for someone. Like an unsuspecting cavalry trooper or enemy tribe.

Smoke. It's dirty, it's second hand, it's generally a big deal for every groovy body these days. But even as dirty as it is, as useless as it is, it rises. Look over at that woman sucking down that ultra-light right now. See her? Sucking hard to filter that smoke through her own, never did anything to hurt her, lungs? Now watch...see her blowing that smoke out of her lipsticked, o-ring mouth? See that smoke curling up from the end of her lipstick-stained, ultra-long, ultra-light? It's rising isn't it? You're goddamned right it's rising, and that's a good thing. Even something as dirty and useless as smoke gets to rise. There's hope everywhere.

Steam gets to rise, smoke gets to rise. In spite of gravity, and life, and all the stupid chatter in your mind, and war in the middle east, it all gets to rise. We all get to rise. That's a good deal. Trust me.

And now it's time to see what's happening with old Dusty Hakilla. Remember him? Three parts Indian, one part Finn? Good guy, that Dusty. Couldn't buy a break with a million-dollar bill, but an all right guy for a smart aleck, I think.

14

Toivo "Dusty" Hakilla stayed in that school in Superior, Wisconsin, the one that he had just missed meeting John Sloan in, until junior high when he transferred back to Duluth. It really wasn't all that bad, well yes it probably was, but not on purpose. The teachers were well meaning but they just didn't get it. Educated hippies, really. It was pretty much like regular school. If you wanted to learn, or could be coaxed into it, it worked just fine. If you didn't, well then it didn't. Dusty *didn't,* but they let him slide. Not because he was special to them or a Helper. He just slid along with all the others who slid. The sliders from his class, the Indian kid's class, and from the regular, mostly white, classes. That's what sliders do, they slide.

The teachers were only human and after being rebuffed enough times they left him alone. Dusty did enjoy reading however, and with his face buried in a book he was less likely to cause trouble, so reading was encouraged.

By the time Dusty entered junior high back in Duluth he was with a foster family. A pretty good one as foster families went. Only three other kids. The two girls, Tina and Terry, (Oh God, please fucking spare me) belonged to the parents and the other boy, Luke, was a foster kid just like Dusty. And Indian just like Dusty. Well not exactly like Dusty. He was two years older and a full blooded Lakota, if you could believe him, and he never let Dusty forget it. So there wasn't much bonding going on there, Lakotas and Ojibwa having feuded for hundreds of years. Especially after the Ojibwe had ran them out of Wisconsin and most of Minnesota. Luke was just doing his time until he reached eighteen and then he was headed back to South Dakota to become a medicine man or a Spirit Walker or some other kind of nonsense that Dusty couldn't quite figure out.

The father, Jim, worked on the railroad. He was silent, often stern, but not abusive. Jim was just doing his time too. He liked to be left alone, so he was. The mother, Goldie, was a chirpy, overweight, born-again Christian. Shallow as the day is long. Everyone could be saved through enough prayer, enough Jesus, and enough eating.

Her one true redeeming value, in Dusty's eyes, were her breasts. They were amazing things. Goldie was maybe five-feet four. Her hips were broad, her waist was thick, but you could still be amazed by her huge tits. Dusty thought they were amazing anyway. He had snuck into her bedroom one day and poked through her bra drawer just to see what size they actually were. Fifty-five EE. Holy balls thought Dusty. Holy balls! No wonder they're so big. Fifty-five EE. Wow. And Goldie had these huge nipples. At thirteen Dusty was a big fan of nipples. Even when Goldie pulled a bulky sweater tight over those beauties you could not only see her nipples pushing the sweater way out but you could see her areolas too. And she had to push through one of those medieval, white, enough-fabric-to-build-a-garage bras too, and she still did it.

Dusty had learned how to masturbate after catching Luke in the act in their shared bedroom one day, and after his experience with Goldie's bra, Dusty masturbated every chance he got. Once even with the bra, but that kind of freaked him out so he just fantasized about Goldie's tits after that. And just because she was Christian and not very bright and almost as interested in Twinkies as she was in her Lord and Savior Jesus Christ don't think she didn't know how her puppies, her phrase for her gravity defying twin towers, affected Dusty. She did. She secretly got an innocent little thrill out of it. Occasionally she'd let him catch a peek as she raced bouncily from bathroom to bedroom, wearing only a towel if they were the only two at home.

She would make sure that he was sitting in the living room watching the TV, which also gave him a line of sight to the hallway where both the bathroom and her bedroom were. She would flop out from the end of the hall bathroom door, *past* her bedroom door and stop at the entrance to the living room where Dusty sat, already erect, watching the tube.

"Oops, I did it *again,* Dusty," she would peep. "I forgot my robe." And she would watch him watch her. His eyes pouring over the postage stamp towel, overworked in its attempt to cover her ample bodies' naughty bits. She would watch for just a moment and then she'd spin and head to her bedroom. The nice thing for Dusty being that, because of the size of those tits she would be turning, it would take a second or two for her tits to catch up with her. So he could give them his complete attention with having to worry about her catching him. And the thing was she really didn't altogether get it. She was a forty-four-year-old woman, who, although she couldn't have done a pull-up to save her life, could have done nipple-ups that would have raised her an inch and a half off the floor till the cows came home, prancing around wearing only a short towel in front of her barely teenaged foster son. Whew! A towel that, because it could barely contain her barnyard appendages, could also barely contain the forest-like patch of hair between her legs. Dusty got a kick out of the patch too, but he had to admit he was a bigger fan of those tits and especially those hypnotizing nipples. After one of her little mistakes he would try to sneak off to his room and choke the chicken. And, swear to God, I don't think she knew what he was doing in there. If she would've walked in on him after one of those episodes she would have been horrified. Like I said, she just didn't completely get it.

The funny thing about it? Or maybe the sad thing, depending on how you look at it. Tina and Terry couldn't fill a B-cup between them to save their lives. Their fronts were like backs...with nipples...maybe. Dusty didn't know for sure and he wasn't interested enough to find out. To say that those poor unfortunate girls were plain was like saying people in Wisconsin kind of liked the Green Bay Packers. They were plain-plus. No, Dusty thought, he'd give his two foster sisters a pass in that area. Even if they were two and three years older than him respectively. For all his Spirit Dancer rap, Luke was sure pretty interested in their shower habits, but old Dusty would just have to give this one a pass.

At least Tina, the younger of the two, could occasionally seem alive. Terry seemed to pass through life as if it, and she, didn't exist. Tina surfaced once in a while just to check in with other humans before descending back into whatever part of her mind she lived in.

One day the whole family was eating supper. Swiss steak and gravy over riced potatoes with canned green beans. Lots of gravy and lots of taters. Very good, Dusty thought. The sisters were bugging their mom about her real name. This is new, he thought. Isn't Goldie a real name?

"C'mon, mom. Tell Luke and Dusty your real name," teased Tina.

"Yea, mom. Tell em," was all Terry could toss in.

"Yea, mom. You wouldn't want to be a liar, would you?" piped Tina.

Not bad, thought Dusty, now a bit interested. Semi OK leverage there, Tina.

Goldie, being the true disciple of the washed blood of the Lamb that she was, finally relented. Maybe she *was* lying to the boys and that would be sinful. She looked at Jim but received no response. His mouth was full of Swiss steak, and his nose was buried in a copy of the minutes from last week's union meeting of the Locomotive Engineers Local 106. "They had better fight for our rights," he was often heard to mutter, " because the Good Lord knows that the railroad won't."

With a blushing look Goldie was prepared to be true to her Lord.

"It's Turleen. My real name is Turleen. Turleen Danbury. Well, Turleen Rayburn now," she sputtered. And she actually did sputter. Old Turleen just loved her Swiss steak gravy.

"Yea, mom. Turleen. Kind'a like a soup turleen," Tina laughed.

"Now you shouldn't tease, Tina," responded Goldie. Not much of a defense there Turleen, thought Dusty.

"Ha, ha Tina. So funny I almost forgot to open my mouth and hoot," tossed in Luke out of nowhere.

Dusty wondered who wound him up. Nice vague owl reference there Chief fucking Spirit of the Mountain. Wouldn't Tina let you fantasize about her last night when you thought I was asleep? Did she sneak into your head and not even let you think about her when she wasn't there? And as long as we're on the subject, could you keep it down just a bit there young Brave With His Hand On His Crank? It's hard for me to sleep with you rockin' into the night in the bed right next to me. Your sheets must be pitiful! Luke had really been getting on Dusty's nerves lately.

Actually, Dusty had to admit that the soup turleen crack wasn't half bad. Especially for Tina. He caught her eyes and mouthed, "good one, Tina." Tina made a snotty face at him, gave her mom a "gotcha that time, mom" semi-sneer, and slipped back beneath the surface. On second thought, forget it Tina. So much for bonding with your family.

Goldie blushed, but being a female stretcher bearer in Christ's Onward Christian army, she soldiered on.

"Hey," Jim piped in, hating to be taken away from his union notes, "knock it off, children. Please."

Jim always added please as if that made him a saint. "See Goldie, I'm Christian. I asked them please after just telling them to eat this here tasty shit sandwich." Jim knew which side his wonder bread was buttered on. And Jim always called them children. Still. Shit, Tina was almost sixteen. Kids would've been better. Brats even. How about *you guys*? Nope, he still called them children. Jim didn't get it either.

All in all, not too bad though. Dusty liked his new home. He didn't have to worry about some whacked-on-speed, merchant marine trying to grope him in the communal bathroom of some flop hotel. Or watch two sadly stooped and drunken, middle aged Indian woman punch each others' teeth out till one of them remembered through the haze that "hey, isn't there a goddam knife around here somewhere?" And the fight being about the above mentioned speed freak sailor. Fuckin' tragic.

Nope, not too bad at all. He ate three times a day, no one hit him, there wasn't much yelling, and there were Goldie's tits. Her glorious, Holy Christ look at those tits, tits. No, life was as close to good as Dusty had ever had it. But even into every marginally sunny life some rain must fall. Sometimes it rains cats and dogs. Sometimes it rains Uncle Lou's. But life was good for awhile.

15

Dusty was fifteen years old before he met another Helper. It happened three days after Dusty had Helped someone. And a month *before* uncle Lou had moved in. When it rains it fucking pours.

Dusty had had a dry spell. He hadn't Helped anyone since moving in with the Rayburns until, boom, there it was again. He was beginning to wonder where it had gone. His Helping. His only special talent. He had to concede that it could be a kick. Even better than the blotter acid he had tried when he was fourteen. Way better really. You just couldn't *count* on it. Who knew when it would happen next?

And you'll never guess who he Helped. Guess? No way. He got a chance to help "Chief Dan I'm Seventeen, but You're Only Fifteen, So Get Out Of My Way." Yep, he Helped Luke and then three days later he met Franklin and then uncle Lou had moved into the Rayburn's house and it had all gone to hell.

Luke and Dusty had reached a silent truce. Dusty left Luke alone and Luke didn't pick on Dusty too much. He didn't dare. Dusty had squared Luke away two years ago when they had first met. They had been talking that first night in their shared bedroom. Luke had already been there for three months so he thought he had better straighten out this little blanket-ass Finlander who was horning in on his territory. In reality Dusty wasn't so little. He had had a growth spurt in the last semester before turning thirteen and moving in with the Rayburns, and now he found himself almost as tall as this stranger Luke who was five-foot ten and fifteen years old.

"You ain't no fuckin' Native American," Luke had said. "Toivo Hakilla? There ain't no Finlanders in South Dakota but I can sure smell a sauna when I see one. They may call you Dusty cuz of your dark skin but that ain't Indian skin. That's fuckin some kind of reindeer Finland shit on you is all, hey!"

Dusty had burned deep red. He was darker than Luke and knew that that must piss the guy off. Dusty was young but when he burned red on the inside people noticed. Some back part of Dusty's mind also noticed that although Luke wasn't from northern Wisconsin he sure picked up quickly on the derogatory slang for Finns. Finlander. It wasn't quite like nigger. It was more like polack. People used it all the time but not in mixed company. And Finlanders said it all the time, to each other and with people who weren't Finn. They took a certain pride in it but didn't like to be called it by a non-Finn.

"I am Lakota," hissed Luke. "Grandson of Gray Hair and nephew to She Wolf. And when I'm eighteen I'll get outah here and go back to Pine Ridge and learn the Medicine."

Oh this is just fucking great, thought Dusty. Just fucking great. Dusty registered that Luke hadn't mentioned any son-of's or much of anythings when reciting his lineage. Pretty spotty there, Lone Ranger.

"How 'bout a little First Nation pride there, Grey Snot?" said Dusty. "Or haven't you heard that phrase yet? Even Native American ain't cutting it anymore, it's First Nation, baby. Indigenous! We're in the same boat here so let's just get along, *HEY*." Dusty emphasized the hey at the end of the sentence to let Luke know not to try to out Indian him, hey. Indians, and some white up-northers, had the habit of ending their sentences with the word *hey*. Kind of like Canadians using 'eh.

This stumped Luke who hadn't heard those phrases yet. First Nation? Indigenous?

"I come from a Rez just like you and chances are if you ain't a true orphan you're a booze orphan just like me so back the fuck off," said Dusty.

Then Luke did something that was just as embarrassing to Dusty to this day as it was then. He slapped Dusty. Right across his cheek. It wasn't a girl slap, or even a sissy slap, but it sure as hell wasn't a man slap. It was only a scared teenaged boy slap. Luke had meant to slap him down and humiliate him as only a slap can do, but Dusty was way past that and it only scared Luke more. He saw that Dusty could have hurt him bad. He saw it in Dusty's eyes. Dusty's medicine, like it or not, was in a whole 'nother league. And Dusty was suddenly sad. Terminally sad. He just stared Luke down and watched him melt. He knew Luke's story then. He didn't know it because he was a Helper, he just knew it because he knew it and he felt sorry for Luke. He still didn't want this dickhead to mess with him, but he saw it all. Luke scared and alone as a young boy. Not sheltered really, just forgotten and alone and shuffled around. Dusty was doing for Luke what Luke should have been doing for Dusty. Their roles were reversed and that made Dusty sad. He's supposed to be the older guy helping me.

Luke didn't cry, which Dusty was grateful for, but he did shrink in on himself. He folded right up. Right in front of Dusty's eyes. Luke knew that Dusty could've owned him in a fight. Owned him. And he knew that Dusty knew he knew. Man, this is too sad, Dusty thought. Dusty also knew that Luke had to save face now, so he let him.

"All right, man, truce," Dusty said. "You don't mess with me and I'll stay out of your way. I ain't expecting anything out of this anyway." And Dusty had let his eyes drop first. "OK?" he asked, giving Luke the chance to have the final say.

"All right," Luke said pausing, " OK. But you just stay out of my way."

Dusty let him slide on that last one. He knew Luke needed it to get this thing moving on. Luke puffed back up a bit but Dusty knew it was a dwelling built on shifting sand. No foundation there, no nothing. Just more of the same shit Dusty was all too familiar with.

Luke would still pipe off to Dusty, from time to time, about Dusty not being a true Indian or about how Luke was going to become a Pipe Carrier and a Medicine Man. Dusty let him. There was a truce. Literally. And Dusty wasn't bothered by that shit now anyway after having seen Luke disintegrate. So who would've thought that Luke would be the next person that Dusty Helped?

One afternoon the social worker was waiting in the Rayburn's living room when Dusty got home from school. Goldie was there nervously wringing her hands and trying to serve the woman tea. No one else was home and Dusty could smell soup cooking in the kitchen. Oh, yea, must be Monday, he thought. Goldie's soup was legendary. She was not only a fantastic "meat and potatoes cook", but her soups were even better. As much a meal as any *meals* she ever prepared. And Dusty loved eating. He loved meals, as only one who has spent a good deal of time not getting any can. Dusty would forever associate what was to happen with the smell of soup. Funny how those little unrelated things become tied in with memorable events.

"Dusty, have you seen Luke? Is he almost home from school?" Goldie asked.

Good, it's not about me, Dusty thought. "Yea, he was about a block or two behind me. He should be home right away," Dusty replied.

"Thank you, Dusty. You should probably go to your room and do some studying for a little while, OK?"

"Oh, you remember Miss Schneff from social services don't you," Goldie said, almost forgetting her guest.

"Sure. Hi, Miss Schneff," Dusty said.

"Hi, Dusty. Everything going well here at the Rayburn's?"

"Oh yea, I like it here. But I should really be getting to my studies," Dusty said, laying it on a little thick, but then they didn't seem to be noticing.

"OK, Dusty, I'll see you in my office next month, alright?"

"You bet, Miss Schneff, see you next month," and with that Dusty high-tailed it to his room. Something big going on here, he thought. And with that the glow started. The Helping glow. Powerful. As powerful as it had ever been. A Helping was coming on and, even being the smart-ass that he was, Dusty opened himself to it with anticipation. His room was full of light and suddenly he was in the living room staring down from the ceiling. He knew his body was still in his bedroom, but he and his Helping were hovering somewhere near the corner of the Rayburn's living room. Oh, let it flow, he thought. He saw Luke coming up the front steps and felt his mind reach out to Luke's. Cold in there, Dusty thought. Lonely too. Dusty's mind was also reaching out to Miss Schneff's and to Goldie's as well. "Hmmmm, Miss Schneff's first name is Charlene", he thought and the fifteen-year-old part of Dusty, tucked in the background of the Helping nirvana, quipped, " that maybe her folks named her after Charlie Chaplin. The mustache is similar. Me and Ralph Malph, we still got it," he thought. "I'm in the middle of the white light of paradise and I still got it." he thought, smart ass that he was. "Now I wonder who I'm gonna Help here?"

Luke entered the living room and saw Mrs. Schneff and Goldie looking up at him from where they were sitting on Goldie's horrid sofa. Plaid green, with a raised flower print. Enough said, you get the idea. Ugly sofa that was.

"Luke, come over here and sit down, honey," said Goldie pointing to the wooden rocking chair that had been pulled over from it's corner and was now facing the two women. "Mrs. Schneff has to talk to you," Goldie said motioning Luke to the rocker. "And I'll be right here too, Luke. I'll be right here for you."

Oh great, thought Dusty. Really breaking it to him gently.

There's a letter Dusty knew. With a picture and a bracelet and then it all broke out at once for Dusty. He saw them down there talking to each other but he didn't hear them. He didn't need to. His grandmother is dead, Dusty knew now. Gray Hair is dead and she was the *only* one left. Every other Rez family had fifteen, mother-lovin', black haired kids and Luke's only got Gray Hair and she's dead. Luke was now the end of the line. Shit, it wasn't even his *grandfather* he was reciting for me when we first met. It was his grandmother and his aunt She Wolf who's long gone now.

And Dusty saw it and felt it as he and the Light crawled into Luke's mind. Like an astronaut's face-plate breaking during a space walk. The vacuum in Luke's mind was sucking him in. A great implosion was happening to what little was left of Luke's broken spirit. Luke was about to be fucking *gone*!

From his mind's perch on the ceiling, Dusty could see Luke looking down and nodding silently while the two women, Miss Schneff mostly, told of receiving the letter of his grandmother's death from the Indian Agent in South Dakota. Fuck, they couldn't even tell him right away. She had been dead for over two months before the agent bothered to mail the letter and the bracelet Gray Hair had clutched in her hand as she lay dying, pleading with the nurse to make sure her grandson Luke got the bracelet. "Please, please, she begged, get this bracelet and picture to him. Promise me you will." The hospice nurse had said yes, she would make sure that her grandson got it. And thank God for that black nurse, who was just as suspicious about the white agent as the Indians. She had to hound the agent every week for two months before he finally got off his government ass and mailed what remained of Molly "Gray Hair" Smith to Luke.

The fifteen-year-old Dusty, that was tucked back in his own mind's corner, made a note that if he ever saw that agent he would mess him up. He might even make a point of it. Christ, talk about insult to injury. Not even a chance to go to the fucking funeral, what with Grandma dead over two months. Bad fucking break there, Dusty thought.

Luke wasn't crying. He was just sitting there, with his head hung and his long black hair hanging down both sides of his face, staring at the carpet. Spent. Resigned. Resolved to something. Resolved to a *bad* something.

Finally Goldie was escorting Miss Schneff, old whisker lip, to the front door. Luke stood up and said to no one in particular," I'll be going to my room now." Goldie looked back with a worried look on her face registering the tone of Luke's voice. Or the utter *lack* of tone in Luke's voice.

"Uh-oh, you better be worried, Goldie," Dusty thought, seeing more of Luke's future. "I didn't know just how close to the edge this fucker was!"

Luke walked down the hall toward the room he shared with Dusty and just as his hand was turning the doorknob Dusty was sucked back into the room and sucked back into his body. The Light was so pure now, and so strong, that Dusty thought he might lose control, but with that concern he saw it harness itself. He felt like he was riding the Light. Like a body surfer just riding along for the rush but he also knew that it couldn't be done without him. It wasn't *him* doing it but it also couldn't be done *without* him.

Luke walked into the room and stared right through Dusty. He was dead already.

Unbeknownst to all, Luke had been secretly squirreling away rat poison that he had been stealing from the hardware store. Didn't know why. He just had been stealing it. Bit by bit and box by box. He kept it wrapped in a towel covered shoebox that he hid in the rafters at the far end corner of the basement.

"This was Monday," the dim recesses of Luke's mind realized, and that meant soup night at the Rayburn's. Goldie would take all of the weekend's leftovers and simmer them all day and tonight was homemade turkey soup with rice and tomatoes. "Goldie could make some soup. But guess what, kids? Tonight was gonna be a special blend of turkey soup. Put *that* in your soup tureen, Turleen," Luke cackled to himself. Luke was gonna burn it all down with the rat poison he had squirreled away, if you'll pardon the mixed metaphor. Burn it *right* the *fuck* down!

He was gonna slip all of that poison into the soup and then, Dusty now saw too, he was gonna wait for the whole family to die, Jim, Goldie, the two T's, and Dusty, and then lay them all out on the living room floor. "Slurp up, children," Luke muttered. "Slurp up some nice death broth."

He was going to go to the bottom drawer in the pantry and find that old wooden-handled ice pick and jab it down into their eyes, pop them out like olives, and, when he had all of their eyes out, he was going to eat them. "Jesus, could you be anymore disgusting?" Dusty wondered.

Dusty was pure light but he still noted what was going to happen in a removed way. He's all the way gone, Dusty knew. Someone turned out the lights and forgot to tell Luke's body, so it's still moving around.

Dusty had Helped people before, but he had never felt it *this* bad. Or maybe it was because he, Dusty, was coming this close to being part of the *this bad*. "Shit, that soup is meant for me too. I could eat some of it too!"

In spite of it all Dusty grooved. "You gonna stand there and tell me there's no *Heaven* when I'm feeling this?" he thought.

Dusty knew Luke wasn't just gonna have an eyeball appetizer with his supper. No way, he was gonna chow down, and then use the ice pick to scalp them all. A pretty tough job too, seeing as how an ice pick sure ain't no knife. At least he isn't going to lick our scalps Dusty thought for some unknown reason. That would be gross. Nope, but he *was* going to take his clothes off, (why do they always take off their clothes?), and paint his body with their blood. After that it was a simple decision. Cut his throat and call the police or just call the police. What was left of Luke's mind, and believe me what little was left was all insane, was leaning toward waiting until the cops were inside and had seen what he had done before slitting his own throat.

Dusty looked Luke in the eyes and some wisp of something flickered there when he saw Dusty. Dusty did the deal. He said Luke's name, in this case Luke's real name.

"Spotted Deer," Dusty said. "Luke Spotted Deer Smith." The light was everywhere now. It was pouring out of and through everything including Luke's and Dusty's bodies. Blowing through them like it was a gale force wind, without the wind. But it was moving, man.

"I am Toivo Dusty Hakilla," Dusty said, "Grandson of Light Heart, Son of Earl Hakilla. But my real name is Light. I am Light. There is a Light and you are Light too. We are brothers." Dusty finished. And just like that, Luke saw the face of God and was changed. Dusty felt him power back up immediately. He felt Luke's mind inside his and his mind inside Luke's and it was good. Shit, it was GOOD!

Luke's new future appeared in Dusty's mind and since it was Luke, and he wouldn't remember much of this anyhow, Dusty shot the breeze with him.

"You almost bought it there, Luke," Dusty said.

"I know. Thank you, Dusty," Luke replied. "Thank you so much. We are brothers, we're all brothers."

"Take it easy there, Kumbaya man. I have it on good authority that you *will* be a Medicine man, but let's not get too huggy-wuggy here, OK? Save it for all those white guys you'll sweat out in your lodge at fifty bucks a donation. And in spite of all the time you spend wacking off to thoughts of Tina's nonexistent tits, you're bisexual, but don't sweat it. You'll learn karate and it won't bother you a bit. Really. Oh and guess what? It gets better and better. You're gonna learn to play the flute. Not marching band flute, you goof, Native American flute. Those wooden, hollowed out, things. And you're gonna make records and be famous as fucking hell and spread Indian love all over the place. No shit, you'll be a regular Yanni, whoever the fuck that is, but take it from me you'll be big, like some Yanni guy, and he's gonna be big too."

Luke stood and stared into Dusty's eyes and became a human being. A human being with hope.

"And you know what?" Dusty said. "I'm happy for you. I am. You will be allowed to remember whatever the Light figures you ought to remember and nothing else. That will be enough. Shake my hand, you are my brother."

Luke grabbed Dusty and hugged him. Hugged him like he could squeeze Dusty into his body and they *were* brothers and it was good. Hell, it was even better than good. It was Light.

Luke wouldn't even have to wait until he was eighteen to head back to South Dakota. His aunt Shirley She-Wolf Johnson popped back on the radar screen a month later and took him home to Pine Ridge. Just like that.

He got out just in time too because uncle Lou moved in shortly after and tore everything up. But that will have to wait a bit because just three days after helping Luke, Dusty met the coolest black man he had ever met. Hell, Franklin was the only black man Dusty had ever really met. He had seen black folks before. They lived in Duluth too, and he had chummed briefly with a black kid in school in Superior, but he had never really met a black man. Three days later he met Franklin Rose. And Franklin was a Helper.

16

On Thursday Dusty showed up for third period history class, which was not something he always did. It was three days after Helping Luke and he still had a little Helping buzz going on. He had to admit to himself that he had been a little worried about not having Helped anyone in sometime and then he winds up Helping Luke. Who'da thought? It was pretty funny when you think of it. Course it would've been real UN-funny had Luke not been Helped, but give me a break. The flute? Both kinds of flute when you think about it. Oh, that was just too much.

Things had been good at home. Luke hadn't remembered too much about what happened but he wasn't the big pain in the ass he'd been before either. He'd even offered to let Dusty ride along with him and his friends when they picked him up in their car for school that morning. Dusty had said thanks, but no thanks. He wanted to walk and think about what happened. And be late, of course.

As a kind of thank you note to this whole thing Goldie had decided to take a shower that morning after everyone else had left. Sometimes the universe just smiled on you. Dusty had been lingering around waiting for everyone else to leave so he could purposely walk to school late and miss the first hour or so. Yep, Goldie had given the old show again this morning. This time, when she paused to gauge his reaction at seeing her wet in only a towel, she had started talking to him a bit. No big stuff, just how's school going, and have you been being nice to Luke and stuff like that. "Jesus she's gotta know I like staring at her tits", Dusty thought. "That's OK with me if she does, cuz I like 'em!" Then after talking with Dusty for a minute or two she seemed to realize that she was barely covered and talking to a fifteen-year-old boy and she got flustered and just as she was turning to head back to her room she dropped the towel. "Wow!" Dusty thought. "I mean fucking, Wow!" He saw the whole thing. All the whole things. Her tits were even better than he thought and being cold after getting out of the shower had those nipples sticking out about two inches. "Holy Christ," thought Dusty. "Jesus!" And there was her thick black bush as well! It's growing up her stomach and onto her thighs too. "YES! Must be dying that thick head of blonde hair, 'eh Goldie? Cuz it's pretty dark downstairs." When she bent over to pick up the towel, Dusty almost had an accident. Almost shot a white little toxic spill into his drawers. He saw her tits from the side and her fertile-valleyed garden from the back. "Man, oh fucking man, but sometimes things are good," Dusty thought.

So Dusty was even a little later to school than he had planned to be that morning. He had made straight for the confines of his bedroom and treated himself to the view again and again. Years later he would still prefer abundantly breasted and abundantly hairy women and he knew why. Some picture postcards stay with us forever.

Dusty bopped on into history class with a spring in his step. He didn't even notice that there was a sub that day.

"There a reason you're late today, son?" the substitute asked.

"Oh yea, I stopped at the office. Here's my note," Dusty told the sparse, middle-aged, balding, black man at the teachers' desk in front, as he pulled the crumpled, already forgotten, note out of his pocket and walked it on up.

"Hope you had a good reason," the man said with a sly smile. A smirk really. "I'm Mr. Rose. Mr. Franklin Rose and I'll be filling in for Mr. Templeton for the next couple of days. Go ahead and find your seat and we'll get back to the subject at hand. Which *today* is history."

Oh great, a comedian thought Dusty, but there was something about this guy that tugged at Dusty's mind. He handed him the note and found his seat and settled in for the rest of the non-eventful class. As class ended, Mr. Rose called for Dusty to stay.

"Could you stay for a minute after class, Mr. Hakilla?" Mr. Rose said as the bell rang.

"Sure thing," Dusty answered and waited for the class to empty.

Something's going on here. It feels kind of familiar.

"Hakilla. That isn't Ojibwe is it, Dusty?" Mr. Rose asked, seeming to know the answer already.

"No. My dad was half Finn, but I am three quarters Ojibwe," Dusty replied. Dusty was opening up a bit here. Almost like when a Helping was coming on. He felt it. Then Mr. Rose shot out a question, but in his mind not with his mouth.

"I always liked big titted women too," he thought toward Dusty. "Ha, ha, and a big hairy bush is most welcomed also," he continued. Jesus, what's going on here Dusty thought and then Mr. Rose opened the curtain in his mind and he knew.

"Fuck, you're a Helper too aren't you, Mr. Rose?"

"That I am, boy, that I am. Sorry for funnen' with you there but sometimes I like to make it interesting," Mr. Rose thought. "Your first time? Not seeing Goldie naked," Mr. Rose laughed already knowing the answer, "but first time meeting another Helper?"

"Yea, it is Mr. Rose," Dusty sent back. And then he rocked back, and almost fell into a chair. Emotions that he didn't know he had felt his whole life flooded through him. About how he was different from other people in so many ways. How he was separate from everyone else. And now, suddenly, he wasn't *as* apart from them—at least not from *all* of them. He almost cried.

Mr. Rose gave Dusty time to settle down. He watched the boy and searched his mind, feeling what Dusty was feeling. And remembering.

"It's kind of scary, isn't it? The first time, I mean. And when we're alone you can call me Franklin."

"Just a little bit," Dusty said, slowly coming back to his senses. "I thought something was crawlin' around inside my head for a second but then I felt the feeling and then I just wondered what the heck was goin on."

"Yep, me too," Franklin continued. "I was a little older too, when I met my first helper. Fifteen, same as you. Like to scare me out of my britches that first time. Was a white man. Hightower Calhoun was his name. What a name, hey? Hightower Calhoun," Franklin sent out, shaking his head a little. "In Knoxville, Tennessee of all places. But he was a good man. Still is. Talked to him last year. We still keep in touch on the phone. He's getting' plenty old now but we still get that good vibration goin' over the phone. You know what I mean? That good vibration?"

"Not really, no. I'm not sure *what* you mean," Dusty thought.

"Well then look around you boy," Franklin said with a chuckle. "Look around you."

Dusty looked around him and he saw it then. "Like a kaleidoscope isn't it?" Dusty confirmed. "Wow." The light was completely filling the room. It was even streaming out all of the windows. And it was coming from their bodies, mostly out of their eyes and their chests. And the feeling. Oh, the feeling was magical.

"Yea, very cool. Very cool," Franklin said and then he just let Dusty wade in the light for a few minutes. "Just let it flow son. Let it flow and enjoy it."

Dusty did too. He even closed his eyes and found that even with his eyes closed he still could see the room and the light AND see into Franklin's mind at the same time.

"Feels just like a Helping, doesn't it Dusty?"

"Sure does, Franklin. Hey, they used to call you Lynn when you were a boy, didn't they? Cuz your name is Frank-Lin, huh?" asked

Dusty seeing more of Franklin's past. "And you liked it when family said it but you hated it when others called you that didn't you?"

"That's right, Dusty. Still not too partial to it. Hite calls me it though," Franklin said.

"Hite is that Hightower guy, isn't he?" continued Dusty. "Wow, I can see some of his stuff too. This is very cool."

"Yes, I kind of think of it as a freebie. Sometimes the Light just figures that we need to bump into each other to know everything is cool and that we're not so alone. Hell, maybe it even charges our batteries a bit," Franklin sent. "Either way it's alright with me. I just enjoy it and count it as a blessing."

'You ready for a little more?" Franklin asked.

"Yea, bring it on," said Dusty.

Franklin opened up his mind completely and Dusty got the whole picture while at the same time Franklin cruised through Dusty's past. Dusty did get it all too. The good and the bad. The Light and the colors were still there and the great feeling was still there even while he experienced some of the very bad things that had happened to Franklin. "The south sucked for a black guy, didn't it Franklin?" Dusty said.

"Yes it did, Dusty, and it still can too. I don't know how people who don't have the gift made it through. I barely made it through *having* the gift," Franklin replied.

"Jeez, and the north wasn't much better," Dusty said seeing more.

"No, but we do what we do, where we do it, with what we have to do it with, don't we boy?" said Franklin getting a full taste of Dusty's past as well. Seeing some of the shit that *he* had already had to put up with in his young life.

"That's a mouthful!" Dusty laughed, thinking about the *what we do, where we do it* thing that Franklin had just put out.

"Shee-it, Goldie now *she's* the mouthful...for a crocodile! See you Helped out old Luke, though. That was a good thing, Dusty. Christ," Franklin continued laughing, "he's even gonna kinda look like that Yanni dude. Whoever the hell he is," Franklin said and they both dissolved into laughter. "Shit, I got to sit down," Franklin said shaking with laughter, "I might just pee my pants and I ain't done that since I was knee high to you. Damn that boy's gonna play that flute... in more ways than one too. And Goldie? The woman's got tits like overloaded ICBM missiles. And I got an ICBM for her too. A big, black, lookin for home, missile. Shoot, Dusty, I'd be taking care of myself ten times a day too with her around. I gots to have a little parent teacher conference with that woman," Franklin continued slipping into a southern dialect that they both knew he was *over-doing* just to be playful and for the sheer fun of it.

"Teach that woman a little something she sure ain't gettin' from old Jim. Damn boy, if my dick was as big as that woman's tits I'd need to get my trousers lengthened," Franklin said, both of them loving that it was getting out of hand, "like Wilt the Stilt and Kareem Abdul Jabbar put together. I'd be the first black pole-vaulter American ever seen and I betcha old Goldie might even volunteer to be the pit. Oh, I just bet she might like that just fine," he smiled, the conversation bouncing from mind to mind.

Beautiful. It was beautiful. And they both sat there enjoying it for the next few minutes. Every so often one or the other would see something funny in the others mind and take off on it and they would break into uncontrollable laughter again.

"Shoot, I'm glad there ain't a class this period. Folks coming in would think we was crazy," Franklin said puffing his eyes out and making a face at Dusty. "But boy it sure is good to laugh isn't it, Dusty? Sure is good to laugh."

Things settled down after awhile and after a fashion.

"I know you aren't going to your next class but you should still clear out of here Dusty," Franklin said this time out loud. "I've got some work to do and I sure won't get it done with you around. I'll be here for the next couple of days. Let's you and me check in with each other. See if we can't charge up the old batteries. Shoot, you're gonna need it living with that Goldie woman!"

"OK, see you tomorrow, Mr. Rose. Man it was good meeting you," Dusty said heading toward the door.

"You too, Dusty. See you mañana."

Dusty headed out the door and left Mr. Rose, still shaking his head and laughing to himself. Life wasn't half bad for Dusty that day. He kept that spring in his step and went to the rest of his classes, even raised his hand a couple of times and joined in.

Franklin Rose continued gathering his papers and reflecting on Dusty. The Light had left but the glow still lingered. He started to see some of Dusty's future and that took a little of the glow off. He knew Dusty had some choices to make. Some would have to be made in the near future. He couldn't see how they would play out either. That wasn't part of the gift. At least not today. Little damn Indian Finlander had a whole chunk of life to chew on coming up. Franklin didn't envy him in the least. He saw some very rough times ahead for the boy. He saw war, he saw death, he even saw John Sloan after a bit, and he saw someone called uncle Lou. That's the boy's next hurdle, he thought. That's a maker or breaker right there.

What he couldn't see was how it would all work out. Have to make sure I leave that boy a forwarding address. He may need a little help and maybe I can give it.

But, all in all a pretty good day for the both of them.

17

Franklin was indeed there the next day and asked Dusty to stay after class again. Dusty usually blew off the entire school day on Fridays but no way he was gonna miss class today. Uh-uh, no way. Too cool for this fool to miss.

"Like to see something interesting?" Franklin asked out loud after the classroom had finally emptied.

"Sure thing," Dusty replied, already seeing and feeling the buzz and the swirling colors and the light building between them.

"OK, cool fool, hang on to your britches," Franklin laughed out loud. "Do you like being a Helper?" Franklin asked out loud and at the same time his mind asked, " and did you get a chance to check out Goldie's beautiful hanging mud pups for me this morning?" he finished.

"Wow, fucking cool!" Dusty responded automatically, both out loud and with his mind. "Both at the same time! I can hear you talking out loud and feel you asking something else in my head. That's a mind blower."

"Yep, it'll blow your mind, won't it?" Franklin added. "We were doing some yesterday but you had so much goin' on that you didn't even notice it and I didn't mention it. No big deal really, almost a parlor trick, but it feels neat the first time doesn't it?"

"Yes it does," Dusty spoke, "and yes I did," he said simultaneously with his mind. Meaning yes it does feel neat and yes he *had* checked out Goldie's tits that morning and he sent an image of the love globes toward Franklin.

Franklin was laughing hard now, "Oh, there's my girl. Dusty you're all right, you know that? Having all that for yourself and still sharing it with old Franklin. You all right boy."

"No problem, Franklin. Just remember she's mine and that means I got first dibs."

"Like you ever gonna get a real taste of that sweet white stuff, boy. Like you even got a chance with old Miss Goldie," Franklin joshed right back. "Dream on, cool fool."

Things settled back down and they volleyed thoughts and experiences back and forth between themselves, sometimes talking out loud as well just for the grins of it all. Just enjoying the motion of the ocean.

"How come you talk in perfect English out loud Franklin, but when we're in each other's heads you talk a different way?" Dusty asked silently.

"Oh nothin' really to that, boy. And it's correct English. I'm a teacher and folks should learn the proper way to speak the language of the country they live in, shouldn't they? At least as best they can. But I guess in my mind, when I'm shootin' the bull with you, I just put my carpet slippers on and get comfortable, so to speak," he said. "You notice how comfortable we are already, doncha?"

"Yea, sure do," Dusty said out loud and inside he thought, "Thank you for honoring me with being comfortable around me."

"You seem to be doin' just the opposite, hey Dusty?" Franklin said. "You funnin' me there?" he said lightly.

"No sir," Dusty said and thought. "It's just that I haven't ever felt this way since I left my folks is all. I *am* honored."

Dusty knew it was true and so did Franklin. All of a sudden big old tears rolled up in Dusty's eyes and he felt like sobbing. The Light was completely washing over him and he felt it as total love. He could only then realize how much love he had missed from his parents, sitting there feeling the love that was coming into him from Franklin. So much missed and so much here right now. He missed his parents and he wept silently.

"C'mere and sit by me," Franklin told him. Dusty did as he was told, while large, Amboy Duke tears slid down his face, feeling a feeling he hadn't known he hadn't felt in almost ten years. He kind of felt like a baby for bawling like this, but sad as it was, it was beautiful too.

Franklin, with tears in his own eyes now, put an arm around Dusty's shoulder, bowed his head slightly and sent as much love as he had toward Dusty. Franklin added his personal love to the great and all-encompassing love that was woven into the Light they were sharing back and forth. Light that was dancing back and forth so fast that it seemed like it could explode the room, heck the whole neighborhood, if it decided to.

"I miss my mom and my dad, Franklin. I really do."

"I know you do, Dusty. I know you do. Just sit here with me and feel the Light. It'll be OK. Just let it go and feel it."

"Hite did something like this for you, didn't he Franklin?" Dusty thought, seeing it happen in Franklin's mind.

"Yes he did, Dusty. He sat with me just like this and passed it on and I'll never forget it."

They spent a few minutes sitting together, heads bowed slightly, Franklin with his arm around the boy and after a bit Franklin started again, "You know, boy, I've been a Helper all my life. Known it for real since I was seven and Helped my first person. And I met a lot of other Helpers in all that time as well and you know what? I ain't never met another Helper with as much of the power in him as you. I mean that. You don't even know it, and you may think I'm just joshin' you here, but it's the truth. Yesterday when our lights pooled together I thought I was gonna faint. I wasn't just afraid I was gonna wet my britches cuz of laughin' so hard about Luke and Goldie. No sir," Franklin continued, "I was almost scared too, scared by the light coming outta you. Jesus, boy, till I got a handle on it I thought you was gonna blow me clear into heaven."

"You really mean that?" Dusty asked and as soon as he thought it he knew it to be true.

"Wow, it is true, isn't it?" he thought. "What do you think that means?"

"I don't know why, Dusty. Don't know why at all. But I do know this," Franklin said. "Even among us Helpers more is given to some than to others. That's just the way it is. Why I met some Helpers that only got a little dribble a light comin' outta them. Like me in the bathroom late at night," Franklin joked, "But it's still beautiful and they still use it. And some of us got a lot more. Me? I know I got a right full tank, but yours is washin' out of the tank all together. That old pump nozzle is stickin' in there pumpin' that tank full and it's gushin' out the sides pourin' all down on the cement."

"Why do you think that is?" Dusty asked not quite ready to leave it alone, it being kind of fun to know that for once in his life he had more going on than the rest.

"I really and truly don't know," Franklin said. "I just think of it like those stories in the bible. About the talents that were handed out and about turnin' your back on the Power. For some of us, more *is* given and more *is* expected and *you* is one 'a them. Me too, a little bit, but not as much as you. If the Light decides to give you five talents you best well *use* them five talents. If it gives you three, well then use them three. And if the Light only sees fit to give you one talent you best not be diggin' a hole and buryin' it. No sir, you better let that little one-talent Light shine," Franklin continued. "And you, Dusty, I'm thinkin' maybe you got even more than five. And don't forget what that other story says about turnin' your back on the Power. Whoa be unto you, or somethin' like that, I forget now exactly, but whoa be unto you that turn your back on the Light. It will come back a thousand times to haunt you."

"Man, Franklin, I'm not sure what to think about all that," Dusty said.

"Don't know that there's much more thinkin' to do on it, Dusty," Franklin said. "It's the knowin' that's important and now you know. And maybe the Light saw fit for me to be here to help you a little bit to know. Passin' it on like Hite did for me. That's more than fine with me. I don't mess with the Light. Uh-uh. I don't mess with it. I'm just thankful for it and I thank God for allowing me to experience the Blessing of it."

"OK," Dusty thought, although he wasn't quite through with it, Franklin knew. Shoot the boy was only fifteen. He was gonna have to toss it around in his mind a bit, but maybe that was OK too. There's a whole lot worse things to be contemplating than the Power of the Light and the gift you've been given.

A minute or two more passed and Franklin said, "OK then, you ready to lighten things up a bit now, if you don't mind me sayin' it that way?"

"Good one," Dusty thought.

Dusty *was* ready to lighten up now, Jesus had he *ever* been Lightened up, although he was a bit overwhelmed by it all. God, it was only yesterday he had met Franklin and now today he was feeling love like he hadn't known he had lost and being told that he had more of the light than anyone Franklin had ever met. Jesus, yesterday he'd just been trying to fight it out and today he was like Gandhi or some Mother Theresa woman, whoever that was. Her name and image had just flashed into his mind—Helper's thoughts sometimes being thrown ahead into time.

Franklin was laughing again now. He laughs a lot, Dusty thought, for a guy who's been through what he's been through. A black man growing up in the segregated south. Sure things had improved some, maybe. Heck, it was 1982, but shit, the man had seen some stuff and he still laughs.

"It's cuz I'm with you, boy," Franklin said reading Dusty's mind. " I feel better than any person's got a right to feel spending time with you. I thank the Light for it. It's been awhile since I had a face to face. And don't worry, you ain't no Mother "effin" Theresa," he laughed. "Not by a long shot. And don't be feelin' sorry for me either, OK? Anybody had it worse than black folks in this country and it's Indians. And in case you forgot, you an Indian even though you got that Finlander last name. You an Indian."

"All right," Dusty snorted, mostly laughter but a few tears still there. "I forgot you were still in there with me. Kind of hard to get used to, but it's cool too. I feel like I don't have to hide anything from you anyway and that's a good feelin'."

"Yes it is," Franklin said. "Now take this handkerchief and dry those crocodile tears, unless you can somehow use them to change you mouth into a crocodile mouth, the better to enjoy Goldie's love orbs with!"

Dusty took the handkerchief and did just so. Crying *seemed* like a bad thing, he thought, but you sure do feel a lot better after you do it. Kind of a conundrum.

"Yea, it's kind of a conundrum alright," Franklin said, not quite out of Dusty's mind yet. "You ain't been *all* asleep in class either, have you son? Conundrum, that's a good one. Keep up with that reading, boy. It's good for you since you don't seem to want to spend much time in school."

"Now clear outa here," Franklin went on. "I don't have a class for another hour but I don't want somebody to walk past and see us two fools sittin' in here weepin' and holdin' hands like we was a pair of school girls out for a walk through the flowers at recess."

"And don't forget to be here Monday," he said. "That's my last day of subbing and I'll be moving on after that, so no skipping. You hear me?"

"No way. I'll be here Monday, Mr. Rose," Dusty said as he grabbed his books and walked out of the room.

Dusty had a great weekend. Nobody was even arguing at the house. The two T's were lost in their own little worlds. Jim puttered in the garage, Luke was reading a book on Ghost Dancers all weekend, and Goldie just bounced around the house to Dusty's private entertainment. It was a good weekend. Kind of like an oasis, or maybe even a pony express outpost—a place for a man who'd been riding hard to sit down and rest and enjoy a good bed and good food before heading out again. Before heading out into the distance where you couldn't even see those storm clouds gathering they were so far off beyond the curve of the horizon. If you could have seen them they would've been shaped funny. Kind of like a guy in a cheap leisure suit wearing too much bad cologne. A scary guy. A mean guy, a vile guy, although he didn't look like it at first. Kinda like Uncle Lou. But shoot, first we gotta go to school on Monday.

18

"Choices," Franklin said as soon as the class had left on Monday morning, leaving only Dusty smiling in his seat already "lighting" up with Franklin. "Choices."

"What do you mean by that?" Dusty thought back.

"You know, I'm not really sure but it just came to me that we should Light up on choices today," Franklin replied with his mind. "Choices made, choices not made, and do we really have any say in the whole matter? What do you think about it, Dusty?"

"I never really thought about it. I guess I never really had a lot of choices to make. They were kind of made for me. Live here, go there, attend this school, live with that family," Dusty said, "you know, stuff like that."

Their minds were completely synched up now, shooting-stars rocketing back and forth. Dusty could see that Franklin was leaving. Not just the class, he was only a substitute after all, but Duluth. "Yep, I'll be heading up to Canada day after tomorrow. Gonna visit my sister in Thunder Bay. Won't stay long, though. My sister may not be the only black woman on the north shore, but she's one of only a few," Franklin added, "and I'm getting the feeling, courtesy of our old friend

Mr. Light here, that it's time for me to hook up with a good woman, so after I visit my sister, I'm gonna start looking for one and I don't know where that will take me. Been a long time for me. Never underestimate the value of a good woman, Dusty. They can light up your life in a good way too."

"Yea, I got the feeling you wouldn't be sticking around here," Dusty said. They both knew Dusty would miss the man he had just met very much.

"Now, I wrote my sister's address down for you and I want you to feel free to keep in touch with me," Franklin said passing the folded piece of paper to Dusty. "I'll be traveling and won't have a phone number but my sister always knows where I am and she'll forward any letters you write. Keeping in touch can be a good thing and I'll always do my best to get back in touch with you right away."

Dusty was glowing from their shared light but he could sense in himself the loss already. It was down there in a little corner of his mind. Not bothering him yet, probably because of the sharing they had going on, but there just the same. He could see it. Funny how when you don't know you don't have something it doesn't bother you as much as when you get a little taste of it and then lose it. Dusty hadn't known how truly lonely he was or how much he missed the feeling of love till meeting Franklin.

"You think I'll ever get a woman?" he asked Franklin. "I'd like to have a family some day and make sure they get all the stuff I didn't."

"It's not for me to say, Dusty," Franklin replied. "I don't know anything about how it will work for you. I sure hope you get some kind of family and a good woman to keep your heart warm at night. Been kind of few and far between in that area myself. That's why it's so nice to check in with my sister." Actually Franklin couldn't see any kind of woman, except for maybe the wrong kind, in Dusty's future but he didn't allow that to escape his mind to Dusty's. Looked like nothing but hard road ahead for the boy. Damn, and he's got such a strong spirit too, but maybe they're the ones that get the hard rows to hoe, Franklin thought.

"What was that?" Dusty said.

"Oh nothing, just got a lot of things zooming around in here. Can't keep track of 'em all myself."

"But that does bring me back to the idea of choices," Franklin continued. "It seems to me we got to try and make the right choices whether or not they matter. They can have a lasting affect on our lives. Now sometimes you can make the right choice and it can still all go in the outhouse and on the other hand, you can make a real stinker of a choice and it still works out fine. Almost like it doesn't matter at all, but I think it still does matter somehow. It's like even when there's no rhyme or reason there's still a rhyme and reason behind it."

These thoughts weren't coming out in sentences in their minds. They were just popping back and forth all at once. The whole idea being grasped immediately. Huge chunks being gulped right down and digested. That's how it worked between Helpers. It was beyond time almost. Just Light and ideas flying back and forth.

"And again, you can make a bad choice and pay for it for a long time. Like there *is* that consequence to pay. It's really beyond my thinking but something just told me to caution you, Dusty," Franklin thought. "You may have some of those choices to make in your future and if you don't make the right ones I'm afraid there might be a price to pay. I don't mean to go scaring you, just wanted to pass along what I thought you might need."

"Well my head's whirling, all right," Dusty said. "Course when we're locked up like this it doesn't really matter cause even if it's something scary it's not as if it bothers me. It's just like it's something over there, contained in a glass box, that I can see and be aware of but it doesn't cause me any fear. Too bad I can't stay in the light all the time, huh Franklin?"

"Well I suppose that's the trick, but for guys like you and me Dusty, we just gotta be grateful that we're getting that taste at all. And as long as we're on the subject of choices, I noticed you wear your hair short," Franklin said. "Everyone else is wearing it long, especially the Indian boys, and you wear it short. Why do you think you make that choice."

"I like to be different, I guess," Dusty said. They both saw that there was just something in Dusty that liked to cut across the grain. If they're all swimming downstream, he was gonna swim up. Truth be told, the same cross-cut saw was in Franklin too.

"But that's a choice you make right?" Franklin asked.

"Yea, I kinda see where it is," he answered.

"You see where I'm going with this?" Franklin asked and they both did. The light was painting pictures for them both. They could both see Dusty in a uniform of some kind.

"Long as you got that short hair already, you may want to be thinkin about joining the service. That seems to be what the Light is sayin' anyways. Nobody joining the service now. Might be a good move for a young fella like you," Franklin continued. "We both know you ain't much for book learning, even though you always got your nose stuck in some kind of book. Just not the right one. Instead of reading your English book you're getting lost in *Catcher in the Rye*. Might be your way up and out. What do you think?"

Dusty could see the sense that the Light was making by way of Franklin's mind. He could feel the seed being planted that would guide his future, and some of his choices.

"The Marine Corps," he shouted into Franklin's mind.

"Hey, easy on the ears there, champ," Franklin thought back, "I'm sittin' right here next to you."

"Sorry, Franklin, just got a little excited there," Dusty said in a quieter mind-voice. "What do you think of that? The Marine Corps, that is?"

"Well it does seem to be about the wildest a man can get without breaking the law," Franklin replied. "Think you'd like to get wild and not have a judge waiting' at the other end of your actions?"

"Yea," Dusty said. "Too wild!"

"Well think about it and see where the Light guides you," Franklin said. "Course you'd probably have to graduate from high school to get in. Think you could do that?" Shit, we might get this boy through school after all, Franklin thought to himself. Thank you Mr. Light.

"Oh shoot, didn't think of that, but yea I bet I could if I had too," Dusty figured.

"Just keep me posted boy and I'll be pulling for you no matter what happens," Franklin sent back. "Now come on over here and give me a hug. I don't know when I'll be seeing you again and I'm gonna miss you."

Dusty walked through the glow and the Light and wrapped his arms around the wiry little man and felt the Power flowing back and forth between them.

"I love you, Franklin," Dusty said both with his mind and out loud.

"I love you too, Dusty," Franklin thought back and then out loud, "I love you too."

"Now you take off and remember you'll always be in my thoughts," Franklin said finally. "No tears, we had them yesterday. Oh, one last thing, if you think of it, if you could send me thoughts of Goldie from time to time I'd appreciate it. Now I don't know if it'll work but if it does I'd surely appreciate it," he joked. "At least you'll be thinkin of me anyways."

"I will Franklin. Bye bye."

"So long Dusty, watch out for those storm clouds and mind your choices, you hear?"

"Yes sir. So long," Dusty said.

Franklin was gone the next day when Dusty came to third period history class and the day after that Dusty could feel inside that he had left Duluth. He just felt a blank spot where Mr. Rose had been. But it was a warm blank spot all the same. It smelled like cinnamon and felt like comfortable shoes. What it really felt like was that third bowl of porridge...just right.

Dusty did join the Marine Corps as we shall see in a little while. It gave him something nice to focus on and he did apply himself harder in school after a fashion. He was focused so hard on that part of the sky that who could blame him for not watching the clouds forming a little closer to him. He wouldn't graduate from high school however. Not even close. Not by a long nose off a short pony. A storm cloud in a leisure suit made sure of that. And one wrong choice. One very wrong choice. Uncle fucking Lou.

19

Dusty had two passions in life. Hockey and boxing. Like most kids in northern Wisconsin and northeastern Minnesota he had skated since he had been old enough to stand on skates. Wobbling around on ponds and rinks, with ankles flopping back and forth, little mittened hands gripping the backs of chairs that steadied them as they learned to skate across the ice trailing behind the chairs. Hand me down skates, but that was what most kids used anyway. You could go to any sporting goods store and get a good pair of used skates for practically nothing, which was good since that's about all Dusty's various families ever had. He loved checking, scoring, and skating with the puck, in that order. Mostly checking. Dusty loved taking someone into the boards hard. Clean but hard. The best thing about it was that it was allowed. Heck, it was *authorized* and he loved it.

Dusty had been boxing since he was twelve years old at Poke's Michigan Street Gym in downtown Duluth. Andrew "Poke" Potek had been a ranked light heavyweight from the Iron Range who had trained in Duluth. Poke had been the real deal. He had even broken the top ten rankings. That's the top ten in the *world*. Poke had speed, power, and a granite chin. He had it all and had been ranked eighth in the world before the accident.

Poke rarely drank but when he did he liked to drive, and one night he had started drinking in Duluth to celebrate his number eight ranking. Poke had gotten homesick and started the hour long drive back to his home north of Hibbing, Minnesota. Nothing overly dramatic happened. Just a patch of ice on a dark curve. Poke's big Buick had almost made it through the curve when it finally gave way its grip on the slippery surface and plunged off the road, down the bank and into a huge Norway pine. Poke's head hit the windshield— no big deal for Poke. Hell, he'd been hit a lot harder in the Terry Davis fight that got him his latest ranking and not even gone down. He had a Stonehenge fucking chin. Unfortunately his knees were only mortal bone and cartilage and when they both met the underside edge of the dashboard they had shattered. Poke didn't box after that. He took over the gym he had trained at and spent his time coaching the occasional up and comer. Mostly he looked after the kids that hung around and sometimes got interested in boxing. He had spotted Dusty the first day Dusty wandered into the gym and had taken a shine to the rough-edged kid.

Dusty spent a lot of time in the gym and he even hit it harder after Franklin left. Gotta stay in shape if I'm gonna join the Corps. Dusty was a southpaw and had already developed power in both hands. He had had a few golden gloves fights and won more than he lost. His only real drawback was his temper. Sometimes he would just see red and start flailing away. Not necessarily a bad strategy but when he went into one of his zones he was not likely to follow Marques of Queensbury rules. He'd head butt, throw viscous elbows and trip his opponents to the canvas and them jump on them teeth bared through his mouthpiece. This didn't score a lot of points with the officials. His fellow boxers weren't big fans of it either.

Poke was trying to break Dusty of this habit, but mostly Dusty just spent his time working out alone in the gym. Jumping rope, hitting the heavy bag, (he loved hitting the heavy bag), working the speed bag, and shadow boxing. He could zone out all he liked on the heavy bag and everyone pretty much left him alone. He had even gone off on the heavy bag one day when he had overheard an older gym watcher by the name of Scratch make fun of his being an Indian Finlander. A Findian. Dusty had used his knees and elbows on the bag for ten minutes straight with Poke watching from the corner shaking his head.

"Hey, you dumb fuck," Poke had hissed at the cigar smoking hanger on, "leave the kid alone. He's got enough shit without some degenerate gambler like you piling it on. Get the fuck outta here before I turn the kid loose on you." Scratch had gotten the message and bailed. Dusty had been oblivious to the whole exchange. He just kept wilding away on the heavy bag until he ran out of gas and the rage had faded.

Dusty headed home after working out at the gym one day a few weeks after Franklin had left. He'd been feeling sorry for himself lately. He really missed old Franklin, and since Luke had left a couple of days earlier, he even missed *him* a little. He thought it was kind of shitty that he had just gotten a taste of some cool stuff and then had it taken away. He was lost in his mind thinking about this when he walked in the door, hair still wet from his workout, and saw a visitor on the couch with Goldie. His first thought was "oh shit, just like Miss Schneff." Not far from the truth really, but he didn't know that then.

Goldie jumped up rather quickly, with more than a little guilt on her face and said, "Oh Dusty, you're home early." He wasn't. "This is Jim's younger brother Lou. Lou Danbury. He's gonna be staying with us for a while maybe." Goldie's sportin' the high beams, Dusty saw, and it's not even cold in here. Uh-oh, what's going on? Her hands were all nervously pulling down her sweater and her skirt much to the slack eyed delight of Lou.

Lou Danbury was forty years old, four years younger than his older brother Jim. He had black greasy hair that he combed straight back and enormous shoulders and arms that made him look even bigger than his six feet. A shame really, built for hard work, but lazy as the day was long.

Dusty got a vibe off him immediately. It was similar to the feeling he would get before a Helping was coming on, only in reverse. This guy is bad news, Dusty thought. Some people are even attracted to that and I think Goldie might be one of them. But they can't see what I see already and Dusty used whatever intuitive powers he had as a Helper and looked into Lou. Nothin there. Jesus. He's bad news all right, but he's much worse than that. Dusty didn't know much about vacuums but that's the image he got.

There was a deep black nothingness inside of Lou. It wasn't even that there were scary images inside of him that Dusty could see. It was the dark emptiness that was the scary thing. Just a great whole deep pool of nothing. He's the kind of guy who started out torturing animals as a kid Dusty knew, but worse than that he would connive other weaker kids, who had no interest at all in things like that, and get *them* to do bad things. Get them to throw a cat off a bridge or pin a puppy and torture it just so he could watch them do it for him. He's not *just* a bad doer, he's a make *other* people bad doers too, kind of a guy. A tormenter because he can, Dusty knew. And Lou could. He could sell ice to an Eskimo if he had a mind to but Lou wasn't interested in anything as harmless as that. What was the harm in that? Take a few shekels from an ignorant savage? Not Lou's cup of tea. No, now if he could somehow ruin the poor Inuit's life and that of his whole family's *and* take them down in a very degrading and dehumanizing way, well then he might just dust off the old ice maker and start to sellin'! *That* was Lou's cup of joe. Take 'em down. Take 'em *all* down. That's where Lou lived. Dusty knew that right off, and he knew that no one else could see it. That's what makes him so effective, Dusty thought.

The rest of the crew started filtering in for the night. First the two T's walked in. Together but not talking. Those two could be together but separate at the same time. Goldie was in the kitchen putting supper together and Lou drew the two girls over to him like powerless moths to a flame. More like a cat toying with a couple of half dead mice. They don't even like him, Dusty saw. They can feel a dirtiness below the surface somewhere but still they sit with him on the couch and let him drape those huge arms around their shoulders. One on either side of Lou. Sinking into the couch and shrinking under the man's probing arms. Tina and Terry were so hypnotized that they didn't even see Dusty watching from the rocker on the other side of the living room, but Lou saw. Lou looked right at Dusty as if to say, "they're mine." See I've only been here a couple of hours and they're mine already. That's power boy." Not *as if* to say. That's what he *was* saying and Dusty knew it. His eyes said "watch out or you'll be next." Shit, you *will* be next, it just takes time is all and I've got plenty of time, and the means to do it.

Lou did have time, and a bit of money now too. He had been born with a muscular build. Some genetic material that just gave him a propensity to grow big and strong. He had added to those oversized arms and shoulders as a digger on the mud gang for Minnesota Power & Light, down in the Cities. Digging and shoveling better than any three men when he had a mind to, which he rarely did. He mostly just bullied the others to do his work for him. Bullied men who didn't bully easy. Not just with physical threats either. Lou used a combination of his build, his attitude, and mostly that great darkness that was in him. Lou had drifted from menial job to menial job before getting on with the Minnesota Power. He had called in a chit that couldn't be refused and got the good paying, blue collar, union job.

Lou had been able to handle the job for about eleven months. The job wasn't the end, though, it was simply the *means* to the end. Lou had an angle, but then again, didn't he always? Something he'd been working on for awhile.

He'd been down in a long hole clearing out mud one day while his foreman had been operating a backhoe. Lou had leverage on the foreman Joe Clark. He knew that Clark was fooling around with Mrs. Ackerly the wife of company vice president Clyde Ackerly. Mrs. Helen Ackerly was the kind of woman that liked to marry rich and fuck poor. And for her, poor was currently the foreman Joe Clark. Dusty would meet many women like that in the Marine Corps. They married officers but secretly liked to fuck enlisted men. Usually NCO's, which Dusty would eventually become. And hell, foremen and NCO's weren't ever *poor* poor in the overall scheme of things. They had managed to fight their way at least halfway out of the muck. But these women didn't know that. To them they were low enough. Marry rich and fuck poor, or fuck mean. And poor and mean quite often went together.

Lou had yelled up to Joe Clark to go ahead and bring the backhoe scoop back down into the hole.

"You outta the way?" Joe yelled, but not loud enough. He should have yelled louder so that the rest of the crew who were now back at the truck taking a break could've heard, but how was he to know that?

"Yea, yea," shouted Lou, "just bring that fuckin' arm down so I can go on break." Lou had been planning this for weeks and now here it was right in front of him. His ticket to the good life.

As Clark was up above lowering the forked scoop down into the hole Lou turned his long-handled work shovel around backward, stretched out his leg so that his ankle was exposed, and waited. And just as Clark got the back hoe's arm to the bottom of the pit Lou used his own work shovel and hit himself hard right on the ball of his left ankle with the backside of the shovel.

"Goddamn you son of a motherfucking bitch! You hit me with the hoe!" Lou screamed, and kept screaming, so that the rest of the crew would hear. "You broke my fucking ankle you dizzy cocksucker!"

The crew was so startled to hear Lou Danbury screaming, almost like a little girl they would say later, all according to Lou's plan, that they arrived at the hole just as Clark was scrambling down from the seat of the back hoe.

"You broke my fucking ankle," Lou shouted again for the benefit of the entire gathered crew. Lou had pulled up his mud encrusted jeans for all to see his swelling ankle. Lou had been careful to not hit himself too hard, shit I almost went too far he admitted, but he had given himself a good enough whack with the backside of his shovel to swell his ankle ball right up.

After that it had been easy enough to get full disability. Clark had squawked a bit back at the shop a few days later but Lou had found out about it and had taken him aside and filled him in.

"Be a shame if Ackerly found out about his little Helen and a certain foreman, wouldn't it Clark?" Lou had whispered in Clark's ear that day. "Be a damn shame, wouldn't it?"

Hell after that it was all just paperwork and Lou had been granted a full disability for life, along with a nice cash settlement for not bringing charges against the company.

Lou had healed completely. He still used the limp when it would benefit him but there was nobody from the company watching. They just wanted it all to go away and Lou ended up with time, and the money type of means. After that he just drifted around stirring things up and today he had drifted into Dusty's orbit.

"Like my new Leisure suit, girls?" Lou asked the two captured T's. Lou was wearing blue jeans but with a red leisure suit jacket on over a blue shirt and tie. "If you're gonna live a life of leisure you might as well wear the appropriate apparel and look darn good doin' it, right sweeties?" he added. "Yes, I think I'm gonna like my new home," he said.

The girls just sat slumped down under his arms like they were doped up. The vile leading the blind.

About this time Jim wandered in the back door and, after checking with his wife in the kitchen, he came out into the living room.

"Goldie just told me you were here, Lou," Jim said in his usual monotone. "Good to see you. Hope you can stay a bit."

"Thanks big brother, I think I might just take you up on that," Lou answered. "I got a couple things cookin' over in Superior and I could sure use a place to stay. Just for a little while until I get my old apartment back, you know? Been out in the Dakota's for a couple of months."

Lou *had* been out in the Dakota's. He'd been in Bismarck stealing money from drug dealers. He knew a couple of losers who'd moved out there and set up shop and he had paid them a little visit. By the time he was done with them they had been more than happy to give Lou their money. Had even watched while Lou fucked their two girlfriends. Lou didn't even need the money. Just needed something to do.

He'd been so charged up after that he had even tried his mojo on some Indian drug dealers out there but they weren't buyin' his brand of shit. Indians had always made Lou a little nervous. He didn't know why but they did. Niggers, as he so eloquently called them, he could shit less about. He'd even fucked up one or two when he had done his first stretch in Stillwater, but Indians just spooked him for some unknown reason. He'd been a little spooked when Dusty had come in but only because he had reminded him of North Dakota. Lou had barely escaped and was still very pissed about the whole thing. Those Indians had almost gotten him and he knew they meant to hurt him bad before they killed him. He could almost appreciate how they had planned on handling it but that only made it worse knowing that there were others out there that could maybe get a jump on him. Lou was very bad on a good day but pissed-off he was worse, and he right now he was very pissed. He might just have to take it out on this little red nigger that had wormed his way into Lou's current territory.

"Stay as long as you need," Jim said. "We got the room."

"Well thanks, Jim, I shouldn't be needin' it for too long but the gesture is sure appreciated," Lou snaked.

Dusty could see that Jim was even blinder than most to Lou's ways. Dusty was starting to get a little glow on as if he had a Helping approaching and he was seeing more. Just a hint of the power. He didn't know if it was a false alarm or not, but he was glad for the extra insight it was providing. It helped outweigh the sense of impending doom he was noticing now as well. It's not that Jim doesn't want to see, although he probably wouldn't, it's that Lou has made him not see. Over the years he had been able to shape and mold his older and duller brother into missing what was at least semi-obvious to everyone else.

Dinner came and went with Jim zoned out over the newspaper and Lou probing the women with his little comments and sly smiles.

Dusty was seated directly across the table from Lou. Every so often Lou would lock eyes with Dusty and show him the emptiness. The fake light in his eyes he was flashing at the women would die and he would give Dusty a dark, observant, lizard look out of those lifeless blue eyes. Eyelids occasionally moving up and down but nobody really home. Nobody like us certainly. Like the north pole, Dusty shivered. Cold, deep and dead forever.

The rest of the evening came and went uneventfully. Well, as uneventfully as things can come and go with a living breathing vacuum of danger in the house, Dusty thought. The Light had been slowly building in Dusty all evening and he was pretty sure now that he had a Helping coming on. When, where, or who, he had no idea. All he was getting was the darkness from Lou and Dusty wanted as little to do with Lou as possible.

The two T's went to bed early and Jim was heading that way himself when Goldie spoke up.

"Well I suppose we should find you a place to sleep, Lou," she said.

Oh fuck, Dusty thought. I hadn't even thought about that! Now where is this fucker gonna sleep?

"You're in luck. Luke, that was our other foster child besides Dusty, just moved out," Goldie purred, "so we've got an empty bed. Lou why don't you grab your things and move on into the boys room. You can sleep with Dusty tonight."

That's how Dusty ended up spending two nights sharing a room with a man who was as close to the Prince of Darkness as Dusty ever hoped to get. *And,* that was how Dusty fell from whatever passed for grace in his young life.

20

The next forty-eight hours were a blur for Dusty and would be for many years to come. The first night Lou had started probing Dusty's perimeter. He'd seen how Dusty had gaped at Goldie's tits when he had come home that late afternoon. He sowed that away and started working on his plan. Gotta have a plan, Lou knew. He didn't know where they came from but they usually bubbled to the surface at just the right time.

"Boy kid, that Goldie's sure got a nice set of jugs on her, doesn't she?" he asked Dusty after they had settled into their respective beds and turned out the lights. Lou found that the best way to plant seeds of opportunity was in the dark. Now a fella didn't always have that option, but suggesting something in the dark, especially right before a guy went to sleep, was the best way. Gives the unlucky recipient nothing but time to contemplate. Really plants those seeds of destruction in deep.

"Man, I'm almost sorry she's my brother's wife," he continued, "cuz I'd sure like to ride that mountain of love she's got perched up there on her chest." Lou figured he'd scored a bull's-eye as Dusty was even more silent than he had been only seconds before. Bingo, Lou thought. Got this little fucker right where I want him.

"I never really thought about it that much," Dusty managed to choke out.

Bingo and bingo, Lou thought. He's hot for old Goldie and he's afraid of me. Carrot and stick thought Lou. Always works the best having some pushin' working on in behind the pullin'.

"Well, couldn't blame you if you did, kid," Lou said. "Not one bit."

Shit, this fake cordiality is even worse than his dead blue eyes shooting out hate, Dusty thought. He could tell by now that Lou was working on some kind of plan to bring everything down in flames, but although he could feel a Helping coming on he couldn't make out the details yet. Nothing there yet but shapes and shadows, shapes and shadows.

The worst thing about Lou, Dusty figured, wasn't even that he was the lowest of the low. Oh, Dusty knew that he was deadly but the worst thing was, that he wasn't the worst of the worse. He was stupid and he made mistakes but he still seemed to be able to survive and fool people. Fool people long enough to hurt them for his own gain, even if that gain was only his pleasure at hurting them. How could this guy have lasted this long, Dusty wondered? That's the worst thing about it. He's so low-budget and yet he keeps on keepin' on. Man, I gotta get outta this.

But even knowing all that, and with the added insight and power that his upcoming Helping was bringing on, Dusty still went to sleep thinking about Goldie. In spite of his extra, Lou had still gotten through to him. That's why he's so effective, Dusty could see now. He combines his dark stuff with other people's weaknesses. Yet even in seeing Lou's effectiveness Dusty still went to sleep dreaming of Goldie. He woke up thinking about her too. That's why he had to wait for Lou to finally leave the room before he got out of bed. Otherwise he would've been busted and embarrassed climbing out of his bed with the front of his gym shorts full with thoughts of Goldie. Dusty was scared.

"Sleep good, did you?" Lou asked before he left the room.

"Yea," was all Dusty could reply.

Lou thought, Yea, I just bet you slept good, punk. Little thoughts of Goldie dancing like sugarplum fairies in that reservation head of yours? Lou was actually whistling as he left the room, in a tattered, silk Japanese robe, heading for the bathroom. This is all gonna work out just fine, he mused. My brother Jim is a dolt, the women are eating out of my hand, and now I think I got this little punch drunk Indian right where I want him. Off balance and thinking. But not, and this was very important to Lou, NOT thinkin about me. Those blind-side Sunday punches were always the best. They don't even see it coming, he thought. And I've been here how long? Less than twelve hours. I still got it, baby, I still got it. Funny, Lou was a fan of Ralph Malph too. Loved that Happy Days show in jail.

"Better get to school on time there, Smokey," Lou said, returning from the bathroom. "Today's Friday. Don't want to get the weekend off on the wrong foot now do we?"

Dusty was about halfway up to full Helping power when Lou said this but he still moved ass and got his tan behind out of the house as soon as he could. He had to get out and away, which all played beautifully into Lou's hand.

Lou puttered around the house humming to himself. Formulatin' his plan. It was all becoming crystal clear now. Eventually Goldie was the only one home with him. No better time than the present to start planting some more seeds. And wonder of wonders, Goldie was in the shower. Now I just bet she's gonna come outta there dressed only in a little towel. Oops, Lou thought. Only it's not gonna be some little foster kid ogling what's underneath today is it? Nope, gonna be old Uncle Lou.

This time when the towel dropped, it didn't get picked back up. Goldie was frozen at the entryway to the living room like a deer in the headlight's of Uncle Lou's lifeless eyes. Overpowering her even as he was seated across the room in the chair Dusty usually sat in. And he wasn't the only one sportin' headlights either. Goldie's seemed to be on full-beam as well. One down, four to go Lou thought. Gonna work out just fine.

Hours after the initial degradations were done, in the privacy of Goldie and Jim's bedroom, Lou filled Goldie in on what he needed her to do for him tomorrow.

"We're gonna have a little party, Goldie, what with Jim working overtime and it being Saturday and all," he told the submissive Goldie. "Just you, me, and the kids. Now I know you're not much for drinking but tomorrow we're gonna make a little exception for the adults. Heck, maybe even a little for the kids too. We'll be supervising them, so what trouble could they get into? So you make sure we've got a few bottles of that good Christian Brother's brandy on hand. The kind Jim keeps for special occasions. You'll do that for me now won't you honey?"

"Sure, Lou. Whatever you want," was all Goldie could whisper.

"Good, baby. That's good," he said. "Oh, and one last thing. Call me Uncle Lou. I want you to call me Uncle Lou from now on."

"Yes, Uncle Lou," she peeped. "Yes, Uncle Lou."

The plan was full on, in effect, and totally cemented in Lou's mind now as the two of them lay satiated in Jim and Goldie's wedding bed, Goldie naked, still covered in sweat, and tucked under Uncle Lou's muscular right arm. Gonna have us a little family party tomorrow, Lou thought. Gonna bring it all down.

Dusty was halfway through his school day when he finally got back into his right mind and back into the flow of the Light that the Helping was bringing on. Lou's working on a plan alright and I don't know exactly what it is, but it's all coming down soon, Dusty knew. The power of the oncoming Helping was stronger now, especially since he was away from Lou. Dusty usually didn't have to spend this much time wondering who he was going to Help. Often times it happened quicker than this and when it didn't he still usually knew who the Helpee was gonna be at least. Then he would just wait for it to happen, guide the flow, and say the words. Goldie possibly. Dusty could see how with Lou around she should be at the top of the list.

Tina and Terry perhaps. Hell, they were topping the charts as well. Maybe even Jim.

What didn't occur to Dusty was that maybe he would be required to help all four of them. It sure wasn't beyond the realm of possibility. They were all in danger of falling pitifully into the depths of no return with Lou pulling the strings.

And there was one more possibility. One that wouldn't have occurred to Dusty in a million years. Maybe he was there to Help Uncle Lou.

21

Dusty lay in bed that Friday night trying not to think and trying not to feel, but it was impossible. Well, not feeling wasn't impossible. That was part of the problem. He'd never sensed his Helping coming on stronger than he did right now. Ever. And yet he didn't feel the good he always felt when he was going to Help. Shit, the Power was there in spades. He felt as if he was sitting on the hood of a super-charged funny car at the Brainerd Raceway. All that unbelievable power just throbbing and rumbling underneath him. He was aware of it being there but only in a theoretical way. None of the joy, or colors, or goodness touched him in any way. He wasn't feeling anything. Well, fear was there. He was feeling fear, all right. Fear, and something brighter and stronger and redder behind that.

Uncle Lou was all tucked in, across the small bedroom from Dusty, in Luke's old bed. Dusty had never wished for Luke's presence more than he did right now. He was sorry he'd ever given Luke a hard time at all. He'd gladly apologize for everything rather than have that dangerous fool laying in the bed only a few feet away from him.

Uncle Lou was humming to himself now. Dusty finally recognized the tune. It was "What a Friend We Have in Jesus." Just as the tune came to him, Lou started singing quietly. Singing just the first two lines. In his own version, of course. "What a friend we have in Jesus," Lou whispered in a dangerous singing voice, "Christ Almighty, what a pal." Then he laughed to himself and hummed the rest of the tune.

Jesus, Dusty thought, I'm all alone out in the cold here.

The family had made it through the evening somehow. Jim had rushed in, packed his grip, and rushed out again. He *had* picked up that extra run and he would be back tomorrow. He had asked Lou to pass this message along to Goldie which Lou thoughtfully did. When Goldie had returned from her last minute trip to the liquor store Lou told her the message and only changed one little detail. Instead of telling Goldie that Jim should be back by three or four o'clock on Saturday afternoon, he told her that Jim might just have to layover and wouldn't be back until sometime on Sunday. Just a little change. No *big* deal but it fit perfectly into Lou's plans. Plans which were now all set. How perfect. Jim would walk into the house tomorrow afternoon and get an eyeful of what Lou had in store for the rest of the household. Jim stumbling in at the wrong time was what made it so right. He would see everything Lou had set up and that would make it all come tumbling down. Lou was downright content.

Lou leaned toward Dusty's bed and whispered through the dark, "You make damn sure you're back from the gym by noon tomorrow, Smoky. We're havin' a little birthday party for your Uncle Lou. You got that half breed? Do not fuck with me," he hissed toward the rigid Dusty.

Dusty was laying under the covers in his bed much like he would do a few years later in boot camp, completely at attention, arms locked down against his legs, hands curled tightly against his thighs. The blankets tucked deeply under the mattress pinned him in his bed.

"I won't," he stumbled, "I mean I will. I will be home by noon."

"Call me Uncle Lou," Lou breathed.

"I will be home by noon,... Uncle Lou," Dusty stammered out hating himself the whole time.

"That's a good little Smoky. Do what I say and you might even get lucky tomorrow," Lou finished and turned on his side away from Dusty. "Saw Goldie drop the towel today myself, boy. Course in my case it was four hours before she picked it back up again. Sweet dreams, champ," Lou said and hummed himself toward sleep.

What the fuck is going on, Dusty thought? I've got full-on power building up here and he's still got me doing it. Shit, maybe I'm the one that's supposed to be Helped, because I've never needed it more in my life. Dusty tossed and turned all night in what was, until then, the longest night of his life. Unfortunately, because of actions taken *and* not taken the next day, it wouldn't be the last long night he would spend. Not even close.

Dusty was up and out by seven o'clock the next morning. Even before Lou was up, but not before Lou had mumbled "Be home at noon, kid," from under the covers on his side of the room.

Dusty raced the fifteen blocks down Duluth's rocky, central hillside neighborhood to Poke's gym. He got there early and waited forty-five minutes for Poke to open up at eight. While he was waiting he could feel the Helping Power full bore but there was not even a whiff of the good feelings. It was as if there was a fog that had settled in, shrouding that part of his mind. And he was getting tired of being afraid. Thanks to being out of that house and away from Lou's grasp he wasn't only horrified. Now he was getting angry. He felt it building up inside of himself almost like it was a Helping in reverse, similar but stronger than what had happened other times that he had "seen" red. Afraid, enraged, and a dangerous young man of fifteen.

Dusty raced through the paint-peeled door to the gym before Poke even had time to pull the keys back out of the lock and was on the heavy bag as soon as he had changed into his gym trunks and hooded sweatshirt. No one else was there and Poke watched the boy flail away. This was as good a time as any, Poke figured. He had been wanting to talk to Dusty about these pugilistic rages and maybe now was the time, but Dusty didn't seem to be running out of gas.

After watching Dusty try to demolish the big bag for an unbelievable twelve minutes straight, Poke was timing him, he shouted for Dusty to stop and managed to drag the boy away from the bag and over to the side of the raised sparring ring in the middle of the drafty gym's floor. He had to shout three times before Dusty even heard him. Poke figured something had set Dusty off, but the ex-boxer wasn't quite sharp enough to grasp that it was entirely more than just a slight that had done it. If Poke had been a little more sensitive maybe he wouldn't have given Dusty the advice he did. Advice that started a chain of events that was to affect Dusty, and those around him, for years to come. *If.* Yea, but if the Queen had balls then she'd be King. But she didn't, so she wasn't. Just wasn't gonna happen.

Poke finally settled Dusty down long enough for the boy to listen.

"I've been watchin' these rages you been havin', kid," Polk told the boy. "These "seein' reds" as you call 'em. They ain't gonna help any boxin' career that's for sure. And ya can't go stormin' around life like that either or you'll end up in Stillwater or down in Waupun in Wisconsin after one of 'em. I seen it too many times, hey" the ex-pug continued. "Now I been thinking that maybe if you can't get 'em ta go away, maybe you can at least get 'em ta help ya.

A light flickered on in Dusty's head as Poke was speaking. Not the light of a Helping. That was still there too, but this was a different light. Certainly not as helpful a light, but a light just the same. Now if Mr. Franklin Rose had been there it might've been different. If Dusty had just thought of his last conversation with Franklin it might have been quite different. Or if Poke had given the suggestion he was about to give at a different time, things might've been different. But it didn't come down that way and now we're back to that queen and her unfortunate lack of testicles. Just wasn't gonna happen.

"Maybe it's not a bad thing, this seeing red you do," Poke continued. "Maybe you just need to harness it and use it the right way is all. Heck it does make ya stronger and quicker than any fighter even close ta your age," Poke went on, his Iron Range accent really kicking in now that he was on a roll. "I dunno kid, but maybe if ya could just make yourself aware of the red when you're in it, you could focus it and control it and just send it in a constructive direction, ya know? It ain't no good when ya go off all crazy like that, but I betcha if you could use it on just one opponent in just the right way, focused like, you could stand up to anyone."

Bingo, Dusty thought and as Poke finished with his advice, Dusty started doing just that. He used the experience he had with focusing and directing the Light during a Helping to start shaping and directing that red ball of rage still inside of him. The Light of his soon to unfold Helping was still there but it was forgotten for the moment. All that was there was the red and Dusty was using every interior muscle he had to direct it where it needed to go. Where it needed to be focused. On Uncle Lou.

Poke saw Dusty's look change, but to his mind it sure didn't look like it had changed for the better. All Poke saw was the resigned look that settled in on Dusty's grim face.

"Thanks Poke, I think that might help," Dusty said as he stepped back from the older fighter and started shadow boxing.

Poke didn't know now that it *would* help at all, but he let it go. He'll either work it out or he won't, Poke figured. Just like the rest of us.

Dusty was workin' it out all right. He spent the rest of the morning running through his training regimen and focusing, focusing, focusing.

Meanwhile back at the ranch, Lou was getting down with the good times. Lou was directing the available players into their places. Goldie, Tina, and Terry. He saw that Goldie had gotten the brandy for them, three large quarts of Christian Brother's finest. Lou also had his little bit of something extra put away too. An ace up his sleeve. He'd just started hearing about Quaaludes a year or so before. "Make's the girls slide right out of their panties," a cellmate down in Ramsey county had told him.

It did too. Lou found that out in North Dakota when he had those two drug dealers tied up watching him take advantage of their girlfriends. Wasn't no takin' advantage about it after the Quaaludes had kicked in. Not for those two drug-addled sluts. Hell they pushed back as hard as he did. Lou couldn't wait to see what it did for Goldie and the two T's. The two T's, not a tit between 'em, he smiled. But mama's got more than enough.

The women had woken up in an even deeper funk than they had been in before. They were putty is all they were. Putty for Lou to shape. By ten o'clock Lou had them all seated around the dining room table. The cake Lou had Goldie pick up along with the brandy was right in the middle. *Happy Birthday Uncle Lou* it said in bright blue letters. Blue strangely similar to Lou's eyes. Nice touch, he thought. Excellent touch.

Lou told them that since it was his birthday that he would serve them. He went to the kitchen and started mixing their drinks. A brandy and ginger ale, weak for Goldie, and two tall glasses of orange juice for Tina and Terry. Being the qualified mixologist that he was he knew that the beverages weren't quite complete. Nope, need a little somethin special to top it all off. So Lou put half a Quaalude in each of the orange juices and a whole cap in Goldie's. A quick little stir was all it took and he carried them into the dining room and served the women. Next he cut them each a slice of cake and sat down to eat with them.

"Eat up, girls, Uncle Lou's party is officially started. Let's enjoy our cake and our drinks and then maybe we can play a game of cards. Does that sound like fun?"

"Yes, Uncle Lou," Goldie said, her voice dull but purring. The two T's only nodded.

Fifteen blocks away Dusty had finished his long workout with more energy than when he started. More rage and more red than he had ever felt before. It didn't go away after the workout. If anything, it was stronger. He treated himself to a long hot shower at the gym and started home. The fucker told me noon, he thought. Screw him, I'll get there early.

Dusty arrived at the sidewalk leading up to the Danbury's house at eleven-fifteen, a full forty-five minutes early, filled with rage. *Catch him a little early, catch him a little off guard.* He started walking up the broken-cemented walkway when he stopped full in his tracks. It was as if there was an invisible wall holding him back. Time slowed and he came back into himself a bit. Suddenly he had a war raging inside himself. His hatred and fear of Uncle Lou versus the White Light of the Helping that was back in full force. It wasn't black versus white in this case. It was red versus white. The full responsibility of Helping hit him hard. Good, Dusty thought, I'll fucking enjoy Helping anyone touched by Lou. He had an image of the actor Slim Pickens in his head—at the end of the movie Dr. Strangelove, where the aging cowboy actor drops out of an airplane riding an atomic warhead like it was a horse. That's what Dusty felt like he had inside, and all around him. The Power of Light and the Power of Red and he was riding it on down.

Recharged he stormed the steps to his house and yanked his way inside the door fully intending to do his duty. To allow the beauty and the Power to flow through himself and Help. And if he got a little satisfaction in the process so much the better.

Many things began happening at once, with little movement involved for anybody. Maybe if Dusty had had his next thought *before* he saw what he saw, things might've worked out differently. Instead he saw what he saw first, and acted accordingly.

Uncle Lou was seated at the side of the table looking at the playing cards he held in his hand wearing his usual jeans and leisure suit ensemble. No tie today. I wonder why, Dusty thought. He had a half eaten piece of cake on a small paper plate in front of him. There was a glass of milk, odd Dusty thought, and a Kodak Instamatic camera with a few already developed pictures lying next to it. Uh-oh, that camera means danger. Dusty wasn't seeing the whole thing the way he usually did during a Helping. Things were jumbled and he couldn't see any of the immediate future.

On the other side of the table, across from Lou, sat Tina and Terry. Their pieces of cake were barely touched and they both had tall glasses of orange juice in front of them. They've had two already, Dusty knew. And Dusty finally saw that they were wearing only their bras and panties. A great sadness settled over Dusty, muting out everything. His eyes slowly turned back to the center where, at the head of the table, Goldie sat facing him. She's had two pieces of cake and three of those Brandy and ginger ales, with something extra in it. The girls too. He could only see Goldie from the waist up but he knew that she was in her bra and panties as well. Not only that but pulled out and hanging over the right side of her bra was one of her massive breasts, nipple fully erect poking out.

In a surly voice Lou said," You're home early, boy. But just in time to see me win another hand."

It was all starting to flood in now, speeding up so that Dusty could hardly think. The sure knowledge of Helping he had had just a few steps ago was gone.

"Now Tina, honey, and you too, Terry, since I won again you need to take off your bras," Uncle Lou ordered. Which they immediately started doing, their slack faces caught in the light of the pale morning sun, shining in through the dining room window shears.

"Goldie, you just flop that other massive tittie of yours out over the top of that huge fucking bra you wear while I get the camera ready for another little picture of my girls. And really, Goldie, you should think of trimming back those long, *unsightly* nipple hairs of yours. Don't want them to get stuck in anyone's teeth do you?"

"Yes, Uncle Lou," Goldie said, her breathing suddenly huskier, as she reached in and pulled out her left breast. All three of the women rapidly took long pulls on their drinks. Goldie even started tweaking her nipples with her fingers.

Jesus Christ! Dusty was overwhelmed. He was everywhere at once but in no kind of a good way. He had the Power of the Helping surging through him. He had the rage too, which was more powerful than anything else at the way this pig was treating these women. Because he *could*, Dusty knew, Lou's doing it because he could. Dusty saw the dark smudges under Goldie's glassed eyes. He saw her fingers tugging on her nipples. Sick, he screamed inside! Fucking Sick! The two T's were taking a lesson from their mother and starting to do it as well—their eyes hot and narrow, and locked on Uncle Lou, their tongues rubbing back and forth inside their closed mouths. Dusty still might have pulled back if he wouldn't have felt the next ping.

Lou turned to Dusty and said, "Like what you see, kid? Want a glass of orange juice?"

And God forgive him, for a moment he *did* like what he saw, in a sickening, below the belt, itching way. The image of Goldie struck him right between the legs and he felt animal lust as he had never, *ever* felt it before or since. God forgive him, he was becoming erect.

"You *are* liking what you see, aren't you, Smokie," Lou quipped. "Oh, I can see that plain as day, boy. You're lucky those britches are loose. If they were any tighter you might break somethin'."

It all came to Dusty and he saw. All that was there and all that was to come. Reds and Whites shooting out of his eyes and his chest. Even breaking through the women's stupor and causing Lou to tilt back in his seat, a brief look of fear in his eyes. This was only the beginning of the day's activities, Dusty saw. How Uncle Lou wouldn't be satisfied until he had everyone in the bedroom doing every imaginable and unimaginable thing in every conceivable combination, in color, with pictures. Dusty in the mix as well, with brandy and Quaaludes and lust running through his system. How Lou would time it all so that when Jim strolled through the door later that afternoon, tired from his midnight run to Cass Lake, Jim would see it all. The family would cease to be. It would shatter and so would the lives of the people in it. A few years from now the girls might still be alive but they would be the unlucky ones. Drug addiction and a series of increasingly abusive men. Goldie would finally start taking those drinks she'd always been afraid to take and wind up existing, for a year or two, in the north end of Superior. Jim? Jim would take the easiest way out. Shit, he worked on the railroad so he'd just go ahead and take the A train. He'd pull their sagging Rambler station wagon around the flashing crossing guards and let the midnight, taconite train from Eveleth catch him square in the driver's car door. Three engines smoking, at full speed, pulling one full mile of brimming hopper cars. Uncle Lou? He'd be gone tonight. On to St. Paul and his next darkness.

Then Dusty saw what had been missing. What had failed to appear to him before this moment. Who he was supposed to Help. The Light was making no mistakes about that now. It was shouting to his mind "save Uncle Lou. Save Lou. He is the one to save." Dusty knew, as only a Helper could know, that the Light wanted Lou saved. And Dusty snapped. "No!" he cried out. "Not a fucking chance!"

Maybe it was because of the power of the rage inside. Add to that the guilt over having been aroused by the sight of Goldie and the girls. Top that off with the brief look of fear that passed over Lou's face, and you have a Helper saying no. No, he said, and no he meant.

"I won't help," Dusty cried, and found he didn't have to, something that would have been inconceivable before. He focused on the red, then hid it, and gave Lou a taste of the white. For a moment he let the Light grow to its supreme intensity and let it envelope Lou. Lou's eyes were opened, he was washed in the Light and he saw just how evil he had been. Lou also saw that this boy that he thought was trash, had the power to transform him into something good. For the first time in his ugly life Lou wanted to be good. He knew what it was to be good. He was clean. Lou felt the Power and was transported.

Dusty was caught up in the rapture and hesitated. This was beauty as even he had never experienced in a Helping before. He was right on the edge. Maybe he *should* Help Lou. He knew the women could be Helped as well and all would work out. All *would* work out. Poised on tip-toes in his mind, he considered. He could very well have made it had he not looked at Goldie at that moment. Looked at her and saw her looking at Lou, hands still stretching her nipples, a look of uncertainty now on her face.

Dusty chose before he couldn't anymore. No thoughts of Franklin, no thoughts on the power of the choices we make and where that can lead us, nothing of consequences. Dusty said no to the Light. He was a Helper who refused to Help. He chose to not *Help* Lou, but to destroy him.

He let Lou bathe in the purity of the Light for another moment and then Dusty inhaled. He inhaled in his mind with all the Power that was in his mind. All of the Power of the Light and the added Power of the Red. He inhaled and sucked the Light back out of Lou. He refocused the Light and the Helping on the women, washing them in the Love, saving them, and he drew up the hidden red beam of the rage's power and focused it fully on Lou. Lou never had a chance. And after turning his back on the Power, neither did Dusty.

22

Well I suppose we could go into all the details of what happened next, but that is all they would be. Details. I could tell you how the women *were* Hclpcd. How thcir lives were saved and changed miraculously. The two T's blossoming into loving, nurturing women. Goldie becoming even more of a bright shining spirit in her church and in her home. Hell, even Jim perked up a bit and he wasn't even there. I could also go into the details of how uncle Lou went racing into the day, barefoot and babbling, nothing left of his mind but torment. Finally cornered by the police hours later wailing in a backstreet alley. But that is all they would be. Details. I think you've got the picture already. Dusty turned left when he should've turned right. Hell, maybe even I would have done the same thing had I been in Dusty's shoes. You too, maybe. Be that as it may, Dusty turned left.

He didn't lose his Helping power. Not at all. As a matter of fact he Helped a plebe firefighter trainee only three weeks later. Dusty Helped him as he wandered past the accident scene where the young trainee was futilely applying mouth to mouth to a dying toddler. Dusty still had the ability. He also now had the burden of his wrong turn. Not something as inconsequential as turning left rather than right on your way out of school in the third grade. No sir, this was turning left instead of right in the big leagues. Dusty was in the big leagues now and he didn't think he could hack it. Fuck.

Franklin Rose had even felt something stir inside himself way the heck up in Thunder Bay. Franklin didn't know the details but he knew something wrong had happened and his mind had flashed back on his last discussion with Dusty. He was so disturbed he had even written Dusty a letter. A letter Dusty didn't answer for quite awhile.

We're gonna skip ahead a bit. There's another character or two that need to be introduced to you and to each other. Way before John can even get a chance to lose his Helping. You remember John, don't you? John's in a world 'a shit, but before we can see what happens there let's take a quick trip down to Florida and then it's on to Parris Island.

23

While Dusty Hakila was dropping out of high school and boxing, in that order, in Duluth, Minnesota and John Sloan was completing high school and wrestling in Watertown, Wisconsin, a young woman was coming to terms with her life in North Miami, Florida.

Deena Morrison was a couple of years younger than John and Dusty. She was an only child who lived with her parents Adele and Jerry. She had darkish, red hair and brown eyes. She liked her hair, liked how it made her different, except when it made her feel different when she didn't *want* to be different. Remember adolescence? Oh yea, the whole shebang, and Deena had it in clubs—the kind you beat yourself with. Her parents loved her and gave her as much as they could, as often as they could, without spoiling her. They had resigned themselves to being childless, when Deena came along unexpectedly and gave them the child they had only dreamed of.

Deena knew she had good parents and knew that she had it so much better than many of her friends and yet she felt she didn't quite fit in. Take her breasts for example. They were almost large. Well go ahead and say it, they *were* large. She was already into a C-cup in junior high and she moved up another cup by high school. Now she liked her breasts and she liked how it drew the boys attention and gave her a certain power over them. And at the same time she would hide them. She didn't just want people to like her because she was pretty, in an offbeat sort of a way, or because she was stacked. She was also smart and quick witted and could be sly as hell, so she often dressed down to hide her physical attractiveness and to see if the other kids would like her for her mind.

Except sometimes she was afraid to show that too. On occasion she could light up a room with her jokes and her sarcasm and her smart-aleckie way of looking at things, but at other times she just felt closed off. In a shell. Afraid. She couldn't quite be a beauty queen and she couldn't quite be a brain. She couldn't quite be anything. That's what she figured her problem was. "I'm too wishy-washy," she'd think. "Too *not enough. Too* much, of *not* much of anything, and not enough of something." Deena had one more difference as well. She was a Helper. Had been since she was five years old. That was the first time she had Helped anyway, and it had proved to her what she already had an inkling about—that she *was* different.

Deena was somewhere in between John and Dusty. She didn't feel the overwhelming joy and goodness of being a Helper that John did. Didn't have that foundation in her that gave John his positive attitude and she certainly hadn't had even a portion of the hard knocks that Dusty had had. Hard knocks and bad breaks that made him cynical and jaded in spite of the goodness of Helping. She couldn't honestly buy into John's thankful attitude and she didn't have the experience to warrant Dusty's horseshit attitude. If she could have put it into words, she would have wished for one or the other. She often wished that she had been adopted. In reality she sometimes wondered if she hadn't *been* adopted, because then she would at least have an excuse for her questioning mind. For her wondering why she just couldn't get it and other people seemed to be able to. Or if they didn't get it, they were at least content with knowing that they hadn't and could live with it. She wasn't too hot and she wasn't too cold but she *definitely* wasn't that old third bowl of porridge either. No, she wasn't *just right* and she wanted to be.

At least her parents were satisfied with who they were. She got a kick out of them, when her teen-aged mind would let her. Her dad, Jerry, worked at Eastern Airlines. He had started out as a machinist, became a shop steward, and now worked full time for the union. He had left Czechoslovakia with his parents as a very young boy. Jerry's parents, professionals in the old country, had never quite adjusted to America. They had hoped Jerry would go to college but were sufficiently relieved when Jerry had expressed an interest in things mechanic and had found a good paying trade.

Jerry *had* picked up their love of reading and continued to read. Often and with varied tastes. He could read a biography of Abraham Lincoln, finish it, and dive right into a Raymond Chandler thriller. From War and Peace to Peace in the Valley to Valley of the Dolls, it didn't matter to him. It gave him a sharp mind and a tolerance for others.

Adele? Adele was a trip. She had been smuggled out of Germany with a younger cousin in the late '30s and had lived with relatives in New York City. Her father had died before even reaching Dachau and her mother had survived a Polish work camp. Adele's mother had made it to the United States after liberation but died shortly thereafter when Adele was about Deena's age now. She often said how she didn't think she would have made it through her mother's death if she hadn't met the quiet, dark haired Jerry at Pullman's Bakery in Brooklyn.

"He bought me a chocolate eclair and asked me to walk with him through the park in our neighborhood," Adele would say, "and he loved me from the start. For some reason I told him my whole life story on that first date and he told me that *he* would be my family. We've been together ever since."

Adele would tell the story in such a delicate and touching way that you could see the scared young woman she had been before becoming the strong, opinionated woman she was now. The woman she had become with Jerry's help and love.

If you didn't know better you would wonder how such a strong woman could be such a softie. Adele could have a stinging tongue and she rarely suffered fools gladly but there were two people in her life that always got the soft end of the stick from her. Her husband Jerry, whom she loved so much it almost scared her, and her daughter Deena. They were her soft spots and they were enough. Way *more* than enough for Adele.

Jerry's thoughts were almost identical to Adele's. Sometimes, late at night while lying in bed, he would review his life and wonder how he had been so lucky. So blessed to have been allowed to be loved by a woman who made his whole world round. How could an average guy like him have been given a woman like Adele? A woman who gave him the love and the strength to be the man he was. More of a man than he had ever had any idea he might be. He had loved her from the first moment he had met her and he loved her still. He would have to choke back a sob of joy, worried he would wake his wife faithfully sleeping next to him, as he considered how God had blessed him not only with Adele, but also, when all hope was lost of ever having a child, how God had given them Deena. He made no mistake about that either. God had given Deena to them. As if she had fallen out of the sky when all of their hopes were gone. Jerry had no doubts about which side of the bread *his* bread was buttered on. His bread was buttered on both sides, and by women. Two women to be exact. Two women, so different and so alike, who made him a man. A good man. The man he was.

Deena *had* been Bat Mitsvah'd at thirteen but had not been raised in a religious household. Any questions about religion always provided Adele with the opening for one of her favorite lines, of which she had many. Are you Jewish, someone would ask?

"My husband Jerry is Jewish," she would reply, pausing and relishing the moment," and I'm," she would pause again with the timing of a Catskills comic," and I.... I'm not," she would finish.

With her punch line delivered, she would regally raise her Benson and Hedges menthol filter-tip to her lipsticked mouth and wait for her well-deserved reaction. Adele *was* Jewish, of course. By birth, but she had never felt a connection with the religion. She wasn't anti-Jew or self-hating. It just didn't apply to her. She didn't feel it or feel any need to force it on anyone, her family included.

She also didn't give other religions a hard time. She didn't dislike Christians, as a few of her friends did, behind closed doors of course. Not hate, but rather, she didn't feel the paranoia or disdain for them as some of her friends did. She never engaged in even the slightest joke that would be at the expense of another's religion. Now, she did love a good, " a Rabbi, a Priest, and a Minister walk into a bar" joke as long as they weren't mean spirited and as long as they were good jokes. She figured if she could laugh at herself, well then by God others could too. But she would never tell tales of their perceived shortcomings. Especially with the Roman Catholic faith. She would doggedly defend them should it come up in discussion.

"They may have had human failings, just like the rest of us, in the past and to this day, for all I know," Adele would respond, with no doubt that she would brook no disparagement of the Catholic church,"and maybe they haven't always acted as they should have, but you can't tell me that they don't care for others too. That they don't look to live a good life, not at the *expense* of others, but by *helping* others. Giving of themselves as any good Jew would do, or Christian or Muslim for that matter."

Gathering steam her eyes would blaze and if the person having the discussion with her had never had it before they would be a bit taken aback at her defense of Catholics. "Don't you even tell me for one minute that there haven't been countless," and here she would repeat," *countless* acts of kindness by Catholics toward other Christians, and Jews as well. There are good works being done by Catholics every second that none of us know about. None of us! So don't you tell me that Catholics aren't as good as anyone else. I won't hear of it!"

Jerry would watch his wife defending a religion, certainly not her own, and a soft look would come into his eyes. Someone watching closely might even get the idea that Jerry shared his wife's views with as much passion as she did. He just didn't feel the need to voice his opinions, but it sure looked as if his were the same.

"She's right," he would say," but let's hear no more of that. Now who needs two tickets to the Dolphin's game this Sunday? I just may have a pair in my wallet that you could talk me out of for the right price."

People who knew Adele would often bait her a bit just because it would raise such a strong response. A strong response from a woman known for her strong responses. Adele was outspoken and, had she been rich, would've been considered an eccentric. And to further her eccentricities, at least as far as her Jewish friends were concerned, she loved nuns. Loved them. Whenever she would pass a nun wearing a habit, or other distinctive apparel, she would make it a point to stop and talk with the woman. On city streets, in the mall, where ever it may happen, she would stop and say hello and pass the time for as long as time permitted, while her companion or companions, whomever they may be, waited patiently or impatiently, as the case may be.

"And people give the Catholic church a hard time," she would whisper afterward. "How dare they, when these women are devoting their entire lives to their God and to others. Don't you *tell* me you go to synagogue on *holidays,* when these women are *living* it every moment of their lives."

Deena had been exposed to Adele's behavior for so long that she never gave it a second thought. She secretly admired it. She loved how her mother took strong stands on things she believed in. You never doubted where Adele stood on an issue. Deena wished she had more of that but, one, she didn't know where she stood on most things, and two, when she did she didn't always express herself. Or if she did, she went overboard and lost control and felt foolish.

Deena missed her parents when she left for college in Gainseville, but go she must and go she did. There was no way that she was not going to go to college. This was something even her father was vocally adamant about.

"If you want to become a fisherman, or fisherwoman, I guess, and cut bait and smell for the rest of your life, feel free and be my guest," her father would say,"but you *will* go to college and you *will* graduate. That is your mother and I's commitment to you. We must see you through that far at least. Education gives you choices. After that you may pursue whatever adventures you wish to pursue. Pursue them with our blessings as long as you're not doing any of those drugs or looking for something for nothing. But you must graduate from college."

Her mother would usually let Jerry handle these discussions. A rarity in the Morrison household. Adele would sit back with a prideful smile and let Jerry talk. You could tell that Jerry was her man. She loved him as he loved her.

Deena grew up in a house full of love. She had the capacity to love and had even had two great loves before leaving for college. The first a puppy love, though no less painful when it ended, and the second a brief and fumblingly passionate tumble with a Coast Guard seaman stationed on Miami Beach. The second had happened her senior year in high school and been broken off right before graduation. He had been the only man, boy really, he was only nineteen, that Deena had gone all the way with. She had loved how his hands had felt on her body. How her breath would shorten and quicken whenever he was around. How he had even taught her how to take him in her mouth, and did it in a gentle, loving way, not in a forceful *you better or else* way. She hadn't even minded how it tasted.

Of course she had been quite surprised after about two minutes when he had accidentally erupted into her mouth, but they had both laughed and he had said that turnabout was fair play and had slipped beneath the covers and performed a similar technique on her. Talk about surprise. She's heard of men going down on women before, but Holy Shit, she thought, I wish I could tell my mom about this! Funny, but that's what she thought. It had just felt so good. Almost like a Helping. She had been totally lost in it and there had even been a bright light. It didn't shine as long or as brightly as a Helping light but it had been there all right.

"Whew," she giggled as she lay panting next to her young sailor," so that's what an orgasm is! We need to do this more often."

They had, and they had used protection and when he received orders transferring him to Duluth, Minnesota, of all places, she had been heart-broken.

She had left for college a girl on the verge of becoming a woman. A Helper not quite sure of her place in the world. A highly intelligent, quick witted, stunning young woman. And she was the last to know. She just knew that she had a nagging suspicion that something was not quite right. That she was missing some part of a bigger picture.

That she would one day end up in Duluth, Minnesota and find love? Yes—but she would find it not with a sailor but with an ex-marine. And he would be a Helper, just like her. And Help her he would. She had no way of knowing all of this when she tearfully left her parent's house on North Miami Avenue and headed out with two of her girlfriends to the University of Florida.

How could she? Did you know? Do you even know, for sure now, what will happen to you tomorrow, or tonight even? You may have a pretty good handle on it but do you know *for sure?* Of course not, none of us do. *Most* of us don't, anyway. Nope, she knew none of this. She just headed up the road like we all do, hoping for the best and fearing the worst. Least of all she didn't know that she would meet John Sloan, be Helped by him, and then leave the best man she had ever loved. Leave him broken-hearted and *Helpless.* Helpless in many more ways than one.

Nope, she knew none of this. She just headed up the highway with her girlfriends, thinking about college and singing along with Tom Petty and the Heartbreakers. Their long hair blowing, windows open, bare feet on the dashboard, singing, "break down, go ahead and give it to me. Break down, baby take me thru the night. (baby, baby, break down) Break down it's all right, it's all right. It's all right." Well sometimes it's all right and then again sometimes it's not.

See you in boot camp.

24

Belay my last. Belay my last? I know, I know, boot camp, Parris Island, John and Dusty meet, they fire up, become compadres, and we further set the stage which will bring us up to date and usher us into the world of the great squirting brown stuff that John's life was to become. Not only bring you up to the present, but then we have to see just what in the hell's *gonna* happen. Now *I* know what will happen. Oh, do I know. I was there. Of course now I'm always there. Where? Well, pretty much everywhere since you asked. But I *was* there and let me tell you I was just as surprised as the next guy. No shit, I was. Who'da thought. Better yet, who'da thought, hey? It shouldn't have worked out that way but it did. Kind of a shame really.

You know, I'd forgotten how much I liked Deena. I liked her mom too, although I never met her exactly. Shoot, Deena didn't even look much like her mom, but she sure could sound like her, when she wanted to or when she needed to.

She had that same delicate streak of love too. Deena would get it when she was with John the way Adele got it sometimes when she was looking at Jerry. Oh man, I have to laugh when I think of how she would look at John when he didn't know she was looking at him. She would *melt*. You knew she was thinking, how did I end up with this guy? Why is he with me? When will the jig be up? Sometimes John would catch the tail end of one of her glances. Love glances, I call them. Kinda like giving someone the old evil-eye, but in reverse.

He would her give the *what(?),* look. The look guys give their women when they don't know what's going on but their women do. *What*, honey? See he thought he was pretty damn lucky to be with her as well. Too bad what happened to them.

So, anyway, I'm gonna screw up the whole chronology, as if I haven't screwed it up enough already, and let them meet for the first time...

John was in his mid-thirties, living in Duluth, and kind of flowing through life. Meeting people, occasionally Helping someone, and just generally taking the journey as it came. He was let down that he hadn't gotten married yet. Really the only true disappointment of his life was not finding a wife and maybe raising a couple of quarter-Swedes.

He had his share of life's small ups and downs. He was bummed when the Packers lost to the Vikings. Saddened when he witnessed the pettiness of people hurting each other. Happy when complimented on a job well done. Overwhelmed with peace when he Helped someone. He wasn't all the way where he wanted to be but he had had enough close calls, and he knew enough people who had had it much worse, to know that he had better not bitch too much. Don't cry hunger with a loaf of bread under your arm.

He worked as a surveyor. Not the phone kind, the land kind. One of the men and women you see out on highways and city streets holding poles and peering through sideways, microscope looking things, wearing orange or yellow reflective vests. Going about their mysterious business of calculations and triangulations while the cars and buses and trucks of life's traffic whizzed close by. John enjoyed it. It allowed him to be outside and it allowed him to move around. He wasn't stuck in one place all day chained to something. He could smoke a cigarette when he wanted and, heck, if you were out of town, you kind of carried your restroom with you, if you know what I mean. Just find a tree and do your business. A guy's job for a guy's guy.

He learned surveying in the Marine Corps, while in artillery school. Yep, they use land survey. Gotta know where you are if you want to shoot where you ain't, at least with any kind of accuracy you do. He was trained as a forward observer but had finished that training so quickly and done so well that he had been allowed to attend the land survey course while awaiting orders.

This proved to be providential as the civilian world rarely called on the talents of a forward observer. Forward looking might be good, if you're part of the president's staff or involved in some think-tank somewhere, but forward observing, no. Wasn't much call for that. Rarely was he in, say, a mall parking lot packing a radio and looking through binoculars calling in 105 millimeter howitzer support. Asking for six rounds of high explosive, that's H.E. to you, jarhead, to be brought in on the map coordinates for the Sears store five-hundred meters away and, by the way, add one-hundred meters left correction, drop fifty, and fire for effect. No, the civilian world didn't seem to appreciate the fact that with only a map and a radio he could contact Marine Corps artillery, air support, or Naval gunfire and facilitate a rain of destruction down on any target that made the simple mistake of being in his viewing area. Death from above, he thought. That he had done, and more, while serving in Panama and Gulf War One.

The fact that he could do all of this while taking incoming fire himself was also lost on, and in, the civilian world. It was appreciated occasionally, should it come up in semi-casual conversation, but it was a generally useless talent outside of the above stated situations. All in all, land surveying was, for John, a nice benefit from a grateful nation.

John was having coffee in a Perkin's Restaurant when he bumped into an acquaintance. He was feeling especially good that day. Almost as if he had a Helping coming on. It had been over a year since he had last been allowed to facilitate his unique talent and he perked up at that idea. Some kind of buzz goin' on anyway, he thought.

His survey crew had stopped in for lunch and he had seen his friend Laura at a booth in the corner of the diner. Laura had worked for the surveying company a while back as a rod person for another crew. They had occasionally shot the breeze after work and had struck up a casual friendship. Laura had been working on survey crews during her summer college breaks after going back to school to finish up her master's degree in social work. She was tall, blonde, a few years older than John, and a bit distant at first, but fun to know once she opened up. And most people eventually opened up to John, given the chance. They had even considered dating but both seemed to know that it would have been a brief dalliance only, and neither cared for that. At least not with each other.

John's food was taking its time getting to his table so he had popped over to Laura's booth to say hello, feeling even more of that special Helping feeling coming on but not really noticing it much. Maybe it's just good to see Laura, he thought. John sensed a millisecond of deep sorrow as well. It was there and then gone in a flash. Barely a blip on the screen and then Laura introduced him to the two women that were seated with her. One of her friends was a dusky, olive skinned woman about his age with a flirting, flashing smile and shining brunette hair. Had Dusty been there he would have mentioned that she also had just a hint of sideburns, but then John liked that. Dusty did too, so he usually let John slide on such matters. Of course Dusty won't be back on this scene for months yet but he did have a way of setting a scene. *Painted, guinea bitch*, Dusty might have intoned, earthy *and* with fuck-me red nails. *Get some a that, Sloantown.*

The other woman seemed almost lost, or maybe hiding in the corner seams of the booth. Maybe not lost or hiding, maybe observing while tucked into the plush plastic folds of the booth.

Some deep sense of *something there* flashed to John. Sadness? A few years younger than John, maybe younger. She had bleached blonde hair with darkish roots, brown eyes, and now she did look to be hiding something. Hiding an impish smile maybe? Like she had a secret and John wasn't in on it. Her name was Deena.

Funny, from that day on John could never remember the name of the olive skinned beauty even though she had been the one that had caught most of his attention. John chatted with the three women briefly, shared a couple of smiles and left. John had thought nothing of it. He wandered back to his crew's table, enjoyed his lunch, and went back to work thinking only of the day and the work ahead. And thinking a little bit about how his Helping buzz was growing. It was a good day. No problems, not a cloud in the sky.

John returned home from work late that night. The team had screwed up on some of their math in the field and John stayed in the office and reworked the problems until they were straightened out. He was greeted by darkness in his small apartment broken only by the flashing of his answering machine light. Blink on, blink off, blink on, blink off. One message only: "Hi John, this is Laura. It was great to see you today. Would you give me a call?" Laura's smiling voice said. "I know someone that wants to date you," Laura sing-songed before saying, "Sloan, you're a studly guy. Better call soon," and she gave her number and hung up.

Now what was that dark haired chick's name, John thought. Gina? Julie? Jackie? I think that's it! Jackie, he thought finally. Maybe that's the buzz I've been feeling all day.

John had no way of knowing just how much his life could be changed by a little flashing light. Or lunch at Perkin's for that matter. It never occurred to him that the machine's flashing red light, the color of his third grade teacher Mrs. Abbott's hair, he thought absently, could have been a warning. One slow, steady, flashing orangeish-red blip whispering to un-hearing ears, "danger, tread softly, step lightly." Flash, flash, flash, "Proceed with caution. Detour ahead."

It was getting late so John had to wait until the next evening to phone Laura. He was excited and nervous about calling. He was also glad that there was a go between. John could be nervous around women he was interested in and it seemed to be getting worse the older he got. Shit, he was still single, and the way he was going, by the time he was fifty, he wouldn't even be able to ask anyone out at all.

There was an inverse proportion thang happening here that gave him a slight case of the willies. The shit he'd seen and the things he'd done, good and bad, and he still got the goofies when asking a woman out.

Caught a break here, he thought. Good old Laura, helping out the cause. Once he knew someone was interested in him, it was OK. No problem, nerves steady for the most part. It had been a running joke around the different survey crews that if John hadn't been so obviously straight, he may have been gay.

"Shit, guys," he'd tell them, "I try. I just don't meet that many women I'm interested in and when I do, by the time I work up my courage to ask them out, I find out that they're either married, engaged, or not interested."

"Sure, John," they'd lisp in unison, men *and* women crew members, " that's all right. It doesn't make you a bad person, honey. C'mon out of that closet you're hiding in, baby. Embrace the love, embrace the dudes."

Good-natured ribbing, in a less enlightened time, perhaps, but given only because of the closeness of John's crew.

He'd pretty much given up talking to them about his few dates. Wasn't worth the abuse so he was very happy to be dialing Laura's number. She answered on the first ring.

"Laura Roland," she said, all business.

"Hey Laura, it's John Sloan."

"Oh, hey John. Good to hear from you. I thought you might have been one of my clients calling to reschedule. Now that I've had my MSW for awhile I've been doing some one-on-one counseling. You almost missed me. I'm leaving tomorrow for a quick vay-cay to Florida and I've still got two more clients to move around. How have you been, John? You looked all studly in your work uniform yesterday. You survey men are such GUYS."

Laughing, John said," I'm good Laura. I see you're still drinking coffee. Good to hear you and good to see you too. Maybe you can slip me in for a little counseling when you get back. Help me touch my inner teddy bear or something."

"Yea, you'd rather be touching something else and none of that's gonna happen here. So what makes you call?" she teased.

John felt guilty all of a sudden, or nervous or something, "Well, I, ahhh, just wanted to get back to you about..."

"I know, I know, I'm just messing with you Johnnie. Do you remember my friend that was with me yesterday?"

"The one with the dark hair? Jackie?"

"No, you goof. You're kidding right. Jenny?"

Jenny. Yea, *that's* her name, John thought.

"Jenny'd chew you up and spit you out. Did you really think I was calling about her?"

"Well I don't know," John said. "I just, you know..."

"No John, my other friend. Deena. Blonde hair, nice boobs, wearing a floral-print, summer dress with the little sweater. Kind of different looking. Did you even see her?"

"Sure, I saw her," replied John, trying to catch up with the conversation. "I mean, I'm not quite sure what makes a dress a summer dress, but yea, I know who you mean."

"What did you think?"

"She looked fine to me, Laura. She did kinda look like she had some private joke going on that she didn't want to let me in on, that's all. She was kind of smiling at the wrong places."

"Well she sure liked you, John. She lit up as soon as you left. She wanted to know who you were and were you married and were you the guy I had mentioned to her before. By the way, I *have* mentioned you to her before. I even thought about hooking you two up about a year ago. I've known her for ages."

"Really?"

"Christ, is that all you can say John?"

"No. Sorry Laura. Sure I'm interested. Is she cool? Is she a good chick? A nice gal? Will she perform oral love on my special parts?" laughed John, finally catching up and enjoying the conversation.

"Shut up," Laura said. "She's cool, and smart, and pretty, although she sometimes tries to hide her looks and her brains. I think you guys might make a nice pair."

"I'm just kidding, Laura. Really. Thanks, I'd love to ask her out. Thank you."

"Well don't give me a hard time if it doesn't work out but she told me to give you her number if you were interested, and if I were you I wouldn't waste any time calling. I'll be out of town for the next week and when I get back I'll want a full report."

Laura gave John the number and they chatted about mutual friends and work for a few minutes before ending the call.

"John, you know that smile you were talking about? Deena's smile?"

"Yes," he replied.

"Well Deena's father died about two years ago and just when she was getting over that her mother died last winter. I haven't seen her smile in six months and I talk to her almost every day. Not anything. Not a joke or a smirk or anything and then you waltz into the diner and she lights up. I think I was almost as happy as she was, so count yourself lucky, John. She smiled for you. Don't screw it up," she said and hung up the phone.

Uh-oh.

25

John left for boot camp in December. He chose Parris Island over San Diego. He had heard that Parris Island was more hardcore than San Diego, and he wanted to test himself. He got the chance.

He probably shouldn't have gotten as drunk as he did at his going away party. His last recollection of that night was of leaning back on his bar stool and falling, chair and all, to the floor. Just like falling into a swimming pool, his drunken mind thought, slowly back and down. After that it was a blur and two days later he was still sick on his flight into Charleston, South Carolina.

He was as nervous as everyone else when he took the cliched, but still effective, midnight bus ride over the levee onto Parris Island and the Marine Corps Recruit Depot. It was just like the first half of the movie Full Metal Jacket, which he saw sometime after boot camp— literally, word for word.

John would have been even shakier going into training but he had Helped someone on the flight down from Milwaukee. He had been seated next to a man that was flying to South Carolina to bury his only son. A son that the man, Tony, had run out on years before. He called himself an ex-drunk and had only just started re-establishing contact with his son two months prior. He had been planning on visiting his son for the first time sober when he had gotten the call. He was using the same ticket to fly to his son's burial that he had purchased for their reunion. To top it all off, Tony's son Ronnie had been riding his motorcycle and had been struck and killed by a drunk driver.

John had been sitting, hungover, next to Tony as the flight took off. The alcohol fumes were still seeping out of John's pours and his hands were shaking. Glad I don't drink very often, he thought. How do people do this? Through the haze John had noticed that the man next to him was hurting but he had been too preoccupied with his own misery to even introduce himself. It had been Tony who had started the conversation.

"I remember what those were like," Tony said, almost as an afterthought. Almost to himself. "Hangovers."

"Man, I sure do," he said, shaking his head slowly as he chucked back a sob that tried to sneak out of his chest.

That got John's attention and he felt the light of a Helping starting to seep in. It broke through the dreck in his mind and started the familiar glow.

"You used to drink?" John asked.

"Yea, I'm an ex-drunk. Been sober eighteen months now, but sometimes I wonder what's the use?"

Now, not only was the light there, but the details of Tony's situation were appearing in John's mind. Tony had been a horrid and pathetic drunk. Not so much violent as absent and heartbreaking. The kind of man whose family kept wondering how such a good, well meaning person could be such a loser. How could he sink so low? John saw the wine sores and the vile living conditions that Tony existed under following his abandonment of his family. He saw his skid row detox and the first light of hope that had glimmered in Tony's mind at an AA meeting. He saw the poorly penciled letters that he had sent to his family in South Carolina after his first six months of sobriety. Heart wrenching in that such a sad attempt at writing could have such power. Could have such *meaning*. Could be so *true*.

John also saw the reason for Tony's current distress—Ronnie's accident, the late night phone call from his hysterical ex-wife. He saw that Tony was waiting only for the flight attendant to escort the drink cart down the aisle so he could renew his vows to booze. How Tony wanted and needed his first love back. How he was willing to do anything if that mini-bottle of vodka would buy him a moment of time away from his pain and his shame.

"My name is John. John Sloan."

Absentmindedly Tony stuck out his hand, and automatically said, " Tony Steros."

Boom! The Light was not only surrounding John and Tony but it was flashing out to the entire plane. The Light was consuming the cabin and pouring out of the small cabin windows. Just like my little sister's Play-Doh Fun Factory John thought. If you jammed a ton of clay into it and then stomped on it with all your might. Sploosh and splatt. The pressure of the Helping being squeezed through John's spirit was forcing it into every nook and cranny in the jet. Forcing it out of the plastic paned, double windows with such force that John wondered how they could withstand the pressure.

"There is a Light, Tony. Do you know that?"

"My God, I hope so," Tony choked out, sobbing quietly now, unseen by the other passengers. "Oh Christ, please. I hope so."

"There *is* a Light Tony. I am the Light, I am in the Light, and you are in It too."

While it was John's voice making these words and these sounds, it was coming from somewhere much more than John. Some place much more than John. It was coming from There. The There which was Here now, as well. And Tony shifted.

John's mind started humming You Are My Sunshine to Tony.

"Your sunshine will never be taken away, Tony. Ever. It's ever present, even when hidden behind great storm clouds. Go, help your ex-wife. Help your family. Be the man you *are*," the voice said, "not the man you were.

Tony was saved and John had Helped. Simple as that. If saving a man's life can ever be considered simple.

The rest of the flight was uneventful. John dozed and Tony, in spite of the circumstances, glowed. Not glowing with the light of joy, but with the light that being useful and whole can bring, even under dire conditions, especially under dire conditions. Their flight ended with only a brief goodbye, Tony's mind already closing in over the Helping.

"See you, John. You be careful in boot camp," was all Tony had said, "and Thank you," he added not even completely sure now why he said it.

"I will, Tony. My condolences."

Now why would he say that, Tony thought and exited the plane.

John's hangover was gone, replaced by a bone tired weariness now that he was facing the unknowns of Marine Corps boot camp. It was a pretty scary ride over that levee but it could have been worse. Much worse.

26

John met Dusty seven days later. John was standing at attention in front of his rack, staring straight ahead at the back of his Drill Instructor's head. Drill Instructor Sgt. Cherico was screaming at the recruit across the passageway from John.

"Hakila? Fucking Hakila?" he yelled in disbelief. "You ain't no Finlander boy, you one of them fucking Indians aint' you boy? You one a them reservation rats, I bet. Runnin' around the woods tryin' to fuck some poor little Bambi, hey private Hakila? Where were you born recruit?"

"Sir, Bad River Indian Reservation, Wisconsin, Sir!"

John noticed something in the voice. First off, a similar accent, Bad River only being eighty miles or so from Superior, Wisconsin. The respect for the DI was there too, but underneath it was something else. Something lacking really. No fear. Almost some humor there. John thought that whoever this Hakila guy was he sure didn't scare easy.

"Bad River Indian fucking Reservation, huh? You think you're a bad man, private Finndian? That's what you are, ain't it boy? A Finndian?"

"Sir, yes sir!"

"Oh, now you telling me you're bad? Is that it? You a bad man, Finndian? You gonna chase me around the woods and try and poke me up the ass?"

"Wouldn't be any skin off my sphinctum if I did, fuck you very much."

What?! John almost laughed out loud. What the fuck was that, John thought? Then he realized that he hadn't heard the reply out loud, but instead had heard it in his brain.

"I'm waitin', Finndian!" yelled Sgt. Cherico, while John was wondering if he had just lost his mind.

"Sir, no sir. The private is not a bad man sir. Sir, no sir, the private does not wish to poke his drill instructor in the ass!... Sir!"

"You a smart ass there, Finndian? Tell me you ain't a smart ass, boy."

"Sir, no sir. The private is not a smart ass, sir."

"Listen up pigs, and listen up loud and fucking clear," chomped Sgt. Cherico to the entire platoon, "I don't give a shit if you're an Indian, a Finndian, a Mexicano-fucking-American or a jig-a-fucking-boo. You are all pieces of shit as far as I'm concerned and I am familiar with pieces of shit, so take my fucking word on it. We do not discriminate in my Marine Corps. No sir! We do not treat anyone different if they are black or white or brown or fucking red-yellow-purple. Here we treat *everyone* like they're black, or in the case of my Bad River maggot, *Indian*. You are all second class citizens. You got that?"

"Sir, yes sir!" the entire platoon agreed.

"We got light green marines and we got dark green marines. We even got Finndian colored Marines, but remember this you pukes. You are all GREEN! And you all SUCK, and you'll be lucky if even one of you makes it in my Marine Corps."

"Shit, the fucker's Indian himself," John heard in his mind. "Little blanket-ass Potto-fucking-wattamii from down in central Wisconsin. Not all that far from your new neck of the woods, hey Sloan." Where was this coming from? *John* wasn't thinking these thoughts. They were coming from somewhere else.

"Surprised, homey?" John heard and thought, "what the fuck?"

"What the fuck indeed," was the reply in his mind.

"Hakila," Sgt. Cherico continued, " your new name is Private Finndian. Got it?"

"Sir, yes sir. The private's new name is Private Finndian, Sir!"

Sgt Cherico wasn't quite done with this little soliloquy. "You are shit, Finndian. I am the only Indian in this sorry ass platoon that anyone has to concern themselves with. And trust me maggots, I am the baddest motherfucking Indian you will ever meet in your life," he said, as he left faced and began pacing in front of the platoon.

John got his first glimpse at the private across from him. Hakila, the one who had just weathered their Jr. DI's most recent barrage.

"He just said maggot. Can you fucking *believe it*? Could we be just a little bit more *cliche* here? Hey Sarge, are you right out of central casting or what? How uniquely you turn a phrase, my three striped Indian brother."

These silent sentences were echoing in John's mind. John searched the eyes of the privates across the squad-bay from himself and was drawn back to Hakila who still wasn't looking at John.

"Name's Dusty," he heard and then Dusty met John's eyes and winked. "Howdy, Helper. Ain't this a little party we got ourselves involved in? Name's Dusty Hakila, and don't you dare call me Finndian or I *will* chase your ass around the woods and poke your little pooper."

John was stunned. He heard Sgt. Cherico chewing someone else's ass at the far end of the squad-bay, but it barely registered and then it all opened up. He knew he had met another Helper.

"Sorry I kept myself closed off," Dusty mind-talked to John. "Just been keepin my eye on you, having a little fun these first few days. You doin OK?"

"Yea man. I guess so," John replied, " and the name is...."

"Yea, I know. Sloan. John Sloan," Dusty shot back. "Glad tah meecha. Good to know ya. We might just get outta this place in one piece. Waddaya think?"

"You bet, we just might at that, hey Dusty?" John said as he felt the glow of contact with another Helper.

27

John and Dusty settled into the frantic routine of boot camp the best that they could. It helped John having a link with Dusty. It helped Dusty too. Gave his mind something to occupy it.

"Fucking Grade-A grins we got goin' here, huh John?", he'd pass along at just the right time.

Which usually was the most inopportune time. As crazy and messed up as boot camp was, it could also be hilarious and even more so when you have a running commentary from a smart ass like Dusty running through your mind. Dusty would get John in trouble. For laughing. John couldn't help it. He would be on the verge of cracking up anyway and then Dusty's voice-over would appear in his mind and he would lose it. Plus, you were so cut off from the world that you lost your humor value. A two, maybe a three at best, on the outside was suddenly a fucking ten-and-a-half inside the cocoon of basic training. Take Private Stenkley for example.

It had been just before lights out and the Senior Drill Instructor, Staff Sgt. Clemons, had them all in a school circle in the front of the squad bay. The platoon was seated, legs crossed, all assholes and belly buttons, pressed up as tightly as possible to one another listening to the

Senior DI talk about, Customs and Courtesies, or VD or the chain of command or some damn thing.

"Any questions?" he barked.

Now you had to be careful where questions were concerned. Even six weeks in, which was just over halfway through, you had to be careful. You couldn't get too comfortable with the DI's. They would use interaction to fuck with the "prives" if they felt like it. You wanted to learn and to get it right so if you asked a question it had better be right. There was no rhyme or reason to it either. It might be a damn good question and still get you in the DI's corner doing bends and motherfuckers 'till *they* were tired. Until *they* were satisfied that the puddle of sweat beneath your face was large enough.

"Sir, the private has a question, sir!" Private Stenkley shouted, jumping to his feet and standing at attention.

"Oh, this should be brilliant," was the voice in John's mind coming from Dusty. "Goofy fuckers like Stenkley should learn to keep their yaps shut."

"Shut up, Dusty," John sent back.

Just looking at Stenkley was enough to get anyone going. The guy just didn't have much going for him. To start with he was overweight. As a fat body, Stenkley was always being put in the corner for "physical motivation". The DI's reminded him constantly that he would be sent back to motivation platoon for non-hackers and fat bodies, and he would have to join another platoon at whatever point they were at in their training. A platoon farther back than the one they were in. John had heard of privates taking six months to complete the eleven-week training.

"Stay away from those motherfucking taters," they'd scream to Stenkley in the chow hall. "It's meat and momma's sweet veggies for you, pig! And stay the fuck away from the bread tray too! Jesus H. Christ, boy, you ain't fit to swab Chesty Puller's colon, you know that, boy?"

You gotta believe me, this was funny shit in boot camp. The other privates would repeat the DI's hazings in private to Stenkley. The one about swabbing Chesty Puller's colon was a favorite.

Stenkley had a weird head too. It was shaped like a fat, scrunched down peanut. A peanut with its shell still on. With his shaved head, from the back, it looked like the bottom two snow balls of a miniature snowman. Kinda like a cartoon head, which was not lost on the Drill Instructors. One day they had even felt the need to point this out to Pvt. Stenkley.

"You got a cartoon head, you know that, boy?" Sgt. Cherico had said to Stenkley in passing. Not even giving him that hard a time. Just in passing, as if it had just occurred to the DI and he had felt the need to share this information with Stenkley.

"Priceless. Fucking priceless," was the immediate response inside of John's head from Dusty. That put John right on the edge.

"A fucking cartoon head," Sgt. Cherico repeated chuckling to himself and shaking his head.

That was all John needed. He burst out laughing. Fuck, it *was* priceless. What wasn't priceless was the fifteen minutes of mountain climbers he had had to do in the corner for laughing after Sgt. Cherico had ordered him to get his little hillbilly Wisconsin ass up front and climb Mount Suribachi until the DI was tired. The DI got tired after fifteen minutes. John had been ready to quit at five but, since the DI wasn't the one doing the exercises, Cherico hadn't been tired for another ten. Just how it works out sometimes.

So anyway, the platoon was in school circle and Stenkley got to his feet.

"Sir, the private has a question, sir!"

"What is it, Stenkley?"

"Sir, the private would like to know,"...and as those words were coming out of Stenkley's mouth, Stenkley farted. A great, loud, flappy fart.

The platoon was stunned. John could already hear Dusty's hooting laugh inside his head. And Dusty didn't laugh all that often.

"Oh shit," John thought, "don't let me laugh. Please don't let me laugh."

Dusty was so busy laughing inside of John's head and his own, that his running commentary stopped for the time being.

"WHO the fuck did that?" the Senior DI bellowed, not yet fully grasping the situation.

And Stenkley farted again. A real fucking beauty this time. All wet and juicy and butt cheek slapping.

"WHO in the fuck did that?!" Clemons re-emphasized.

Whole groups of the seated, squeezed together, platoon were shaking as they tried to hold their laughter in.

Stenkley was frozen at attention and he almost made it. Fuck, he almost made it. But almost...horse shoes and hand grenades and all that. The DI focused his attention on the seated platoon and took it off Stenkley. The Senior DI was moving his eyes up and down the seated ranks of his platoon and Stenkley relaxed. A big mistake. He thought he was in the clear so he snuck his right hand around to pull the back of his utility trousers out of the crack of his ass. A move that was definitely needed in Pvt. Stenkley's little world, but *now* was perhaps an inopportune moment to perform the much needed act. Just as Stenkley was pulling his camouflage trousers out of the crack of his ass he farted again. Just as SSgt. Clemons had begun eyeing Stenkley again.

By now it was tightly controlled pandemonium as the platoon tried desperately to not laugh.

Dusty was laughing uncontrollably in John's head. The surprise of *that* was the only thing keeping John's laughter in. A few of the platoon were snorting snot out of their noses, heads ready to explode, little squeaks and squeelies, escaping from their compressed lips and red, shaking faces. This was a bad situation. SSgt. Clemons was not a DI to be fucked with even among DI's. He had more ribbons on his chest than the battalion Sgt. Major. *Three, count 'em three,* tours in 'Nam. He looked like he could make Sgt. Cherico piss his pants with the look he was wearing right now. He was the baddest in a world full of bad motherfuckers.

The platoon was on the verge of losing it completely when Clemons spoke quietly.

"Boy, you gonna stand there and pick your ass when you address your Senior Drill Instructor?"

"Uh, oh," John and Dusty thought simultaneously. Even Dusty was no longer laughing.

"Boy, you gonna stand there and pick that nasty ass of yours, and *FART* while you address your Senior Drill Instructor?!"

The platoon was silenced. Clemons had a look of pure evil on his face, as if he was holding back the entire rage of himself and all DI's that had ever worn the smokey-bear cover. His face was scarlet and he was shaking.

"Sir, no sir!!!" Stenkley voice squealed out. And, as long as his voice was squealing, his ass decided to join in the fun one more time as well by farting. Farting long and almost musically. Less moisture involved now, more of a tonal quality to it. Almost as if his ass was singing   the   Fa   part   of   Do   Re   Mi. "Faaaaaaaaaaaaaaaaaaaaaaatuuuumphufffff," Stenkley's ass sang out in a strong, proud voice.

"Faaaaaaaaaaaaaaaaaaaaaaaaaaaaaasqeeeeeetomphfffff." Again.

And SSgt. Clemons lost it. He lost it, but not in the way the platoon would've imagined in a million years. His face looked like it would explode and then the most unexpected thing happened. He laughed. No shit! He laughed. Senior Drill Instructor SSgt. Clemons laughed uncontrollably and the platoon went from the gallows to paradise in one brief moment.

Clemons was trying to speak but was laughing so hard he couldn't. The platoon even laughed and the most outrageous thing was, Clemons let them. He allowed them to laugh. The two Junior DI's, Sgt. Cherico and Cpl. Flood, came out of the DI's hut trying to figure out just what in the fuck was going on.

Pvt. Stenkley figured out that it was OK for him to laugh too, and he did. Which brought one last and final toot from his ass.

Finally Clemons sputtered out, "Boy, I guess you *are* gonna stand there and pick your ass and fart in front of your Senior Drill Instructor. You are sure one stinky ass private, Private Stenkley...one stinky ass private. You just got yourself a new name, boy. Private Stinky."

"Sir, yes sir! Private Stinky, sir!" the newly renamed private offered up, which brought more laughter spilling out of Clemons. The two junior DI's joined in as well.

"Well, Stinky, you best get your ass in my corner and begin. If you last thirty minutes I might just let you stay in my Marine Corps."

"Sir, yes sir!" Stinky said, running over to the corner and beginning his mountain climber exercises.

"You either got balls or you are the stupidest recruit to ever wear a uniform. You might just make it, Stinky. You might just make it."

It's funny but Pvt. "Stinky" Stenkley *did* make it. His whole world turned around that day and he eventually became squad leader and graduated PFC. His parents didn't even recognize him at graduation because of the amount of weight he had lost. Of course he got kicked out of the Marine Corps two and a half years later for smuggling contraband American coffee, cigarettes, and booze off base to the locals in Okinawa, but for a short while his star did shine.

As in life, things shift quickly and suddenly in boot camp. Clemons let the platoon have their head for a minute or two and then he was back to business finishing his Marine Corps Customs and Courtesies lecture. (A rather ironic lecture, now that it comes to me.)

Dusty and John were listening to Clemons *and* reliving Stinky's most recent adventure in their minds together. John should have seen it coming but he let his guard down, just as Stenkley had done. He relaxed and forgot that not only did he have to watch out for Clemons he also had to watch out for Dusty. Clemons was lecturing in the background and John and Dusty were shooting smart-assed remarks back and forth.

"Holy shit. I think Pvt. Rogers, (who was sitting directly behind Stenkley at the time of the incident), got some on him. He almost got himself a big wet kiss from old Stinky. Fuck, if Stenkley got himself a vocal coach, he could teach that ass of his to sing the Marine Corps Hymn at graduation."

Shit like that. Just two buddies kicken' it back and forth. Except these two buddies could do it in their minds. Dusty had John on the verge of laughing out loud again. Something he wanted very much *not* to do since their brief reprieve was over and laughing was no longer allowed. Definitely not allowed.

John was right on the edge when Dusty sent him this sweet tidbit.

"No shit. The crazy thing is, Clemons's fly was down the whole time. Look, it's still fucking unzipped. Pvt. Stinky got an ass singin' like a nightingale and Clemons wants us all to peek at his mighty sword."

Dusty *had* timed it perfectly. John started laughing and stole a look at SSgt. Clemon's fly, just as Clemon's zeroed in on the laughing Pvt. Sloan who was now staring at his crotch. Farting, at certain times and in certain situations, may be allowed in SSgt. Clemons's Marine Corps but copping a peek at another man's crotch, *especially* your Senior Drill Instructor's, was not allowed. Not in *any* world. Busted!

"What in the fuck do you think you're lookin' at?" Clemons spat at John. The ha ha voice was *all* gone now, this was his regular *I killed more fucking gooks than you got hairs on your head* voice.

"Gotcha," piped up Dusty in John's mind before disappearing.

"Just figured you'd steal a little peek at my dick and have yourself a little chuckle, hey Pvt. Sloan?"

"Oh fuck," John thought.

"Sir, no sir!"

"Wanna see this dick do ya, Pvt. Sloan?"

With that SSgt. Clemons pulled out the largest dick, white or black, and SSgt. Clemons was white, that any members of the platoon had ever seen in their young lives.

"Fuckin cock on that guy, hey Johnny," Dusty whispered, back in John's head again. "Hate to be on the business end of that."

The platoon was more in awe of their Senior Drill Instructor than ever. Clemons stuffed his huge manhood back into his trousers and honed in on John.

"You're a Private Eye, ain't you, Pvt. Sloan? Yea, you're a regular fuckin' *Columbo,* sneekin' and peekin' around there, ain'cha? Well detective Columbo, you just met Private One Eye. Now get your ass in the corner with Stinky and fucking begin!"

"I wonder if the irony of Peter Falk only having one eye is lost on our Senior Drill Instructor?" Dusty sang into Johns mind. "What do you think, Columbo?"

"Fuck you, Dusty," John shot back.

"Got you good, bro," Dusty finished and left John to his mountain climbers.

From that point on, John was known as Columbo in platoon 3339. Sometimes Private One Eye, but usually Columbo. Years later in his Marine Corps travels John would bump into fellow members of platoon 3339 and they would still call him Columbo. He had to admit that Dusty had gotten him pretty good. John took the good with the bad and he was glad for the good and for Dusty. They were buddies on their way to becoming life-long friends. Dusty had to admit *himself* that John was a good friend too. Best one he'd ever had. Shoot, other than Franklin Rose, John was the *only* friend Dusty had ever really had.

28

Tight friendships were often formed in boot camp, but even other members of the platoon could see that John and Dusty were becoming peas. Two peas in a pod. Butt buddies. A *real* buddy. A real buddy is someone who goes out to town and gets two blow jobs, then comes back to the barracks and gives you one, or so the saying went. Now of course that never happened, but everyone knew what it meant. In a platoon filled with guys who would cover your back, a butt buddy covered it even more.

John realized this first and pointed it out to Dusty to see if he was feeling the same way. It sure felt like he was.

John noticed SSgt. Clemons and the series commander, First Lt. Braddick were peas, after observing them over a period of weeks. Clemons should have been at least a master-sergeant but had been busted down in rank twice in his career. Lt. Braddick was a mustang (an officer that had started out enlisted and then become a commissioned officer somewhere along the way) and because of this he was older than other lieutenants. Hell, he was as old as Clemons. The two had served two tours in Nam together and they were tight. John would watch them together when he could. The platoon would be out at the grenade range, or on bivouac, and Clemons and Braddick were together whenever possible. Just shootin' the breeze or not even talking sometimes. Just hanging together and being grateful for it. Clemons was white, Braddick was black. Didn't matter. They would occasionally trade war stories and let the platoon listen in. There was an ease and comfort between the two men that was noticeable to John and he liked it. Clemons didn't always use the usual courtesies around Braddick either and Braddick let him, if he didn't think the platoon could hear. They would call each other by their first names and their brotherhood was evident.

"You ever notice how Clemons and Braddick are together?" John asked Dusty one day. "Do ya see the groove they've got?"

"Yea, man. They been through it," Dusty silenced back.

"I'm not trying to get all mushy but I get some of that being with you," John went on. "Not queer or anything but I just feel a click with you."

"Yea, me too," Dusty sent back already knowing that John wanted to talk about it, but feeling uncomfortable. And knowing John was wondering if Dusty felt it too.

"Even among other Helpers I've met, I just feel like we were destined to meet or something," John thought.

The two young men had already opened their minds to each other in this area. Letting the other experience their personal meetings with other Helpers.

"And it's deeper for us, I think."

"Yea, John, I feel it too," Dusty said, serious for once. "It's good to have another Helper around or I don't know if I'd make it through this shit," Dusty admitted. "If I couldn't keep it grinny I think I'd go off. But you helped me figure something out too. How we don't take it personal when they dog us. I figure I don't because I've seen too much bad to let it get to me, and you've kind of got a handle on the good from all your Helping experiences, and that keeps it from getting to you."

John had opened his mind to Dusty completely by this time, and Dusty had experienced much of John's life and certainly all of his Helpings.

John knew not to probe too deeply into Dusty and he was amazed by how serious Dusty was allowing himself to be. John knew that he didn't see all of Dusty. He could see what was there, and what *was* there amazed John. He'd never met another Helper that was as powerful as Dusty. He could tell that right off. He could see the Light in Dusty and it was broader and deeper than anything John had experienced before. Limitless, it seemed to him. But it also felt too clean to John. He knew that Dusty was holding some stuff back, shadowing things. He could see how Dusty had been raised and that was painful. What he couldn't see was all of Dusty's Helpings. He sensed that all that was there wasn't all that was there, but he didn't push. Friends didn't need to do that, right? Not all the time anyway.

"Man, Dusty, I never met another Helper as deep as you," John told him. It wasn't a jealousy thing, just a reality. "Sometimes it seems as if you've got almost as much power as the Power."

"Don't make too much out of that," Dusty said. "It doesn't seem to be doing me much good. I think I've got some debts that I'll never be able to repay. Not just mistakes, but debts."

Dusty had come to trust John by now. He carried the burden of his *not* Helping Uncle Lou with him every minute of every day. John sensed something, but didn't know what to do about it, so he was surprised when Dusty opened up.

They had been cleaning the head. John scrubbing the shitters and Dusty the pissers. They were alone, and it was just before lights out.

"I did a real bad thing, John," Dusty sent to John. "I haven't even told Franklin about it." John did know about Franklin. "And I'm a little scared to tell you about it."

John just listened with his mind and opened up. "You can tell me about it if you want," he said. "Just open it up a little at a time."

Dusty did start opening it up, a little at a time. John had known about Dusty's last foster home but not what had happened there. Dusty had polished it up into a generic kind of reading for John. This time he allowed John to watch it unfold. The whole Uncle Lou thing, one instant at a time. "I turned my back on the Helping, John. I was supposed to Help and I didn't, and it's killing me."

John saw and he was shocked. It had never occurred to him that you could *not* Help someone. He didn't even know that it was possible. He wasn't sure it was possible for him, but he could see how Dusty had done it, all the same. It must come from his having more power than most of us, John thought.

"That's why I was afraid to tell you," Dusty said. "I knew you'd be blown away." He could see John wasn't pissed at him. Just confounded. "I'm bad," Dusty said. "What good is the extra power, or any power at all, if it doesn't do me any good?"

John didn't know. What he did know was that Dusty was his friend in spite of what he had done, and Dusty could see that.

"I don't know, Dusty. You're my bud anyway, I know that. I guess we all make mistakes and maybe yours was just bigger than most, maybe cuz you got more power. Who knows?"

Dusty mustered all of his courage and crawled out on the cliff and asked what he was suddenly terrified to ask. "So, are we still buds, John?" Sounds like a silly question doesn't it? It isn't and it wasn't. Especially when you've got as many walls built as Dusty did.

John pushed all of his not inconsiderable light and power into Dusty's mind and said, "Yes. Of course we are." And Dusty saw that it was true. "Like it or not, we're asshole buddies. Even if you did get me busted checking out the Senior's crank," John finished, knowing that now was the right time to lighten things up a bit. He saw that in spite of Dusty's power, there was an emptiness in him that seemed to run almost as deep. Relief surged out of Dusty like a river. A great big fucking river, with water in it and everything.

"You know, I'd die for you, don't you motherfucker?" Dusty said. "Just don't make me have to do it!" he finished, adding his own lightening touches to the moment.

"Well you may have to if Clemons ever catches me staring at his crotch again," John joked.

They *were* peas, they now knew. Bonded, attached, together.

It occurred to John that maybe Dusty should write to Franklin Rose and tell him what had happened, and he told Dusty this. "He's worried about you," John knew. "Put his mind at ease."

"I will," Dusty said. "Man, you just saved my bacon. You know that if there's ever anything I can do for you I will, don't you?"

"I do," John said. "Just stop making me laugh. That's a start."

"Well shit, I don't know if I can go that far," Dusty said, "but I'll try."

They both knew that Dusty wouldn't stop, and that that wasn't really the point. For them it was a kind of competition. It was fun and it passed the time. Dusty did write to Franklin and both benefited from it. Dusty felt more relief from being able to unburden himself. Franklin just felt relief to hear from Dusty. He worried about that boy.

John and Dusty both graduated from boot camp meritorious PFC's. They both got orders to Forward Observer school in Fort Sill OK, although even with John taking the land survey course, Dusty still graduated from school three weeks behind John. Something to do with Dusty fighting an Army corporal over a woman of shady repute. They both served their first duty assignments at Camp Pendleton and were attached to different batteries in the same battalion. They ran together and partied and cemented their friendship there. They even bumped into each other on Okinawa.

After that their paths drifted apart and they didn't run into each other again until years later in Kuwait. Gulf War One. Right after Dusty had annihilated six men with his M16. Just cut them down when they were in the open. The first four had been easy. All shot in the initial bursts of his rifle fire. The last two had been the tough ones. He had had to pick them off one by one, using all of his skills to sneak up on them until he had finally killed the last soldier up close and personal. They were not the first kills he had in the war. He had called in fire missions and wiped out whole platoons, and he had used his personal weapon on multiple occasions to kill the enemy. These last six were different. His effort was nearly heroic. He would most certainly have earned a decoration if not for one small fact. The men he had ambushed were not Iraqis. They were Americans.

29

John made a point of calling Deena the day after speaking with Laura. He hated to admit it, but it was all he thought about all day at work. The crew even remarked about the extra spring in his step.

"Feeling good today, Johnnie?" more than one had remarked. "What's up?"

"Nothing, just having a good day," he told them not wanting to jinx anything by mentioning Laura's phone call or his meeting Deena. He'd had too many of these things go sour to blow his horn before it was actually time for the concert.

Even knowing that Deena had wanted him to call, John was still a little nervous dialing her number. He went through the whole "should I call right away when I get home, will she be home yet, don't want to call too late" thing. Funny how he'd Helped countless people, felt the Power of that anonymous Good, been in combat situations, and he still felt on edge calling a woman. He didn't know if other folks went through that or not, but he didn't like it. He felt it was some kind of weakness that maybe prevented him from hooking up with a good woman.

He eventually did call her. It must've been at the correct time too since she answered on the second ring and they seemed to hit it off immediately. He felt comfortable talking with her right from the start. No pregnant pauses, no worrying about if he had enough things to say, realizing how she was right there with a question when the conversation lagged. All in all, a nice start.

They chatted about regular stuff. His job, what part of town he lived in (North 28th Street in Superior), her job (dental hygienist), and where she lived (downtown Duluth with a nice view of the lake), that kind of stuff. Good, first conversation stuff. After twenty minutes or so he asked her out to the movies and maybe a drink afterward. She said yes, they discussed what they wanted to see, and made a date for the next evening.

"Good, no waiting around wondering what will happen," they both thought. They were ready.

Their first date went smoothly, after a rocky start. It was Friday and John knocked off work early, and decided to take a little nap so he'd be fresh for the date. It was a good idea, until he overslept. He had to race around his apartment and even nicked himself shaving. They had decided to meet outside at the front of the theater and when John finally raced up late, but not *that* late, she was waiting for him. No summer dress on tonight. She was wearing jeans with fringed moccasins and a dark blue, man's dress shirt tucked into those jeans.

"Yea," John thought. "All right, very sexy."

She was standing alone in front of the box office, most of the crowd having already entered the theater. Not angry, John could see. She had more of a forlorn look than anything else. It broke his heart. She did get a little mad now that he was here, but he explained truthfully what had happened and she didn't make him pay too much for leaving her standing there. Fair enough, they each thought. Then that smile came back to Deena's face. The one he had seen in the diner. They were half way through the movie before he got it.

"You're a Helper too!" John sent to her mind. "No wonder."

Her mind was immediately in his, laughing, "Yep," she said grabbing his hand in the dark and snuggling right up against his side. That got to him too. First the lonely look on her face outside the theater, and now her holding his hand and fitting right in next to him in the theater.

"Land me and bag me," he thought," cause I am hooked."

Deena sensed this and sent, "Mmmmm, me too," back to his mind. John had a hard time following the rest of the movie. Good thing it was almost over by then. His mind was racing between the "wow, what's gonna happen next" and the "Mmmmm, me too."

They decided on going to a twenty-four-hour Embers instead of a bar. John liked that too. He didn't drink very often and found it hard to meet someone else who didn't want to party all the time.

"Coffee and pie is good for me," she told him.

They had a great time at the diner. John had a way of speaking directly without stepping on people's toes.

After they were seated and given their menus, he told her how sorry he was to hear about her parents. He hoped she didn't mind that Laura had told him, and he wanted to convey his deepest condolences to her. His parents were still alive and he couldn't imagine what she must be going through. What could've been a real downer as a conversation starter wasn't. Deena opened up to John and they talked. Out loud. John had made sure that his Helping was opened to Deena as well, but he could see that she wasn't roaming around in his mind that much. He also saw that she wasn't opening that part of herself up completely, but that was OK. This was something that might go somewhere and he understood. He'd never even considered what would happen if two Helpers were romantically involved, so he let it be.

They talked for two and a half hours in Embers. They finished two pots of coffee (both decaf), two pieces of pie (peach for him, apple for her), and one brownie (which they split). They both seemed to be on similar pages. They talked about dating only being a means to an end, not an end in itself. How you dated to see if this was a person that you wanted to be more involved with, and if it was there was no sense fooling around.

John gave her a hard time about "hiding" herself from him when they first met. A woman's prerogative, she told him. She teased him a bit about being naive or maybe too open. He misquoted Mark Twain to the effect that if you always tell the truth you don't have to remember as much. And they stared into each other's eyes. There was a lot of staring into each others eyes going on.

By the time they kissed in the parking lot next to Deena's car, they both knew that they wanted to see where this thing was going to go. Deena had wondered to herself when, if ever, she was going to get out of the darkness she had been in. First her father, then the bomb that her mother had dropped on her, and then her mother's death. A death that came before she could really talk to her mother about what had been revealed in that dropped bomb. That was part of the reason she was not opening the Helping side of herself up to John completely. She wasn't sure where she was inside, and she wasn't ready to let John explore all of that before she had come to some kind of terms with it.

The other reason was that she felt like John did. She had never considered that she might fall in love with another Helper, and although it was too early in the game to be talking about *that*, the potential was there with John.

They made love three nights later. They had gone for a walk along Wisconsin Point, enjoying the breeze coming off Lake Superior (warm, even for summer), sand between their toes, the whole bit. They held hands and opened up a little more to each other. Talking more with their minds than they had before. Enjoying the sunset and the seagulls and the touch of each other's hands. They had the big buzz working. You remember that kind, don't you? The *big* one, when you're thinking that, "you know what, this might just work out. Not only does it feel good now, but it may last." At least Magic Eight-Ball is telling you that all signs point to yes.

They went back to John's apartment and started kissing before they even made it in the door. From there they moved to the couch, things starting to get unbuttoned now. Feeling right. Feeling good. Mumbled, but sincere, questions about birth control (she was on the pill) and then he had her shirt off.

"MMMMMM, nice breasts," he thought. Of course she was right there in his mind with "Why thank you, handsome." Wow, more things to consider. Neither had ever made love to a Helper before. They both kept their minds open anyway. Not all the way, even John held back some, but enough for each of them to know that they weren't thinking of anything or anybody else.

"Whew," they both laughed to each other.

John was cradling her breasts, still inside her bra, when something popped up in his mind and he sensed that she had a little something going on too. He had almost forgotten about it. Before he had a chance to bring it up she spoke.

"I have herpes, John." They finished the rest of the conversation in their minds.

"Me too," he told her. Relief washed over them both. They had both had trouble finding a partner, and now both hated the idea that something like this could prevent it. As the song says, it's the little things that make a house a home.

"I almost forgot to bring it up," he said. "Although all it really means is that you've had sex at least once before meeting me," he told her. "That's all it takes. Not that hard to be our age, single, and have it. Just the luck of the draw and we both drew the special card. But it looks like we've drawn it again and it's jokers wild this hand."

He could tell she was relieved that he didn't think bad of her for having it. That she was a "less than". She thinks about that a lot, John knew. And not just in this situation either. So he was tender and she was loving. It didn't take long for her bra to come off, and then it was Katy bar the freakin' door. The proceedings carried along a little farther on the couch, and then he picked her up and carried her into the bedroom.

"Yea, I'm corny," he sent to her.

She laughed, "Mmmmm, I love corny." He was, and she *did* too. Good match, hey?

They made love. Twice. She opened up a bit more the second time. Good thing too. He needed it a bit. He was horny yes, but hell he wasn't a kid anymore. They smiled and moaned out loud and into each other's mind's.

"Wow," was all they could say. "Fucking wow."

Deena spent the night and for the next three months they only spent two nights apart. One night John was out of town for work, and one night Deena was just too tired to head over the bridge. That was two nights too many for the both of them. After three months Deena brought up what was already on John's mind. Something he had been too nervous to bring up.

"Why don't you move in?" she asked him.

He had thought that he should ask her to move in with him, he being the man and all, but she did have the nicer apartment and that view of the lake was sweet. Plus she had definite ideas about how she like her apartment decorated, couches, etc. and he could care less. His apartment was month to month anyway so he waited two weeks and moved in. They were in love. They were Helpers. How could they lose?

30

Deena was a thinker. Now you may or may not place a value judgment on that but, let's face it, some people just think too damn much. It was almost as if she couldn't help it. Her mind was on *on, all the time*. It thought. A lot. It went over everything. This was often beneficial. Sometimes brainstorming was problem solving at it's most ruthless. But why think when there's no need to?

John was often amazed at how her mind worked. When she would let him in, that is. He didn't have carte blanche in her head. They always seemed to have their "pilot light," Helper's connection going, but Deena didn't allow John to just roam around willy-nilly in her mind. She would hide the things she hadn't or couldn't work through.

Fear was the first thing she thought about. The first thing that created turmoil in their relationship. Imagine the nakedness of two Helpers being in love. Being able to roam through each other's minds and experiences at the most intimate and vulnerable moments. Like when they were making love. It was beautiful. She really was in love with John. During moments of passion she would find herself in his mind and feel the joy he felt at being with her. Sometimes it made her feel unworthy. Did she love him that much? Or did she just love him because he loved her? Bummer shit. Something that everyone goes through but multiply it by about nine zillion, they being Helpers, and it can get to be a burden.

And fucking Oprah Winfrey didn't help either. Deena watched an episode of Oprah and the topic was men fantasizing about other women while making love to their wives. She just couldn't get that out of her head. She only thought about John when they made love. Oh, once in a while she would think about some problem that was bothering her. She'd lose her love-making train of thought and slip into some little stumbling block in her life. She would catch herself and jump back into the moment. This created guilt. Why wasn't I thinking about him? What if he's in my mind and sees that I'm thinking about how I need to get my beige blouse dry cleaned cause I need it for Laura's party? What if they can't get the stain out? But mostly she worried that she would peek inside his mind during love making, and find he was thinking about someone else. Or find him not pleased with some aspect of her body. That created fear, which made her close herself off to John. What if he was thinking about her friend Laura while he was making love to her? You see the problem here? She thought too much.

John liked being open. Not that he was a saint. Far from it. He liked it because he wasn't a saint, and he had found that the best way through that stuff was by being open. It seemed to solve problems, so he used it. He thought that the two of them being Helpers was an asset. Deena wasn't so sure. Sometimes it just made her feel naked. You won't like who I am if you know me. And if you do like me, I can't respect you because I know how unworthy of your love I am.

In spite of herself, Deena did force herself to open up to John as the months progressed. She did see the benefit in it. So far, the little scrapes they had gotten into only made them stronger, once they had gotten through them. It did bring them together. She did see that he wasn't just putting up with her. That he did love her. *So far anyway,* her brain told her, thinking, thinking, thinking. Hell, the two people that loved her more than anyone else lied to her. Why wouldn't John?

Her parents *had* lied to her. That was the bomb her mother had dropped just before her death. A bomb that her mother and her had never really had a chance to talk about.

Not that Deena was the shallower of the two. If anything she was much deeper than John. It wasn't all just beige blouses and hair coloring. No, she had some unexploded bombs working in her that she couldn't let John in on yet. Some UXB's lurking, half buried in the rubble, waiting to be dismantled or detonated.

John would often laugh and admit to her that he wasn't the deep thinker that she was.

"I'm the dog," he would say. Then he would add quickly, before she had time to think too much about that, "not in *that* way. Not that I want to jump and hump every woman I see. No, I'm like a dog because I like to keep things kind of simple, I guess. What you see *is* what you get. I don't have any hidden agendas," he told her. "Really. Look and see for yourself."

She would. She would search his open mind and see the simple love for her there. But then she would *think* (there's that word again), "yea, but if I hide stuff, well then maybe he is too."

"I love you, baby," he would say. "Just point and click me. I love doing stuff for you. Not cuz I'm trying to trick you, although if washing your car gets me a roll in the old sack-a-roonie that's cool, but mostly because I get such a kick out of it. Like a dog. A very smart and handsome dog," he would add, joking and making handsome "Alec Baldwin on Saturday Night Live" poses.

Finally, if they were having a state of the union discussion, he would say, "Deena, I just love you. You're my woman. I wasn't sure if it was ever going to happen to me and it has. Maybe I'm a little over the top, but if I am it's only because I want to try my best. I just want to be your man." This would invariably end the discussion on a high note. Deena would be able to laugh at herself and admit, "Maybe I think too much, huh Johnnie? Well maybe just a wee bit," he would say and it would pass. Just the ups and downs of a couple getting to know each other and getting comfortable with each other.

Funny, but it was hair coloring that initiated what was to come.

Deena colored her hair. John loved it. It was blonde with dark, kind of reddish, roots. He would joke with her about how it smelled up the apartment when she did it. He'd cry dramatically for his gas mask and gasp around the apartment on his knees doing his best Audie Murphy war movie imitation. "Tell Deena, I.... love...her. Tell...her I did...my best," he'd say and then crumple the rest of the way to the floor in the hall outside of their bathroom. He'd peek up at her out of the sides of his eyes and then exhale and lay still. John enjoyed this more than Deena, but not by much. She got a kick out of how he liked to play.

John came home from work early after working only a half day one Saturday. Deena hadn't expected him home for another two hours. He walked in the apartment and heard the radio cranked. KQDS kicking out some excellent classic rock jams. Not the same old tired "Zep-quarter-after-ten-o'clock" bullshit that passed for classic rock on most stations. Nope, KQDS, played them all. Not just the hard, classic rock nuggets that should get played, but classics from Jerry Rafferty and Steely Dan too. Rock and roll for grownups, and they did it well. The next thing John noticed was the smell. Uh-oh, hair coloring time, and he searched his mind for how he could pretend some little skit and make Deena laugh. He loved making Deena laugh. It bubbled up out of her and her eyes would shine. Making her eyes shine could keep him going for a whole day. Just the sound of her laugh echoing in his mind, playing over and over in his mind like a classic, flip-side ELO deep-cut on KQ.

John walked quietly down the hallway toward the bathroom. The door was slightly ajar and he could hear Deena absent-mindedly singing along with the radio blasting from the living room. John stood outside of the door and grabbed his throat with both hands, getting ready to do his best choking scene for Deena. He held his throat and nudged the door open with his head and what he saw amazed him.

Deena was in fact coloring her hair. Kind of. She was sitting on the side of the bathtub with one leg up on the toilet and the other splayed out on the floor. She was naked from the waist down. Cool, was his first thought. MMMMMM, his next. Then he saw what she was doing. She was coloring her pubic hair.

"That's kinda weird," John thought. Especially once he saw the embarrassed look on her face when she saw him looking at her.

"Hey, get out!", she startled.

John was frozen in the doorway, feeling things slipping away.

Deena got very nervous and told him again to get out. She said it a little more forcefully than necessary, but what the heck, he hadn't knocked. She slammed the door and John went to the living room and tried not to think. Tried to hum along with Rikki Lee on KQ. Felt the first scary feelings of a fight or a discussion coming on. Felt what he hoped wasn't a *shift*. The shift that came in some relationships where all was fine, and then suddenly it wasn't.

Deena spent five more minutes in the bathroom. John heard the shower running and then Deena going into their bedroom. After five more minutes she came out.

"Should I ask about anything?" John said. "I mean, I'm sorry I walked in on you and it's really not that big a deal."

"No," she said, "that's all right." It sure didn't *seem* like everything was all right, but OK.

"I like your secret garden any color you decide it to be," John said trying to not make things too heavy.

"No, it's not that, John," she said.

"I am curious, though, what is your natural color," he said.

Deena told him the story. "Red, John. I'm a redhead." She told him how she was sorry if she freaked him out. Shit, he had freaked *her* out walking in like that. Yes, she *did* dye her pubic hair. She knew it was kinda weird but she thought it would be weirder if the hair on her head was one color and her pubes another. John opened up and then Deena opened up too. It started spilling out of her. How she always felt goofy as a kid. Like she didn't fit in. Like she was different. Hell, like she was adopted. How she was a redhead and her dad had dark hair and her mom had bleach blonde hair. (and her mom's natural color wasn't red) She didn't even fit in with them that way. So she figured if her mom dyed her hair she would too, so—she started doing it as a young teenager. How her first lover had mentioned the red hair on her pubes and it had made her self-conscious, so she started dying the hair down there too, just combing it through. "Plus I overheard some stupid boys in high school. They were talking about another guy they had seen in gym class. Another redhead. They were joking about how they had given him a hard time. *Red on the head, like the dick on a dog*, they would tell him. Ughhhhh, what an obscene thought." The image kind of freaked her out and made her even more self conscious. Like she hated how her own pussy looked.

That's what she called it too, pussy. John got a kick out of that. He was always curious about how women referred to those special parts of their own bodies. Sure, guys said tits and pussy, but it was still a wonder to him that women used those same words sometimes. It made him less uncomfortable using those words around them if they were intimate.

John was following along listening to the story unfold, curious. Nervous, but enjoying learning more about Deena. Enjoying how Deena was opening up. How she was letting her mind open up. Letting him root around in there with her, while she told him the story. It almost slipped by him. He almost missed the not quite invisible wall she had up.

"There's more to it than that, isn't there," he said. "I mean, that's the truth, but there is more going on now. I can sense it."

Deena hesitated. She kept the wall up in her mind. Protecting her truths from John's mind. He saw it and she knew he saw it and she knew he knew she knew. Whew! Lot's of work keeping secrets from each other. Deena had been afraid of this moment. She had had an idea that it may come out, but she didn't think she was ready for it. She kept the wall up but haltingly started telling John the story out loud.

"You know how I've mentioned that I always thought I was adopted when I was younger? Even thought about it as an adult? Well right before my father died he told me that he really wanted to talk to me about something. Something important that he hadn't told me, that he thought he should."

John felt something opening up. Maybe a Helping, but maybe not. There was a sense of foreboding. A little orangeish-red light flashing in his mind. Like that answering machine light. Like Mrs. Abbott's hair for some darn reason.

Deena continued, "Well he never did tell me. He died before he had the chance to tell me and it killed me. It drove me nuts, so I drove my *mother* nuts. I pestered her and pestered her. I was grieving my father, and the knowledge of his hiding something from me was killing me. I forgot that my mother was grieving too. She would just say, I don't know what you mean. I don't know what you're talking about. And then *she* started dying. I finally said, *Mom please tell me what dad meant. Please.* She wouldn't, but then a week before she died she sent me a letter. All it said was...Honey your dad was right. We didn't want to hurt you. Please believe that. Things were different then. You were adopted. We adopted you as a baby. But you were our daughter. Please forgive us. Come and see me soon..... That was all it said. I was sooooo goddamn mad and hurt that I didn't even call her. Guilty too, cuz here was my mother and she was dying and I was mad at her."

Deena was crying now. And more beautiful than John had ever seen her.

"I hated them at that moment. And my mother died a week later just before I was to visit her. I can't forgive them and I can't forgive myself. That's why I was so happy to meet you, John. You were the first nice, good, clean thing to come my way in too long. You made me smile. And I fell in love with you, but now it's all creeping back in and I don't know if I can keep it together or if I can even stay with you. I'm sorry, John, but I'm just so lost."

John saw it all. She opened that part of herself up to him. She really *was* lost. She really didn't want to lose him but she didn't know if she could stay either.

"Baby, I'm here for you," John told her. "You are my love and I love you. If I can do anything at all I will." He was crying now too. He hated this helpless feeling he got when he couldn't fix something. He held her in his arms and rocked her back and forth. They swayed together on the couch and finally kissed. Kissed with an intensity that was part passion, but part something else. The something else part was holding on tightly to each other while they were slipping away. Like falling in a dream. Not wanting to, but not being able to stop it. They made love. Intense, frightened love. As they fell asleep John couldn't help feeling that something was unanswered here. There was something he was missing. Maybe something that Deena didn't even know about. Something nagging at his mind behind the scenes. Hidden behind the curtain. That there was something he could do if he could just figure out what it was. He was sad. Deeply sad and yet he felt that glow that an upcoming Helping often brought on. Only this time it offered no solace. Yes, there was a Helping coming on somewhere in his near future. Where and why and for whom he didn't know. And frankly, Scarlett, he just didn't give a good God-damn. He just didn't want to lose his baby. He drifted off to sleep with KQDS playing in the background. Steely Dan. Or was it Donald Fagen's solo stuff? Either way the last line he heard before he slept was, "I think I just got the goodbye look."

Deena didn't fall asleep as quickly as John. She was still thinking. She knew John was on to something. That maybe he had an inkling that he could help her even if he didn't realize it. She also knew something that she didn't let on. Something she had kept completely hidden. She was pregnant. John was the father, she loved him more than anything or anyone in the world and, in spite of all of this, she didn't know if she could stay.

186

31

John was standing in the Regimental CP tent in Kuwait. He was hot, thirsty, dealing with the reality of killing others, and trying hard to compartmentalize that reality, to be dealt with at a later date. He had been sent back to the rear by the commander of the infantry unit he was attached to. No shit, over some paperwork SNAFU. Unbelievable, even in war some assholes worry about crossing their T's and dotting their I's. Even the pogues at regiment understood how goofy it was, but it might as well be taken care of now, and maybe John could grab a shower somewhere and spend a night in a cot at base camp.

He wasn't worried, as some of the battalion staff were, that the war was moving so quickly that it would pass him by. Nope, he had seen enough already to take care of that little concern. Once you actually kill some people you realize that it isn't always the big boner you thought it was when you were just a cheese eating newbie. And having the man, the buddy, the fucking pal who got you drunk in Jacksonville, North Carolina when you were broke and lonely, the guy who gave a SHIT about you...when you had this marine standing next to you one second and splatters of his head exploding all over your face and body the next...well that's when you started to lose the old "win one for the Gipper", "ain't I gonna be a stud Marine" attitude. That's when you just wanted to kill them all to get it over with. Kill them before they killed another buddy of yours. Or killed your Gunny. The guy who had literally saved your boot ass from marrying that twice divorced, former Korean bar-girl now living in Twentynine Palms, California, who only wanted a divorce and a portion of your already tiny pay.

John was *glad* that it was going quickly. The quicker the fucking better, as long as they didn't get moving so fast that, in their haste, they killed some of their own in doing so. No, John didn't mind taking the night off at all. May even cop an extra shower in the morning. Plus he was getting that old feeling again. He had an idea that Dusty was somewhere close. Man, it would be good to see Dusty and thank God for paperwork.

Desert Storm, or Gulf War One as it came to be known, was moving so quickly that the rear positions barely had time to set up *their* positions when it was time to tear down and move forward again. This was before GPS devices were available to even some troopers in forward areas. Things were much more static then, moving in a slinky-like way across the sands. A lot less communication than today. Maybe that's why for every one grunt in the field it took ten pogues *in the rear, with the gear.* Christ, they needed that many just to keep track of where all the little "*ones*" were that were out there ahead of them. And from the little that John could see at regiment they had their fucking hands full doing that. It was a "kind of" war in that sense. We *kind of* knew where our troops were. We *kind of* knew where the enemy was. We *kind of* knew where those zillion dollar bombs were going to land.

Not that John was bitching. It's only in hindsight, and with the benefit of ever advancing technology, that we can compare it to anything. At the time it was the best thing going. But in spite of the sense of impending victory and the Ooh-Rah effect of slaughtering one's fellow human beings, John could see a look of worry on some of the faces in the rear. Some of them knew that they didn't know where everybody was. War is like that, but when you have technical killing abilities far outreaching your technical *detecting* abilities things could get hairy indeed. The shit that used to take a while to get there now got there immediately. Maybe before someone figured out that it shouldn't have. That was the worried look John saw in some of the officer's and senior enlisted men's faces.

"Just don't let 'em get me," John thought. "It's not my worry," he compartmentalized, "but just don't let 'em get me by accident."

John had taken care of as much of his paperwork problem as he could, so he roamed around base camp. He bumped into marines he had served with in the past. By late afternoon he was standing in the sweltering heat of a tent, filled with cots, shooting the breeze with some jarheads who knew some buds who knew some buds that he had known. Just "fucking the dog" as the saying went. Killing time and waiting.

The rear guard all wanted to ask their "how does it feel to kill a raghead?" questions, but weren't quite sure how to ask. The guys who knew how it felt sat back and wanted to rest. They would sit near each other, somehow knowing the others who had shared their similar experiences. Same as it ever was, same as it ever *was*...sang the Talking Heads.

John finally bumped into a guy that both he and Dusty had served with at Pendleton. Luis Ortega. Fucking Louie. Still only a corporal.

"Guy's been in as long as me," John thought.

Louie had EFSD embroidered on all of his jackets back in Oceanside and John saw that he had the same acronym on the olive-drab, dust 'kerchief that was tied around his neck and hanging below his chin. He loved to jump out of planes. Doing it in the military wasn't enough for Louie. Nope. On weekends off, back in California, he would seek out the little airports where people jumped out of perfectly safe aircraft for no particular reason at all but the thrill. Eat, Fuck, and Sky Dive. That was Louie's motto. It was good to see him.

"Sergeant John goddamned-Columbo Sloan," Louie spit out in his accented English. "Fucking good to see you, bro."

"You too, Lou. Stayin' safe?"

"Sheeit," Louie replied, " safe as these broke dick (which came out deek) rear guard motherfuckers'll let me be. These broke dick motherfuckers almost dropped a whole sheetload of weely fucking peter on my pos. They were trying out some new computer motherfucking thing, and they tried sending the fire mission I called in right fucking down on me and my company. They wouldn't let me send it back to my battery direct. Noooooo, it had to be routed through fuckeeng regiment first. By the time those limp dick motherfuckers sent it back to Echo battery it was all fucked up. If me and my Lieutenant hadn't been listening in on the comm we would've gotten blown away by our own battery. And that's why we're back here now. Those shitty motherfuckers tried pinning it on me and the Lieutenant. Can you fuckeeng believe it, man?! Cocksuckers!!! Fuck John, I'm getting the fuck out after this one. I got my ribbons, now I'm gonna be a scuzzy-ass civilian."

Louie's voice would get higher, and his accent thicker, when he went on one of his tirades, and John let him rant. He'd never been in a war zone with Louie before but John could tell that Louie was a little shaken. Just like he was himself. John just nodded and cussed at the appropriate moments and Louie was happy to fill in all the other blanks inserting cuss words at their accustomed every third or fourth word place. In a military world of premier cussers, Louie was still a star.

As Louie ran out of gas their conversation changed to reminiscences. Who was here? Who wasn't? Did you hear that Sergeant Kennedy, now Gunny Kennedy, got it, Louie mentioned? One of those fucking ragheads didn't shoot himself in the foot with his Tow. He somehow managed to launch the hand-held missile and it blew Kennedy's jeep and life to shreds. Poor fucker only had four to go too, Louie said. Four more years and he would've had his twenty with a check for life and nothin to do but smoke dope and jump rope. Grow a fucking beard and act weird, man.

"Man, that was too fucking bad," Louie finished. "Sheet, I almost married his sister too, bro. Fuckeeng war sucks."

Their conversation went on for an hour or so when Louie remembered somewhere he had to be.

"Sheet bro, gotta fucking meet my El Tee. He said as long as we was fucking back here he'd try to score us some fucking brew, man. Come by my tent tonight and weel get shit-faced, man."

"Cool with me, Lou," John said. "I'm gonna grab some shut-eye, and try to score another shower, and I'll check with you later."

Louie flipped back the tent door's flap and was heading out when he stopped and turned back in toward John.

"Fuck, bro, I almost forgot. I seen Dusty, man. Your bro is *kicking ass,* dude. No shit, they got him up for the fucking silver star, bro. He was *way* fucking forward with some recon ranger motherfuckers and like single-handedly saved the whole fucking day. Killed a bunch of the raggies and saved the squad or some shit like that. I heard El Tee talkin' about it with some Captain. No shit John, your homeboy did some John Wayne shit. He's the craziest motherfucker I ever met."

Oh man, John thought. I knew I felt him around here somewhere. John really wanted to see Dusty. He was realizing that he was more shaken up than he had thought he was. He needed to hear Dusty's smart-ass comments. He suddenly needed Dusty to cover his back.

"You seen him?" John asked.

"Yea, right before jump-off, I did. And someone said he's 'sposed to be around here somewhere. If not now, at least soon. They're gonna give him a medal or some shit right here in the desert. President Bush (which came out Boosh) or some fucking big cocksucker is gonna show up with cameras and shit. He's one crazy motherfucking Indian," Louie said laughing and turning to go. "Shit maybe your boy'll show up tonight just in time for the beer. That'd be just like him. Fucking Dusty, man."

With that said Louie headed out into the dust and heat.

Now that he thought more about it, John had the feeling that maybe Louie was right. He could feel Dusty around. He could feel Dusty's Helping reaching out to his. Right on time, John thought. Man I could use a hand. I think this shit is gettin' to me. It's getting' dark, too dark to see, quoteth Dylan. I can feel it.

It *was* getting dark too. But what John didn't know then was that it wasn't just his own darkness he was feeling. No sir. It was fixin' to get "way past midnight" for Dusty too.

32

John hit the chow tent for some hot supper and bumped into another guy who knew Dusty. The staff sergeant told John that Dusty was in fact to receive a medal. As a matter of fact he would've gotten it this afternoon but he had stayed out in the desert and gone on some kind of sneak and peak the night before.

"Fucker was supposed to report back last night, but instead he headed out to a supposed hot spot with some gung-ho young lieutenant," the marine said. "All I heard is it got very hairy. Like *freaky,* fuckin' hairy and no one's heard from Dusty since. They broke radio contact after engaging and it went silent after that."

Sounds like Dusty, John thought. Always going against the grain. The bigwigs tell him to get to the rear and he immediately heads the other way. John had had a nightmare the night before and he hoped it had nothing to do with Dusty. He was very nervous all of a sudden. In the dream he had been naked and out on some kind of patrol in the desert. Nothing too crazy about that. People were always naked at work in their dreams. Of course most people's occupations didn't involve killing the other guy before he killed you but that *was* John's current occupation so it made a certain amount of sense. John had been naked, wearing only his helmet and flak jacket, and been caught in the middle of a sandstorm. He had lost his bearings and he had thought he had lost his weapon. He kept seeing shapes moving through the blowing sand. Shapes that scared him deeply. Shapes that made his ass and balls pucker up tight. He realized the shapes were the enemy and with that realization his M-16 had appeared in his hands.

Dusty's voice had come to him in the dream. "Careful, bro," it said. "Don't make the wrong decision." The shapes had suddenly came charging at John and he had opened fire on them. He had woken up growling and screaming, sitting up and still firing the dream rifle cradled in his arms. He was terrorized by the thought that he had shot his own men and not the enemy. It had freaked him out and was adding to the underlying fear that was gripping him the next day.

John killed some time after chow and finally headed over to find Louie's tent at about twenty-hundred hours. The hot chow still weighed heavy in his gut adding to his discomfort. "My first chance at cold beer and I'm filled up with chow," is what he thought. He found Louie and a party was indeed raging in his tent. Three different boom boxes battled each other from different parts of the smoky and stifling tent. Drunken marines, in various stages of hysteria and dress, were alternately screaming and laughing. Sweaty, athletic bodies punching and wrestling each other too. Business as usual with combat marines.

John found a spot off to the side and nursed a beer, watching the festivities. If you could call them that. Nothing festive really going on. Primordial was the more appropriate word. All that was missing was a fire and a cave with primitive drawings on its walls and they could've been hunters back from a raid in Neanderthal times. Christ, they almost looked like apes. Primitive looks on their faces and brows, their shadows dancing on the walls of the tent. More growls than words. The boom boxes taking the place of sticks and drums being beaten.

John started to panic and he left the dimly lit tent for the darkness outside. He needed to get at some *fresh,* desert hot air, instead of the stifling, *smoky* hot air inside. He felt Dusty now. Felt him close and his feeling of panic increased. He had to find Dusty soon or he was toast. He saw a lone figure in the dark, walking around the perimeter of the tent city. Head down, weapon cradled in his arm, war gear on. John had never seen a wearier trudge than that of the man now heading in his direction. Just like I feel, John thought. *Weight of the fucking world* kind of walk. The man looked as if he was just circling the tents aimlessly. Like he had been doing it for hours. He was about thirty yards away from John, and even with him, on his circle tour. Just as he was about to pass by John's position his steps swayed drunkenly and his head came up. John still couldn't see the man's face. He could just make out his outline. The man swayed, turned, and started slowly plodding toward John and the tent. Night of the living dead, is what occurred to John. The man seemed out on his feet and only heading toward John because of some basic, stem impulse.

John's Helping was screaming now. Out of nowhere it had kicked into high gear. None of the radiant brilliant light this time. But it was some kind of a Helping coming on, none the less. The man's figure started coming into view more and more. At about ten yards John recognized him. It was Dusty. Covered in blood and sweat and the never ending grit and sand of the desert. Dusty slowing continued his plodding and, even though their eyes were locked, he was looking right through John. Doesn't recognize me at all, John knew.

"Dusty," John called. "Dusty, man, it's me. John. John Sloan. Columbo, man."

Dusty stopped directly in front of John.

"Dusty, you all right man?"

Dusty blinked slowly and opened his mouth slightly, then closed it. He opened it again and then seemed to recognize John.

"John," he said in a hollow voice. "We should stay out of the desert. It's too red. We should go back home to the woods. It's not good here."

The Helping in John was working overtime now. The light blasting into every crevice of Dusty's being and yet John still couldn't see anything but a blank darkness. Nothing there but nothing.

Dusty turned and brushed past John toward the tent entrance. He turned back toward John and his face had changed. It was coming alive again but in a horrible way. Not alive, just animated. Horribly animated.

"The red is everywhere, John," Dusty said and flipped open the tent flap and slipped inside, his rifle slung over his shoulder, but with magazine inserted, and one round in the chamber.

John was too stunned to do anything at first. He finally snapped out of it and hurried into the tent. The music was not as loud as before and everyone had noticed Dusty's entrance. The drunken crew were welcoming Dusty. For Dusty's part he was full on red. That's what John thought. He looks like Uncle Lou is what rocketed through John's mind. Laying a trap.

By now everyone knew that Dusty was to receive a medal. A Silver Star, or maybe even the Navy Cross, was what the scuttlebutt had said. Fuck, the only thing higher than those two awards was the fucking Medal of Honor! They peppered him with questions.

"Fucking-A, redman. Get some!"

"Dusty, you are one motherfucking badass jarhead, dude!"

"Heard you said *fuck'em* and got some last night too, huh, dude!?"

John watched as Dusty took it all in. Dusty's experiences were starting to appear in John's mind rapidly. His desert experiences rolling out from start toward finish. John saw what Dusty had done to deserve the silver star. Felt his fear and his exhilaration. His lack of thought once he had started. Just acting and reacting, not trying to be a hero.

"Just like the old timers say," John thought. "They didn't try to be a hero, they just acted."

John made his mind call out to Dusty's, but Dusty couldn't, or wouldn't, listen.

"How's it feel to kill some ragheads?" one drunken newbie shouted.

This got Dusty's attention and he swiveled his head, body, and *weapon* toward the FNG, the fucking new guy.

"How's it feel to kill?" the newbie asked again, in spite of himself.

He wanted to know but had been afraid to ask any of the veterans before. His excitement and his drunkenness had gotten the better of his fear.

"Well now," Dusty replied in almost a whisper. "That's two different questions isn't it?"

The tent was now very quiet. Everyone sensing a danger that had suddenly appeared. They could see now that Dusty was off. *Way* off. So off that he was ON in some kind of violent and dangerous way. John's mind was rapidly inputting all of Dusty's experiences trying to catch up to this moment. He had caught up to the night before. How Dusty and his lieutenant had gone way out in the desert. As forward observers their job would be to call in artillery fire on the enemy. Enemy troop movements had been reported. Heavily armed, enemy troop movements. That's why the young lieutenant had volunteered for this sneak-and-peak.

The duo humped up on a small sand dune and as they reached the top they had to suddenly drop to the ground as they saw a small group of soldiers making their way quietly through the night desert. The lieutenant had their one night scope, but it was malfunctioning, so the view was poor. Dusty had to stop the over-anxious Lt. from banging it against a rock.

"Gotta watch our noise discipline there, El Tee," Dusty hushed to the nervous lieutenant. "Just follow my lead."

The boot lieutenant couldn't wait to get some kills. Had dreamed of confirmed kills since his days in NROTC.

"Fuck, El Tee, we don't even know if they're the enemy," Dusty hissed. Dusty had already seen how fucked up troop movements were.

"Yea, but it was a fucking raghead jeep abandoned just down that trail," the Lt. had said.

"I know," Dusty said, "let's just wait to be sure, OK lieutenant?"

All of this flashed in John's mind in a breath, while the newbie was questioning Dusty. John was having a hard time keeping track of everything. He had the situation in the tent that seemed to be developing out of control, *and* the situation in Dusty's mind from last night that definitely seemed to have gotten out of control.

The lieutenant had gotten antsy. Too antsy. Dusty had scrambled a little farther over the berm when he heard a squawk. An unmistakeable squawk. The lieutenant was keying his radio and calling into base.

"Knock that shit off," Dusty hissed. "I'll fucking kill you myself, you fucking brown bar."

Dusty hurriedly crawled back to the lieutenant and that's when their position had been located. The small patrol below them opened up with automatic fire. The lieutenant's eyes were the size of full moons by the time Dusty got back to him.

"Just trying to get some confirmation," the lieutenant said, right before an enemy round found one of his full moon eyes. It entered into the surprised target and exited out the back, removing the rear portion of the lieutenant's head. And now base camp *was* radioing back and the radio was under the lieutenant's body and loud enough to give the attackers a perfect location to fire at. Dusty didn't know who was fucking dumber...the lieutenant for giving away their position or the enemy for opening up on what to them had to be an unknown amount of enemy. There were only six of them, and for all they knew, I could be up here with a company, Dusty thought.

Dusty grabbed two grenades and threw them to either of the enemy's flanks to give them the impression of a larger force. Three of the dumb motherfuckers' were standing up, and Dusty could see through the now-working night scope. He cut them down quickly and headed back down the berm before changing direction to outflank them. It never occurred to him to retreat. Just as it had never occurred to him to not save the men he had saved, or kill the enemy he killed in the action that had won him the silver star. He just acted and reacted.

And he was angry. So very angry. Red angry. The dumb fucking lieutenant and those even dumber fucking ragheads down there.

Back in the tent Dusty finally seemed ready to address the newbie.

"How does it feel to kill rag heads?" he asked the newbie. "Feels like fucking victory, you young little pig," he said, echoing Robert Duval's classic line from *Apocalypse Now*. A favorite of the war hungry marines. The classic line should've raised a cheer from the group but it didn't.

The new guy was practically shitting his pants. Dusty had his war face on. That and the fact that he was covered in blood had the new guy near tears. All the other marines were backing off too. Even the old salts were nervous.

John suddenly realized part of Dusty's new plan. He didn't know it all but he did know that if something didn't happen soon Dusty was gonna dust the new guy. Shoot him square in the face with his M-16. Right in *his* fucking full moon eyes.

John saw Dusty back on the dune crawling his way toward the enemy's position. One by one he set about picking them off. Three down, three to go were his thoughts. He threw another grenade to their opposite flank and shot two more when they ran toward him away from the blast. One left. Dusty was seeing red now and full on. He silently slid his K-Bar from it's sheath. A long bowie knife type of blade that he kept sharpened to a point where he could shave the hair off the back of his hand. Gonna kill this one up close and personal.

"And now to address your other question, piggy," Dusty continued. "How does it feel to kill?"

Dusty crawled quietly toward the remaining enemy. Dusty could see him without seeing him. He could smell him and the smell made his mind try to take back control from his rage. The smell was familiar.

"Fuckin' raghead smells like mashed fucking potatoes," he thought. "What in the fuck is with that?"

Fuck that, his rage told him. Kill the motherfucker. Dusty could hear the radio still squawking under the lieutenant's dead body. "Come in, romeo two," it called over and over.

"Even that motherfucker sounds uptight," Dusty thought. "Fucking comm maggot back at base camp's wetting his pants."

Dusty had the lone man in his sights now. He threw his remaining grenade in behind the man's position to get him to come back toward the kill. Dusty realized how green these troops were. They couldn't even hear at night otherwise he never would've thrown the remaining grenade over the man. He would've used it to kill him perhaps, but he never would've given him a chance otherwise, had they not been so green and obviously inept. It seemed like Dusty's "full-on red" wanted to toy with this last enemy soldier. The man had lost his weapon and was running directly at the crouching Dusty.

"How does it feel to kill in general? Is that what you're asking, my baby-shitting young friend?"

Dusty towered over the young PFC, who had scrunched back to the far end of his cot.

"I'll let you in on a little secret," Dusty said to the marine, and to the entire tent, his voice rising now.

The lone enemy soldier was running full tilt, and panicked, right into Dusty's position. At the last second, Dusty rose up and spun the young soldier, choking him and holding his K-Bar to the man's throat.

"Victory," Dusty thought as he slit the man's throat and twisted his head, blood cascading over both of them. It was only then that Dusty noticed the man's uniform. US Army. Transportation company.

"It feels just as good," Dusty hissed. "Even when they're your own," he said, knowing that it was true. Dusty quickly un-shouldered his weapon and raised it into firing position.

The radio hissed down at Dusty from the dune. Muffled by the dead body covering it, but audible just the same. "Romeo two, romeo two, CEASE FIRE, CEASE FIRE, possible friendlies in you area! I repeat cease fire, cease fire, possible friendlies in your area. Do you copy, I say again do you copy?"

"I copy," Dusty registered, "oh, I fucking copy."

Dusty painted his face with the blood of his last kill and shouldered his weapon and the radio. The jeep he and the lieutenant had ridden out in was forgotten as he started the walk back to base underneath a blanket of stars shining brightly as only a desert sky can allow.

John was up to speed now and knew something needed to happen fast. He saw that Dusty had killed six Americans and that Dusty had gone around the bend. He also saw that Dusty meant to kill the PFC and then turn the weapon and kill himself.

The Helping opened up in John completely. Time stood still, and all movement stopped.

"Dusty," he yelled both out loud and with his mind. "Dusty," he said again as he walked over to his friend. Dusty paused, not just in action but in mind as well.

"I don't think that will work, John," Dusty's mind told John.

"Shake my hand, Dusty. Shake it," John said as he reached out.

John felt a chink in the armor inside of Dusty's raging mind. He saw the Helping attack that chink as fearlessly as Dusty had attacked the men the night before. It slashed in through the crack and illuminated Dusty from the inside out.

"There is a Light, Dusty. Even for you. I am the Light and you are the Light too. It *is* in us all, Dusty. Feel the Light. Embrace it." John grabbed Dusty's now-raising hand and felt the Helping passing through them.

Tears were now pouring from Dusty's eyes, leaving wet trails of blood and dirt streaking his weary face.

"It works whether you think it can or not, Dusty. It's the fucking *Light*."

John saw how Dusty had worked his way back toward base camp and been spotted, and had brief contact with an American patrol at dawn. How a separate team had surveyed the damage Dusty had wrought. How news of what was quickly coming to be realized as a friendly-fire incident had made it back to the higher echelons at base camp before Dusty had made it back. Dusty had walked the twenty-five miles back to camp in eight hours, lost in soul and spirit.

Dusty was stunned and couldn't believe he had been Helped, but he couldn't deny it either. He could *feel* how clean he had been made. He could feel how forgiven he was, no matter what the military decided. His spirit wept and joined the Light.

"I was gonna kill that fucker, John," Dusty said. "Kill that boot motherfucker dead, and enjoy it."

"It's over, Dusty. Let's go outside."

Both John and Dusty knew that the exchange between them would not be remembered by the platoon inside the tent. The Helping would erase that and smooth over just how out of control the situation had been.

And just like that the tent came back to life. Everyone laughed nervously as Dusty said "bang" toward the PFC, lowered his rifle, and turned to go with John. The noise level escalated and the party was back in full swing.

"Hey, boot, better watch out! You don't ever want to fuck around with a salt like Dusty."

"Shit, you almost shit your pants, Templeton. How you gonna be in combat?"

"You a bad motherfucker, Dusty. *Bad* motherfucker."

The two friends made it outside of the tent. Healed, both of them.

"Shit, I was hoping to see you and have you help *me,"* John said. "I've been freaking out! Sorry man. You had it worse than me. Helping you helped me. Thanks, Dusty."

"Thank me?" Dusty said. "Man, I owe you my life bro. Again. Shit I'm supposed to be the big powerhouse. How come you keep Helping me?"

"Shit, I don't know, Dusty. That's just how it's worked out. You know it's not up to us, it's up to the Light. What was I supposed to do? Not Help you?" John said as they put their arms around each other and hugged as only the best of friends can do. Peas, asshole buddies. Each trying to lift the other off the ground.

"Well all I know is that I owe you big time, man, and I'm gonna pay you back if it takes the rest of my life. I swear to you, John," Dusty said now serious, "I *will* pay you back."

The friends walked toward John's tent basking in the peace. In the midst of war, glowing in the peace. Come what may, military inquiry or not, guilt or not, Dusty knew that he had been Helped and that he had been saved.

"Man, I wish we had some beer," Dusty said. "I *need* a fuckin' brew."

"I can maybe score us a bottle of brandy," John thought toward Dusty. Conversation unnecessary now. "There's a Captain from Milwaukee owes me a favor. He keeps a case of Five Star in his jeep."

"Maybe later. First things first. You got any tobacco?," Dusty said, solemn now. "We need to do something."

John pulled an unopened pack of Old Golds from the side pocket of his desert cammie trousers and flipped it to Dusty. "Will these do?"

"Yea, they should. I need your help for one more thing John. Let's go back out into the desert a ways."

With that Dusty led John back outside of the camp's perimeter, murmuring to himself. A low-throated chant beginning. The two marines found a slight rise in the dark desert sand and Dusty broke open the pack of smokes.

"Let's see if the old ways can help too," Dusty added.

Dusty began chanting and dancing slowly. Circular movements, feet going and knees going up and down, head going up and down. Offering tobacco to the six corners of existence. All four directions, then up to the sky and down to the ground.

John felt out of place immediately. Like he didn't belong and was witnessing something that he had no right to.

"Knock that shit off," Dusty's mind shot to John, his dance and his chant never hesitating. "I need you here. You belong here. You are part of the ceremony. Who gives a shit if you're white? Fuck, I'm *part* white. You are needed and you're my bro. Who else if not you?"

John first witnessed Dusty's ceremony and then joined in. The two friends lowly chanting, dancing in a circle, first praying for the souls of the Americans Dusty had killed, and then all the others. The men John had killed as well. Each offering up tobacco, silhouetted against the dark desert sky. Stars blazing overhead. Murmuring, chanting, dancing. Praying for forgiveness and for the souls of the dead men. Praying for themselves, for each other, for mercy. Offering all up to the Light. The old ways, the old way, the Light.

33

In the infinite wisdom of military madness Dusty *did* receive his silver star. And he was found not-guilty of negligence in the killing of the six U.S. troops. What could you do? It may not feel like justice but it was. He was, *unofficially*, found temporarily unfit for combat duty. *Too fit* was actually how the Battalion Sgt. Major had put it. The battalion's top enlisted man had whispered in the colonel's ear that what Sgt. Hakilla needed was some R&R and then maybe a training position back in the states. He's too *good* to be wasted, the Sgt. Major had intoned, but maybe a little too *sharp* to stay up here.

John had been able to hang in the rear long enough to see Dusty's medal presentation. But not long enough to find out about the inquiry, although news filtered forward to him about it almost as soon as Dusty was sent back stateside—the military grapevine working almost as quickly as direct, technical communication. Often quite better.

Dusty's time in the war was officially over, and John's may as well have been. And thankfully so. John rode the spearheading advance with no further troubles. A troubled mind, perhaps, but that too had been eased by his Helping of Dusty. His elation at the time of victory was tempered with a weariness to get back home. He, for one, was glad that they didn't roll right in to Baghdad, as some had thought might happen. He was done and he knew that it was time to hang up his boots. His military service had to end, even though he had considered making it a career after he had voluntarily extended for Panama, and had been involuntarily extended for Desert Shield and Desert Storm. The wormy-worm had turned and he knew that he needed to get out of the military for good. He couldn't just drift in and out of the Marine Corps. He was done. Next chapter... time to move on... the shift had occurred.

34

It had been the goddamned shift, John now knew. When he had caught Deena coloring her pubic hair, unbeknownst to him, the precariousness of their relationship had shifted. Things were quiet for a bit and then what *could've been* the really good stuff, the Helping stuff had happened, and it had still all gone to shit.

Deena had started drifting away slowly, and finally, when things could've gone either way, she had chosen to bail. Hadn't had a choice in her mind. She *had* to go. And it had all started with a conversation. Why the fuck did he have to open his yap? Fuck, if he hadn't said anything maybe the Helping wouldn't have occurred and they would still be together. And if Dusty hadn't shown up out of nowhere...yea, yea, yea, and if the queen had balls...

John's feeling of a Helping coming on had gotten stronger and stronger as the days passed. He and Deena had established a truce. They were feeling each other out again almost as if they had just started dating. Hard to do when you're living together. Walking on eggshells, and checking each other's emotional temperature every five minutes. The big think had led to the big talk. Of all things it had been Deena's answering machine that started it all off.

He had gotten home before Deena and had walked into the dark apartment and seen the blinking light of the answering machine. Off and on, off and on. "Why doesn't she get voice-mail?" was John's first thought. Could we rocket out of the 20th century here, or what?! Mad all of a sudden, and with images flooding his mind. Red orange, red orange. Mrs. Abbott's hair, nuns, and the shimmering light of a Helping. Not seeing clearly but knowing there was a path to follow.

Deena walked in five minutes later to find John sitting in the dark.

"Whatcha' doin, Johnnie?"

"Been sittin' here thinkin', honey. There's a Helping coming on and things are all a bit jumbled in my head right now. Hoping you'll help me sort it out."

That's what was nice about being with another Helper. You could talk with them about things that couldn't have been brought up with a civilian. And it occurred to bot John and Deena that neither of them had Helped anyone since they had gotten together. What would that be like? That thought brought fear creeping back in as well. What if we can't Help like we used to because we're together? The fact that John most definitely had a Helping coming on did nothing to alleviate that fear for both. Shift.

"But can we turn a light on, John? It's a little spooky sitting here in the dark like this."

Deena turned on some lights and put away her lunch things from work. Her little routine. Tupperware containers in the sink, ice pack back into the freezer, and her cool-pack lunch box underneath the counter. Hidey, tidy, all in a row.

"All right, John, what's going on?" she said settling down on the couch.

John wasn't sure how to start so he just opened his mind and at the same time started jumbling out the images to her with his voice.

"Nuns, I keep seeing nuns," he said. "What's that mean to you?"

"My mother always loved nuns," Deena replied.

Click, shift.

"She did, didn't she? I can see that now."

Red hair, orange hair. He told her about this.

"Well, my real hair color is dark red," she told him, "but I don't know about the orange."

Click, shift. Lights and colors shooting out between them as their dual conversation continued. And then the image of Mrs. Abbott solidified in his mind. Mrs. Abbott's orange hair.

"Who's that!", Deena shot out quickly.

"My third grade teacher. You've seen her before haven't you? When you've cruised my mind?"

"Never," was the reply.

Click, shift. Now an image of a younger Mrs. Abbott in the hospital ward with the nuns. Both John and Deena's minds locking on the image. An answer hovering just below the white light shooting between them. The scene slowly unfolding of a baby being handed from mother to nuns, of a Light passing between mother and daughter, of the Helping being passed. But this time the scene didn't stop with the baby leaving the room and the remaining nun comforting Mrs. Abbott. John had never known anything past this point before, but now his mind rolled out new visions that both he and Deena were watching with amazement. John was almost to the point of knowing, Deena a bit farther behind.

"Do you see this Deena? Are you getting this?" his mind shot.

Deena's mind only nodded absently back to John's.

The nun with the bundled baby now walking down a corridor, sunlight streaming through the windows. Her praying and cooing over the baby. Walking past the care-giving portion of the hospital into the administrative area. Into the office of the head nurse and Mother Superior. The two nuns were waiting for something or someone. It was all on the tip of John's tongue now but he couldn't quite spit it out.

"What's going on here, John?"

"I don't know, Deena." Which was correct but not completely right. John knew that he knew, he just couldn't access the information.

The buzzer on the Mother Superior's desk juzz-janged and both of the nuns jumped, startled.

"Send them in," the head nurse said into the plastic box of an intercom. They both rose, one with a baby in her arms, as a couple walked through the door.

Deena recognized them immediately and knew. So did John.

"Those are my parents, John. My mom and dad. Oh God, that's me being adopted!"

Click, shift.

35

Deena's dad Jerry had worked with a guy, who knew a guy, who's sister was a nun up in Milwaukee. The guy Jerry worked with, Tony, had known about the Morrison's childless situation for awhile. Shit, he and Jerry had worked next to each other for over seven years already. Side by side, hit the break-room for lunch together, the whole shebang. Tony had been able to read beneath the lines and see the pain this caused both Jerry and Adele. So when Mike Dabney, an usher Tony knew from church, mentioned that his sister was a nun working at a hospital/orphanage in Milwaukee it just seemed natural to pass this info along to Jerry. Come to think of it, Mike was always mentioning that his sister was a nun. Always. And Tony was even pretty sure that he mentioned the orphanage adoption part of the story as well. It had just never clicked in before. The time must be right, Tony thought. God's time, maybe.

It had all happened very quickly. A few letters, some background checking, a big helping of recommendation from Tony and Mike, and before you knew it, Adele and Jerry were on an Eastern Airlines flight to Chicago, followed by a train trip to Milwaukee.

The Morrison's were as surprised as anyone. They hadn't mentioned it to any of their friends. Adele couldn't bear the thought of having it all fall through and then having to explain it all, over and over again to her friends. The fact that it was a Roman Catholic organization allowing them to adopt surprised them even more. They were helped in this by the fact that they had an inside track via Tony, Mike, and Mike's sister, Sister Mary John Ignatius. Sister Mary and the Mother Superior were two peas in a pod and they had to do a little plotting to keep the Monsignor's nose out of everything. 1970 was a very different world than the 21st century. Through the Grace of God and Greyhound, well actually Pan American Airlines, they were given a beautiful baby girl.

They took their new daughter back to Miami, and this again being 1970, not many questions were asked. Adele mentioned it to a few of her friends and that had been that. Adoption being something usually talked about in hushed tones, if at all, at that time. Better for the child not to know had been the general consensus. Plus, the Morrisons decided they needed a bigger house and had found one within two months after getting their baby. A bigger house in a different neighborhood. Nothing was planned on purpose, but this led to even fewer questions being asked. On their new block in North Miami Beach, they were just the new family—Jerry, Adele, and baby Deena. Deena was a name Adele picked out. Mrs. Abbott had been told to not even name the baby for fear of developing even more of an attachment to the child before having to give her up so the naming was up to Adele.

Adele had always felt sorry for the anonymous mother who hadn't even had a chance to name her child. She understood the reasons, but still felt a sad connection with the woman. A debt owed for the joy she already felt at being a mother. Adele had a long memory and she understood debts. And she paid her debts.

"We're calling her Deena," she had said as they walked down the long hospital corridor and stood waiting for the elevator. "She's our beautiful little Deena."

"Where had that come from?" flashed through Adele's mind. Adele had absolutely no idea where that name had come from, but she had recognized it immediately. She recognized it as their babies' name. I guess that's how people name their kids, she thought. And she liked it. Deena. Something perfect about that name. Something complete, somehow. Better still, she *knew* it was their new baby's name. She had no way of seeing the residual Light still connecting their sweet little baby, no, suddenly their sweet little *Deena*, to her mother. Not realizing that one more thing had been passed on. From mother to child. From mother to mother to child. From Dianna Abbott to Adele to Deena.

Jerry understood that the baby's name was not a subject open for discussion. Adele had spoken because Adele was convinced.

"Deena is a beautiful name, Adele. She's our little Deena now. And thank God."

"Oh Jerry, thank you so much. I am so happy, Jerry. You don't know how happy you have made me right this moment."

Jerry hugged his wife who was cradling their baby. Hugged her and thanked his lucky stars. Oh he did know, but he didn't say. Oh yes, he did know how happy he had made his wife. Because his life suddenly felt just as complete.

36

Deena and John sat facing each other in the dimly lit living room. A chasm seemed to have yawned open between them, despite all of the powerful thoughts and experiences they had shared.

"She didn't even get a chance to name me," Deena finally replied. "Dianna, Mrs. Abbott, shoot, my mom, I guess."

Deena thought of her real mom, Mrs. Abbott, then of her *real* mom Adele, and then about the baby she herself was carrying. Sad and empty. That's how she felt. And sadder still because she had kept her new pregnancy hidden from John. All that's left is the decision, she thought.

"What was that?" John thought back.

"Nothing, baby, I just feel so sad about it all. My real mom having to give me up, and then my other real mom having to keep it all secret from me. And now I feel as though I'm left without anybody."

Ouch, John thought, and Deena wished she could have taken that back. Not that it wasn't true, she saw that now more than ever, but the last thing she wanted to do was hurt John. And she was beginning to understand that she was probably going to have to.

"Sorry, John. I didn't mean that. It's just all so confusing. I don't even know who my real mom *is*."

"You had two real moms, Deena. Even though that may be hard to believe, can't you see how they both gave you as much love as they could? Mrs. Abbott gave you so much, and gave up so much for you. She made your life possible. All of it. Your life with the Morrisons, your Helping ability, everything. And your parents...you have to know how much they loved you. How much they gave to you. Even I can see it and feel it so powerfully."

Deena did feel it. She did see it. And she was still so empty. A change was coming on and she knew it. It was all too much for her mind to handle. She cursed herself for even considering aborting her baby. After all the two women in her life had done for her, she had up until that point been considering an abortion. She knew now she wouldn't do that. No matter what happened, she *couldn't* do that. Not that she was against abortion, either in the abstract, or in practice. But that was suddenly an option not available to her. She must have her baby. There were some other musts coming into focus in the recesses of her mind, as well. They weren't clear yet, but she had a feeling that her life was soon to become overwhelmed with *musts*.

John was sensing Deena's internal struggle but not seeing the details. He felt like his world was tilting, disorienting. The presence of the Helping was stronger now as well, but he was feeling more than a little sick. Light was throttling up inside of him and he became aware of a subtle panic too. He was sensing that somehow he was going to lose Deena. She was going to leave him. He didn't know what to do. The only thought that occurred to him was that maybe the Helping *was* for Deena. And that maybe by Helping her he could keep her. He *had* to keep her. He knew that now. He must. He couldn't lose her. He saw how completely and utterly he loved her. How empty his life had been before meeting her. The contrast stood out in stark relief. Before and after Deena. He opened his mind.

"Can you see the Light, Deena? Can you feel it?"

Deena could feel it and yet she had never felt farther away from John or anybody than she had in her whole life. She was adrift, not knowing what to do.

"I feel it, John." She could see his panic mixed in as well.

John was scrambling now. All caught up in the Light and in his own fear. This had *never* happened before. Light surging out of the Source, through him. Whistling up through the hollowness of his spirit. "I'm losing her," he thought. Deena could feel that too, and she became enraged. Enraged at the unfairness of it all. Mrs. Abbott not being able to raise her. Adele and Jerry having to lie to her. Her love racing away from John. Carrying John's baby and being too weak to tell him. Too weak to build a life with this good man. This loving man. "Screw it," her soul cried out.

"No, Deena! No! See the Light, baby. See it. See it for me." John was in a dream, falling and falling without being able to stop. He felt the Power of the Light too, but he felt powerless at the same time.

"There is a Light, Deena. We are the Light too." Words and thoughts and fear spilling out of him. And through all of their fear and anger, the Helping still took hold. Images formed and rocketed back and forth. Mrs. Abbott's true situation became clear to Deena and was understood. This was the first forgiveness. Deena truly knew that her mother had done the best for her. It could *not* have been any other way. Next the Light shown on her anger toward Adele. How Adele had truly had no other way to respond to the situation and how it had torn her up. How, in spite of that, Adele had poured her life and love into her daughter. Deena was seeing, and, more importantly, having all resentments and rage taken from her.

"Do you see, Deena? Can you see it?" John was in tears now. John felt the healing taking place within Deena, yet felt no solace. His panic was subsiding, replaced with a helplessness. The Light continued to wash over them. The idea that it was time for one last push came to John. One last contraction.

He suddenly saw how Adele was passing the torch back to Mrs. Abbott. Giving Deena another chance. Replacing her own, sickened and dying body, with a healthy, loving one. How she hadn't *taken* from Deena but was giving Deena the chance to have what most people would never have. Another mother. Another *true* mother. Giving Deena the chance to replace her, all passed along by a few words sent in a dying letter. John saw the sacrifice she made. Felt the love she had for her daughter, to give her up to another. Pure Light now. Pulsing, cleansing, Helping.

Deena saw it too. She was uplifted. She saw how she was being spared a lifetime of "what if's." How she was being made to see, and to understand, and to be truly accepting of what had happened.

"My mother gave me back to my mother," Deena thought. She was in tears now as well. Deena was protected. She wasn't overjoyed, but she was completed. She was in a safe place within herself, looking out at all that was. Not knowing all that was coming to pass, but insulated from it. Seeing the parting that was happening between herself and John but not feeling the pain of it. Not exalted, but safe and cocooned. And she felt grateful.

"John, I see it all so clearly. Thank you so much, Johnnie. I've been given another chance. I love you so much."

John was too spent to respond. He felt like he had given all he had to give. "I love you too, Deena."

"The hand of Providence, John. I truly see the Hand of Providence."

John saw it too and felt nothing. In a detached way, he heard the distant rumble of impending doom. An unsettled, drum roll being played on a great timpani off in the distance. He was empty.

Click, shift.

37

Deena watched the gulf between herself and John widen. She could see it clearly, didn't want it to happen, but still felt detached and separatc from it. She was starting to sense a new purpose. A new goal. A dual goal. She was thinking more and more of the baby she was carrying. For that was what it was now, a baby. It hadn't truly been that until John had Helped her. Before that it was just a possibility, a missed menstrual cycle. She didn't know now how she could have ever considered aborting it. But she had, when it was just a missed period. It was infinitely more now. She was also thinking of her mother. Her birth mother.

Deena felt like a link in a human chain. Caught between her unknown mother, and her future baby. Suddenly it all seemed to be about possibilities. She wasn't overjoyed about them, she was still separated by this imposed detachment she was experiencing, but she was witnessing the blossoming of future possibilities.

She felt terribly saddened by the fact that John seemed to be disappearing from those possibilities. And from her. She saw a muted shell-shocked-ness to him. He was going through the motions, saying all the right things, but something was missing. Some spark of the previous tender attachment that was theirs, was gone. She had tried reaching out to him, both inside and outside, but that had not helped. She also found that she was less and less interested in directing her efforts toward John. This added to her guilt. She felt that she was the linchpin in a mythical tug of war. A link in a different chain. One that had John on one side, and the concerns of motherhood on the other. *As* a mother, and *for* her mother.

Deena still hadn't told John about her pregnancy. And that was how she was thinking of it, as *her* pregnancy, not theirs. She felt guilt over this, as well. Here was the man of her dreams, a man that needed her help, that would be a father for their child that she had only dreamed of, and yet was beyond reach.

John felt himself slowly disengaging. He sensed that something was different about Deena, something *physically* different, yet it was beyond his grasp as to what it was. He also knew that their relationship was crumbling. It was drifting beyond the point of no return and he seemed too tired to prevent it. This caused a distant pain that John did not know how to respond to. There was nothing specific about it that he could grasp and try to solve. He reflected on his many experiences in life. The panic and terror of war, the loneliness that he now knew he had experienced before Deena, the many people he had Helped. None of that was of any use to him. He kicked himself knowing that others had had it worse and survived, while he was helpless to stop this descent, this separation, that was happening.

He went through the motions. He went to work and tried to keep a positive front up for his crew and toward his coworkers. This was becoming less and less important to do. They were starting to mention John's attitude, or *lack* of attitude, among themselves. They *too* became watchers, just as John and Deena had become. He went through the motions with Deena as well. Bringing home his twice weekly bunches of flowers for her to place on the dining room table. Still leaving little hand-written notes on her pillow some mornings after she had left for work. Making an effort to include play in their life together. Their frequent showers together. Their love making.

His only hope was that if he could hold out long enough something would shift the momentum back the other way. He *knew* that not only was something wrong, but that something was missing too. Something important, something right in front of his eyes, but something he couldn't put his finger on.

His family had noticed it too. His sister Theresa had called out of the blue and been so worried that she had told John to come to Minneapolis for a quick weekend visit. Had *ordered* him, actually. It had been so evident to her upon seeing him, that the first chance she had to get John alone she had bluntly told him that he looked like shit. Theresa had gotten Deena to take Theresa's daughter out into the backyard immediately after their arrival.

"Sherry, show Auntie Deena your new swing. She's just loves her new swing-set, Deena."

Theresa took charge when she needed to, heck she took charge when she didn't need to, and she saw right off that she needed to here. So within five minutes of John and Deena having entered the house, Theresa had John backed up into a corner of the kitchen. "You look like shit, John. What the hell is going on?"

"I don't know, Theresa. We're just going through a little rough patch, me and Deena, ya know? Work's been a little crazy too, I guess. You know how it goes."

Theresa had been able to see through John ever since he was a little boy, and she was able to do so now. They had been closer than any of the other Sloan children, in a family known for close ties.

"Bullshit, Johnnie. What's going on? Mom says you haven't called her in over a month and nobody else in the family has heard from you either. What is going on? Is Deena OK?" Theresa had noticed something different about Deena too. Something she couldn't put her finger on. Something she didn't figure out until the couple was pulling out of her driveway the next day.

John told her the truth. "I don't know, T. I can't figure it out."

Theresa saw that he was telling her the truth and it scared her. She could see that he really *didn't* know what was happening and that he was mired in depression. Slow moving, slow to smile, and not seeming to care.

With a half-hearted grin John said, "I think it'll all work out. Small price to pay to be one of the world's finest, I guess."

Theresa let that pass and John noticed.

"Well, get your shit together, John. Please, and let me know if I can help in any way. Oh, and speaking of world's finest...I heard Dusty is back in town. Somewhere around back home. Cousin Linda told me he was on leave before heading to Afghanistan."

Theresa looked, hoping this would bring a spark to John. It even brought a little spark to Theresa. She was happily married now, but she had spent a wild week with Dusty in her younger days. John had brought Dusty for a visit to the Sloan homestead and something in the younger man had caught Theresa's eye. When she saw him again two years later she didn't let it pass. Dusty was much too wild and polygamous for Theresa, but they had shared a whirlwind week, both knowing that it wouldn't last. Theresa saw no such spark now in John.

"Oh, that's cool, T. I hope he stops by Duluth. Man, I'd like to see him." although it really didn't sound like it.

Theresa let that pass as well. She did what big sisters did, she watched, she registered, and she made up her mind to do what she could, when she could, to help her brother.

She hadn't been able to get much out of Deena during the weekend either. While Deena didn't actually seem to be avoiding her, the chance to really talk hadn't presented itself.

It had only been as John and Deena were walking out to their car to leave that something had tickled in the back of Theresa's mind. Something about the way Deena was carrying herself. She looked a little fuller, a little healthier, a little brighter. There was an imperceptible something there. And then as their car was pulling out of the driveway it had occurred to Theresa. "Oh my God. I wonder if she's pregnant." And next, "I wonder if John knows."

38

From Theresa's lips to God's Ears. Five days later, who should show up but Dusty.

It *had* registered to John when Theresa told him about Dusty. At first he had been lightened but then the fear had crept in. He knew Deena didn't care much for Dusty. They had only met once and Deena had been very stand-offish. She had been turned off by Dusty's direct manner and wild eyes. Also by the undeniable bond between John and Dusty. It was as if they operated in a whole different manner from other people. Even from other Helpers. Not just starting and finishing sentences for each other like a couple would. She knew they weren't *gay*. That was part of what pissed her off. They had a shared connection that seemed to edge Deena out, even though she could see they were both trying not to. She could see the bond and the love they shared. It was if they were two parts of a greater whole. She had to admit, she was jealous.

And, she was scared of Dusty. She had never really known anybody that had lived the life Dusty had. She knew that John had war experiences, but with him it was easy. Those experiences never came between them. If they did come up it was no big deal, and when they did it was always so gentle with John.

Dusty had stayed three days that time and that was long enough. Longer than a trio of Helpers would usually spend together anyway, although Deena could tell that Dusty had kept a lot of his Helping ability keyed down. Still, she had never felt the Power of a Helper so strongly as with Dusty. He only let it out when he saw that it wouldn't get in the way for the three of them. He was also holding part of his edgy personality back. Trying, for John's sake, to get Deena to like him. This added guilt to Deena's mind, which added to the gulf. All three were relieved when Dusty moved on.

Five nights after coming back from their visit to Theresa's they heard a pounding on their door. It was 10:30 on a rainy Friday night. Wind off the lake and colder than shit, as the local northlanders put it. A ragged boom, boom, booming on their door. John and Deena were both in bed, but with the lights on. Deena reading something from work and John laying on his back trying to recapture feelings of when this picture of the two of them in bed like this would've warmed his life. John's first thought was "police. What are the cops doing here?" Deena even ventured a frightened look his way.

"Open up, it's the fuckin' police, man," boomed from the front door.

As Deena stayed back, John headed toward the front of the apartment thinking about the muffled voice. "Well it's sure not the police."

Boom, boom, boom again. "What the fuck?" John thought. Even though their downtown apartment was on the second floor, it was still a walk-up and drunks and meth-heads were known to knock on their door from time to time, lost in their inebriated worlds thinking they had a different apartment. John had already checked the perimeter of the apartment before heading to bed with Deena, old habits die hard, so he knew the door was locked and chained. He opened the door as far as the chain would allow and through the dim hallway light he was greeted by the site of a drunken man with a very drunken woman. Dusty.

"Hey, Columbo, let me in. It's colder'n shit out here," Dusty said, wearing a lopsided, rain-drenched grin.

John let the two into the front room of the apartment. By this time Deena was in the room too, standing well back, clutching her robe to herself, watching.

Dusty and a woman. An obviously drunken, Indian woman. John's mind stumbled up through his recently acquired haze to find a solution to this situation. Not only was Deena not fond of Dusty, but he knew that she was generally afraid of Indians as well. Especially drunken ones. Living in Miami may have been a much broader, and ethnically diverse, experience for Deena, but she had never spent time around Native Americans, and they scared her.

"Hey John, man, 'ja ever meet my cousin Candy? It was so cool, I was drinkin' on Tower Avenue over'n Superior and I bumped into her at Al's." Al's Waterfront, not the most comely of bars. An equal opportunity establishment, perched on the north-end, port area of Superior. Boat slips so close, the thousand-foot freighters looked to be parked right alongside what beat-up cars could be found in the parking lot. Dwarfing them. You didn't have to be white, black, or red to drink there. Being helplessly alcoholic was all that was required.

"Candy, say hi to my bro John."

Candy somehow managed to raise her hanging head and peer out at John from under her long, rain-slickened, coal-black hair. Her head was tilted and she had only one eye open. Her one opened, but glazed, eye *did* seem to register a little.

"Hey young buck, wanna fuck?", was all she was able to manage, slurring and trying her best to look demure.

Oops. Not a bad line maybe, but definitely the wrong time for it. This even penetrated Dusty's semi-drunken head.

You didn't have to be a Helper to see that Deena was both scared and pissed.

"John, I've got to get up early. I'm sorry but you'll have to entertain your friends." Entertain being the last thing Deena had in mind, John knew. Deena turned, walked down the hall, and shut the bedroom door behind her.

"Shit bro, I'm 'm'sorry. Fuck! We'll go, man. I'm gettin' ready ta ship out an' I just hadda see ya. I knew I just hadda see ya."

"That's alright, Dusty," John said putting his arm around his buddy. By this time Candy had plopped down in a chair and was pondering unconsciousness. "She gonna be OK?"

"Oh sure, Candy'za trooper, man. We'll go, we'll go. Gonna see ya tomorrow. We'll talk. Gotta see ya man. I got a room at the Androy, seven-hunnert somethin', I think."

John was able to hail a passing cab, stuff some bills into the cabby's mitt, and bundle the drunken couple in.

"Call me tomorrow, Dusty. OK? We'll get together tomorrow. You better come alone, though, OK?"

"Sure John, whatever ya say. Gotta see ya. Somethin' wild goin on, man."

39

After John had gotten Dusty and Candy off, he went back upstairs to check on Deena. She was tucked into bed with the lights out, breathing evenly. John had stood in the dark and watched her, gauging whether or not she was awake. "Just what I need now, " he thought. She looked peaceful, a long lump in the bed, the covers rising slowly up and down over her stomach. Peaceful, insulated, separate.

John mumbled an apology to Deena in the morning. He was less and less able to approach Deena about anything. He was finding it harder and harder to start conversations, to connect with her, to live a life of two. They seemed like two life-spheres floating through the same space, but interacting less and less.

"Baby, I'm sorry about last night," he whispered, the two of them still deep under the covers that morning. They both lay listening to the early morning rain trickle down the window panes and rain gutters of their apartment. Next to each other in bed, touching side by side, but no longer quite one.

"You know, it's just Dusty," he said.

"I know, John. That's OK. They just startled me. It was so late, and that woman was so drunk." Deena didn't add that she was finding herself to be more and more protective of herself, and her child. A daughter she knew, (hoped?).

"I'll talk to him. He's shipping out to Afghanistan so I suppose he's letting loose before heading back into the shat-storm over there."

John snuggled up to Deena, attempting again to break out of the separation between them. Trying again to bring them back together. They made morning love, something they both enjoyed doing frequently. It was sweet, and it was nice, but it wasn't them. It wasn't the them that had been, but it was what they had, and they took it. It was the them that they were now.

Dusty showed up two hours later. The last of the breakfast coffee was cooling in cups, the dishes from their simple breakfast of toasted English Muffin bread and homemade juneberry jelly drying in the dish-rack. John had just come back upstairs after his morning cigarette, smoked outside, down under the eaves on the front stoop—s taring out at the rain and the low fog hugging the harbor below, Lake Superior drifting in and out of view down below the rooftops on steep hill in front of their apartment that led to the waterfront. A thousand-foot lake-boat's horn forlorning through the mist. The boat making its way under the aerial-lift bridge coming from one unknown port to another.

Tap, tap, tap this time, not a cops bang, bang, bang, "let me in" knock. An apologetic tapping. Dusty stood sheepishly in the doorway. Dress-Blue uniform buckled tightly under his military raincoat, his white barracks-cover tucked under his arm, its black bill polished to a brilliant black. Obviously a different uniform than the disheveled one he had appeared in the night before. Two bouquets of flowers wrapped in his arms. Two dozen red roses tucked against one shoulder, a huge mix of wild flowers against the other.

He greeted John, shrugged off his raincoat and handed it and his cover to him, and then headed straight for Deena apologetically. He stood in front of her, almost standing at attention, again so different from how he had looked the night before. Now her eyes were drawn to the dark blue sleeves of Dusty's uniform with its red and yellow, three-up and two-down gunnery sergeant stripes, and below that the five, red and yellow hash-marks indicating length of time in service. But mostly her eyes were drawn to the row upon row of multicolored ribbons on Dusty's chest.

"Deena, I am so sorry about last night." Gaining strength, and because Dusty was never too far away from bullshit, he got down on one knee and presented the flowers up to Deena, as if presenting his sword to the queen. This instantly started to dispel the distance Deena had in place to enforce security around her spirit.

"Please forgive your loyal, yet erring, subject," Dusty said, now taking the opportunity for a quick glance up to gauge her reaction. And he was in. Their Helping walls came down, as much as Dusty and Deena allowed their walls down, and the lights and colors of a gathering of Helpers commenced.

John let out a sigh of relief, his first in quite some time. At least *this* may be OK, he thought. And it *was* good to see Dusty. He needed back-up now like never before.

The three Helpers sat and chatted for hours. Because they were in a *three* they automatically withheld most of their mind chatter and just shot the breeze like normal folks. Occasionally brilliant flashes of light would burst forth, but for the most part they just caught up.

Dusty sensed the growing distance between John and Deena. He sent his mind out surreptitiously to probe their defenses. John didn't even notice, which bothered Dusty. He really wasn't getting much of a picture from John's mind. Not a lot of reality, more of a stage-front setting. Like the town in a western movie. Store-fronts, all with windows and swinging saloon doors, but with nothing behind them. That wasn't the case with Deena's mind. Dusty snuck around in there as best he could, but she had her shields up and caught him once. Her mind spanking him lightly in a good-natured way. "Uh, uh, uh, don't come in without being asked," her mind parried. Dusty got a feeling of Deena being larger than normal. More than herself. And it was quite obvious, even if you weren't a Helper, that the couple was going through a rough patch in their relationship.

At Deena's request John left to walk down to the Central Hillside Bakery for fresh bread for lunch, and Dusty had a chance to be alone with her.

Their minds started up immediately.

"What's really going on?" Dusty asked while they stood in the kitchen waiting for the fresh pot of coffee to brew.

Deena opened up and let Dusty see what had transpired. Thoughts Dusty should've gotten already from John. As a rule their minds downloaded instantly upon meeting. Dusty wasn't quite sure how to respond so he just let his mind bathe in the experiences Deena was sending. His thoughts lapping back from time to time.

"Well at least you had two mothers, I never really had even one," he sent. Not dismissively, but to allow her to view another part of the reality.

"I know, Dusty," Deena thought back, "but now I feel compelled to find her. My real mother. Now more than ever."

Dusty could see the "now more than ever" in her mind, he just couldn't see the why. At least not yet. He also knew something that he couldn't allow Deena to see yet. Something he had to think about first. Something that Deena sensed but couldn't grasp. Dusty *knew* where Mrs. Abbott was. Exactly where she was. Hollywood, Florida. Not far from where Deena grew up. Teaching at a private school. An Indian school on a reservation smack dab in the middle of the peninsular city-mass of Miami/Fort Lauderdale that was south Florida.

"What? Do you know something?" she probed. "Hollywood? What's that mean?"

Dusty automatically sent out a laugh, (camouflage, cover, and concealment second nature to him) "No, I was just thinking how goddam Hollywood-ish this all is. It's a damn movie of the week. Oprah would squirt to break this baby."

"I know, I know," he added, hands raised in supplication, "I'm not making fun here. It's just how my mind works."

Deena bought the fabrication.

To change the subject he asked about John.

"What's with Columbo? It's like he's not all there."

"I don't know, Dusty, and I can't figure it out and I'm growing tired of even trying."

"You *know* how much he loves you, don't you?"

"I do, Dusty, but things just seem to be happening so fast, and I'm afraid it's all gonna fall apart."

Here she started crying quietly. And Dusty used the opportunity to probe deeper into her without her knowing it. He almost got it. He could wrap his mind around it but he still couldn't figure out what it was. What she was protecting. He saw the image of a mother bear. That was all. The front door squawked open and John's return broke the spell.

"Don't let him know I was crying," Deena said, and hurried into the bathroom.

How could he not know, was all that Dusty could think? You're both Helpers.

They spent the next few hours eating and sharing stories. Sandwiches and coffee, old friends and new. Almost as if nothing in the world was wrong. Mostly catching up on Dusty's travels and his imminent departure to Afghanistan.

"I think this is my last one," Dusty said and even John could tell that it was true. "I'm out after this. I already have my twenty in, shit I've got over twenty-one years now, but they involuntarily extended me. I'm just gonna skate through this one and get the hell out while I still can."

"I have to leave day after tomorrow," and the trio made plans for the following night. John and Deena walked Dusty to the front door and said their goodbyes. It was in the cab crossing the High Bridge back to Superior that it came to Dusty. "Shit, she's pregnant," he knew. "Jesus, and John doesn't even know."

40

Dusty called the next morning and asked John to pick him up. He was having to talk to John with his voice more and more. He hardly felt a link with John's mind and that was freaking him out. He knew he had to bounce the whole Mrs. Abbott thing off John before approaching Deena with it, to see if he should even say anything to Deena at all. His first allegiance was to John. Deena might be a Helper but John was the one that needed the help right now.

Wearing civilian clothes, Dusty was waiting for John under the awning, on the street in front of the eight-story, brick, one-hundred-year-old Androy Hotel. After hopping into John's pick-up, Dusty waded right in.

"John, I'm not sure exactly what's goin on with you, but I'm worried. Shit, I can't hardly read anything in your mind, and it's not like you're blocking me. Shit, you could never do that anyway. Not against my superhuman powers!"

John shrugged and said nothing. All good humor gone, no malice, just more of the same. More of the nothing.

With neither the frontal assault or the humor working, Dusty waded on. "I know where Mrs. Abbott is."

At this John perked a bit. Not perked *up*, more of a twitch really.

Dusty knew that John may allow what he thought was the right thing to be done, even if it was not to his benefit. Hell, even if it hurt him. And that twitch looked more like a flinch to Dusty.

"Long story short...a few years back I was trying to get my shit together and I did some volunteer stuff for the Seminoles down in south Florida. I worked out a few months away from the Corps before renewing my last enlistment. The one that would get me my twenty. So anyway, I somehow wound up down in Florida. Franklin Rose was down there in one of those little trailer parks and I spent some time with him. He's gettin so old I was afraid I wouldn't see him again. He sent me over to the Seminoles to get me out of his hair. That's what he said anyway, but he was really trying to stir something in me. I was there a week or two and I saw this white lady, with orange hair, walking down a hallway and I flashed on you. Then I flashed on her, and then she flashed on me. You know how it is...two Helpers and all."

John did, or used to, he thought.

"So anyway, we fired up. Man, what a cool lady. I even got Franklin to meet her. I thought she might keep an eye on him."

John said nothing, just stared out the windshield of the car, as they headed north on Tower Avenue toward the waterfront.

"She's still down there, John. I know cuz Franklin wrote me. I know where she is."

John continued driving, the wind buffeting the car as it crossed back over the mile-and-a-half-long High Bridge, that towered over the gray, choppy harbor waters below, connecting Superior to Duluth.

"Are you gonna fucking *say* anything?" Dusty lashed out, trying to shake John from his lethargy. Also, in part, because Dusty was scared. He didn't know what to do and he needed John's help. "Should I fucking tell Deena or not? I've kept it hidden so far, and I'm sure I can 'till I'm gone too, but maybe I should tell her. It *is* her fucking mother, for Christ's sake."

"Tell her, Dusty," was all John said, never taking his eyes from the road. "We'll tell her as soon as we get back."

And that's what they did. John opened the front door, told Deena to sit down, and told Dusty to tell his tale. A voice in the back of John's mind said that maybe this is the answer, maybe this will bring us back together again. John found that he didn't even care all that much. The panic was gone. He was just tired, and maybe this was the right thing to do.

Deena sat silently on the quilt-covered sofa, hands folded in her lap, blue-jean clad legs tucked up underneath herself, gray light feebly washing in from the front-windows behind her. Dusty opened up and told her both vocally and with his mind. A conversation that seemed to be going on above John's head. He simply sat there, watching and listening.

Deena wasn't mad that Dusty had held this back from her. She saw why. All the telling did was solidify the actions she now felt she must take. What she must do and who she must, or mustn't, do it with. She was surprised, and baffled, and amazed. Dusty didn't stop to watch her reactions, he just rolled it out. Showing Deena more of himself in five minutes than Deena had ever seen of him before. Seeing more of John too. And that hurt, knowing now where she must go.

One thing did surprise her though. The last thing Dusty slipped in before he made an excuse to leave abruptly.

"I know you're pregnant, Deena. And I know that John doesn't know." They both could see that this image hadn't penetrated John's haze. "Shit, I don't even know if he wants to be a Helper anymore. He's not even *in here* with us," Dusty continued. "And I'm not gonna tell him. And I don't think you should either. It'll kill him. And unless you feel a Helping glow coming on, which I sure as hell don't, neither one of us is gonna be able to Help him if he falls any farther."

Deena nodded and agreed with her mind.

"Now I figure you're gonna leave his ass and go to your mom. I guess I can't blame you. If I had a mom to go to I'd probably do the same thing, but don't you hurt him anymore. I'm gonna try to leave some protective mojo with him. I don't know if it will help or not but that's all I've got to give. Shit, look at him, he isn't even seeing us."

And he wasn't. John was sitting there watching but not seeing, and more importantly not joining them with his mind. His eyes glancing from their conversation to the slate sky outside the front window. Back and forth, slowly.

Dusty wrapped it up quickly after that. He floated a lame excuse about having to find his cousin Candy to give her some money. Even John figured it was a lie, but they all accepted it. Half-hearted plans were made for the next morning, but those too went unheeded. This was it for now.

"Bye, Columbo," Dusty said at the door. "Send me some Reiki healing voodoo while I'm in Afghanistan, OK? I may need it."

"Sure thing, Dusty."

"And get your shit together, Columbo. Now gimme a hug."

Dusty hugged John, who sluggishly responded.

Deena followed Dusty out onto the stoop and the two of them spent more time saying goodbye than John and Dusty did. That was the only thing that registered with John. He wasn't jealous, he just felt screwed. He watched from the window as Dusty walked down the steep sidewalk toward Superior Street and the downtown Fond-Du-Luth Casino, where he said he was going to look for Candy. Deena stood on the steps and watched till Dusty rounded a corner.

Dusty left the next day. There were no more farewells.

The day after *that,* John returned home from work. He had wandered the lonely apartment for over half an hour before he found the note on Deena's pillow. "I'm leaving you Johnnie, before either of us gets hurt anymore. Please don't try to find me. Love, Deena." Not, "I love you," John noticed, but just "Love."

Deena had left as well.

John sat in his bathrobe in his favorite chair, next to his favorite window, and looked out at the downtown buildings and the big lake below them. Silence was all he felt and all he heard. He felt coated with a thick layer of oil. Muted, cut off, unfeeling. The great horn of a thousand-foot lake boat bellowed in the distance and his mind searched itself. Dusty was gone, Deena was gone, but something else was missing too. It took him awhile to figure it out.

His Helping was gone.

Click, shift.

41

Well we've finally come just about full circle, haven't we? Back to whence we started. John Sloan, a Helper, finding himself bereft and Helpless. Not only reeling from Deena's abrupt departure but also realizing that he is no longer a Helper. Before we come back up to full speed on John, a bit on Dusty and Deena.

Deena did leave abruptly. She figured it was the only way out. She knew that John, as detached as he was, would eventually find out she was pregnant. There wasn't going to be any way to hide *that*. She was already starting to get looks from her non-helping friends. About her glow, her increased womanhood. Her friend Laura was on her back about it constantly.

"What's with you?" she'd say. "You look like you have some kind of secret. Mind sharing it?"

Deena did mind, and she didn't share.

Deena had gotten Franklin Rose's phone number from Dusty. Dusty had slipped that into Deena's mind when he told her of her lost mother. The day after Dusty's departure she had called in sick and hurriedly packed two bags while John was at work. She quickly turned her credit union account into Travelers Checks, over $2500.00, and gassed up her pale blue Toyota. She could've flown, heck she had over two-hundred thousand dollars in an account, conveniently located *in* south Florida, from Adele's estate, but she knew she needed the long ride to sort things out. And to deal with the fear she had at both meeting her mother for the first time, and the fear of life without John. And it would be life without John.

When Deena closed a door, it stayed closed. She had a glass-like edge inside of her that quickly sliced off any dangling entanglements. She could go cold and damn the torpedoes when she felt she had to, or when cornered. And she was cornered now. She knew she couldn't keep all the plates spinning in the air this time. Her pregnancy, the possibility of meeting her mother, the fact that she and John were drifting apart *anyway*, and the fear. The fear that she was a fraud and that John would just dump her anyway when he found out. Dump her *and* leave her with the baby. *No way* was that going to happen. John had to go and so did she.

Deena hid the packed bags in her closet and spent a last night with John. She didn't allow herself to think that this would be the last time she would ever see him. For his part, he helped. John was more oblivious than ever. Dusty's visit, and his subsequent revelation to Deena, had rocked John, leaving him more disoriented than ever.

She did do something that she hadn't done in a while. As they lay in bed just before sleep she had lain with her arm across his chest and whispered child-like in his ear, "I love you, John." A nightly ritual that had been lost somewhere along the way in their growing distance. John had enough stem activity left to complete the ritual. "I love you too, Deena," he said aloud. A small relationship tradition that usually brought a smile to both their lips. One, because they had once loved loving each other, and two owing to something Deena had said early on when John had first told her he loved her.

They had been standing in John's candle lit living room, swaying and dancing to a Nora Jones song on the radio. Something that Deena had loved about John. How he would extend his arms to her and invite her to slow dance even if they were alone at home.

John had bent back from her and slowed their dance. He looked into her eyes and said, for the first time, "I love you."

Deena had immediately echoed back, "I love you, *Deena*. Say, I love you *Deena*, John."

John had been caught a bit off-guard. It had been hard enough just to say it for the first time and now he had gotten it wrong. But he did love her, so he had said it and meant it. "I love you, *Deena*."

"I love *you*, John," she said. "Oh, I love you too," she had whispered into his right ear.

That had become one of their little "lover's secrets." Owing in no small part to Deena's insecurity. She didn't want "I love you" to be just a line. She needed to know that *she* was loved, hence she needed to hear her name attached. Not that big a deal really. Until or unless it creates the need to drop a spinning plate, and *you* happen to be that plate in question.

So they completed their ritual, but this night without the accompanying smiles. Deena had even looked at John's darkened face to see it, but it wasn't there. And without it there on his face it couldn't be on hers.

She saw him off to work without a kiss and a hug (that would've been too much for her to bear) telling him that she was scheduled to go in later than usual. She turned off the coffee, poured out her cup and the pot, unplugged the toaster, took one last look around and grabbed her bags. All that was left was to pop the trunk and hit the freeway.

Deena allowed herself exactly fifty miles to think about John. She timed it on the odometer. Fifty miles and then she moved on. She was like that. She could do that. That is not necessarily a good trait to have.

Dusty's trip was a bit different, and his trip home was a *trip and a half.* And he thought about what had happened for a lot more than fifty miles. A whole lot more. He caught a flight from Duluth to Minneapolis/St. Paul. Then a flight to San Diego and a bus back to Camp Pendleton. A week later his unit C-130'ed down an undisclosed runway to a series of undisclosed stops, to a final undisclosed destination somewhere in Afghanistan. His trip home took a lot longer.

42

And just like that, they were one. Deena, and the little biological package she was carrying, disappeared into the mists in her Toyota, headed south. A one now, even with the baby she was carrying. Dusty disappeared into the various mists that were to take him back to where he found he hated to be. Also a one. John just disappeared into the mists. Going nowhere, doing nothing. Alone, and a one.

John went through the well known stages of grief. Depression, anger, then depression, then anger. His was more of a two-stage, revolving door process, as opposed to the better known five-stage process that at least allowed for acceptance at its conclusion. Depression, anger, depression, anger, with liberal amounts of grief thrown in for flavoring. A two-and-a-half stage process that, much like a revolving door set on spin cycle, prevented the occupant from escape.

It should be noted here that Deena made it to Florida. Trepidation mixed liberally with morning pains and diarrhea highlighting her journey. She found Franklin Rose with no trouble whatsoever. She found the Seminole Reservation school that Mrs. Abbott was teaching in. Then she made the long walk down the school's hallway toward the *room* Mrs. Abbott was teaching in. It seemed to her the long walk down the school's corridor was much like the walk Adele had made after adopting her. Filled with the same love, fear, and anxiety. Deena felt mixed emotions. As if she was being disloyal to Adele by finding Mrs. Abbott. Like she had to trade one in on the other. As Adele had felt guilty about taking another woman's child.

Deena stood by the door's window and peered in. She saw an adult and a child standing at the chalkboard laughing, with their backs to her. They were slapping erasers together and sneezing. And the light, oh Deena could see the Light between them. The barrage of colors and thoughts and Power that flowed between two Helpers meeting. The woman had braided, flecked-gray, orange hair, running half-way down her back. The boy was Indian and the spitting image of Dusty.

Suddenly the woman's carriage stiffened. Her back still to Deena, Deena still standing outside the door, she held herself completely erect, so swift a change that Deena could see the young boy notice. He looked up at the woman hesitantly, as if asking for directions. The woman bent toward the boy and whispered something, the boy's face caught in the gravity of the moment. Deena still couldn't see the woman's face but she could see the boy's. His face was serious, as if watching a movie that he couldn't quite figure out, then his eyes flew open in surprise and he nodded his head. He put the erasers back on their ledge, touched the woman's arm and headed toward the door. On his face now a look of wonderment. The woman still stood with her back to the door.

The boy walked solemnly to the door, eyes piercing through the door's thick-paned window, looking directly into Deena's. He opened the door as Deena took a step back into the empty hallway.

"She says you should come in," the boy said.

Deena was too stunned to say anything. She just looked at the boy, felt his connection as a Helper, felt his connection to her as a Helper, and mouthed thanks.

"You're welcome," he said, and started walking down the hall, where he then stopped, and looked back at Deena still standing outside the closed door.

"Go in. It's all right. Mrs. Abbott says she's been waiting for you."

The little push from the boy gave Deena the impetus she needed. She looked through the window one last time, drew a deep breath, opened the door and walked into the classroom. The woman, Mrs. Abbott, her mother (Deena finally thought), still had her back toward Deena. Deena could see the woman breathing deeply, pulling herself up to her full height. She finally turned, and spoke before Deena had a chance to.

"Do not," she emphasized, "feel disloyal to your mother. Adele loved you in a way I never got the chance to, and she will always be your mother. Do not feel guilty about this."

Deena was stilled. She saw the woman now that she was completely facing her. The slender, tallish woman was standing with her arms crossed in front of herself protectively, throat moving up and down, tears pooling huge in her eyes. The woman opened her arms to Deena. And Deena felt the hesitancy there. Not a hesitancy of wanting to embrace Deena, but rather that once the offer was given it could rejected. The woman motioned with her eyes, and sent out a bolt of love to Deena. A brilliant streak that went from one Helper's mind into another's.

"Mom," was all Deena could choke out as she rushed into Mrs. Abbott's arms. "Oh mom, I missed you so much."

"I know, Peach," Mrs. Abbott said, embracing her daughter. "Oh baby, I know."

The emotions in Deena's mind flowed into Mrs. Abbott's. The feeling of missing Adele and of missing this other mother that she had never known. The guilt and the confusion and the love washing and rolling all together. Deena also felt the love Mrs. Abbott had always had for her. How she did not love Deena any less because Deena loved Adele. How she loved her more because of this.

As Deena's mind was forming her next question, Mrs. Abbott's ricocheted back with the answer. "You can call me whatever you like, Peach."

And Deena's mind whispered it for the first time.

"Mom?"

Mrs. Abbott's tighter embrace was all the confirmation Deena needed. They stood, tightly locked, swaying to the light and the music of homecoming bouncing between them.

"Now what we need is chocolate ice cream," Mrs. Abbott said. "Because you're gonna be a mom, and I'm gonna be a grandma."

After a pregnant pause Mrs. Abbott added, "How could I not know?" Answering Deena's unasked question.

With that they walked out the door, mother and daughter and future granddaughter.

43

John only attempted to contact Deena once, and by then it was too late. He waited until he could stand it no more, which in his case was ten months. Ten months of what he thought had been the worst torture in his life. Caught up in a web of self-pity and remorse. Back and forth, back and forth. If only I had done this, if only I hadn't done that. Why me? And why the fuck can't I be a Helper anymore? He swore at God. Railed and stormed against whatever Power had deserted him.

He couldn't stand being with other people and couldn't trust himself to be alone. But alone he was, most of the time. His work suffered, but luckily it was a hard winter and his survey crew was off work much more than usual. Thank god for that he thought, purposely using the small "g". He was drinking too much, smoking too much, and swearing almost more than even his survey crew could tolerate. Plus there were the "S" thoughts. The ones he couldn't tell anyone about. Not his sister Theresa, not Dusty who was long gone, and not the 24-hour mental health nurse he had confided in late one night.

He had pulled out his health insurance card and spotted the twenty-four-hour, toll-free number for mental health. After his seemingly ten-thousandth sleepless night he had dialed the number and been connected to a nurse. A woman who, obviously experienced and tender, knew just what to say and what not to. Even at quarter to four in the morning. *Especially* at quarter to four in the morning. But what was he going to tell her? "If I can't get these thoughts out of my head, if my fucking mind doesn't stop running me into the ground, I'm gonna have to put an end to it? Oh yea, and by the way, I'm a Helper. I have super-power skills from above, or beyond, or from some fucking place, that enable me to save people. I mean *really* fucking save them! Shit you and your shrinks couldn't even think of doing in a million years. And now not only is the love of my life gone, but I've lost my super-human powers and I might just have to take a swan dive off the High Bridge into the ice chunks of Lake Superior." John was sick, not stupid, and he didn't think that even *this* nurse could handle that. "Fuck," John thought, "they'd never let me out of the rubber room, let alone off the Lithium if I told them that." So he told her what he could and let her off the hook. The same hook he was left dangling on.

It all came to a head on the way back from his sister Theresa's in the Cities. He had come at her guilt-laden insistence, and had barely made the trip down. Theresa meant well, but the sight of her and her happy family only made John's pain worse. He made it a day and a half before leaving late one night after the family was asleep. He even left the prerequisite, and quite cliched, note. "Sorry T, I gotta boogie. I'll be fine. Don't worry, and kiss the kids for me. I'll call you soon. John." He didn't even notice that he didn't write "Love, John" at the end. That pissed him off when he remembered, thinking that Theresa would notice that and be all over him, worrying.

He felt a little better after leaving, but twenty minutes into the darkened freeway ride back home he almost lost it. He couldn't shut his mind up. The radio was of no use and silence was even worse. That was when he started eyeing bridge abutments. Here was a new thought, joining the others, that wouldn't leave his mind. "Just jerk the fucking steering wheel," it said. "Ooh, there's a good one. Fuck, you missed it, you chicken-shit. Wait now, there's another one coming up." John was afraid that he was going to do it without even knowing he'd given the command himself. What if he did it without even thinking of it? Whoever said that you can't hold more than one thought in your mind at one time was full of complete shit as far as John thought.

Laura, the one who had gotten this whole mess started in the first place, had actually said that to him. "You can't hold more than one thought at a time in your head, John, so focus on your future and find another girl. She just wasn't right for you, that's all." "Yea, fuck," John knew, you *could* hold a myriad of thoughts in your mind at one time. Especially if they were all *bad* thoughts."

The only thing that saved him was the airbag.

Fooled you there, didn't I? What, you think this story ends here? Puh-leeze, you must be crazier than John.

John's mind was persistently coming back to the bridge abutments when the thought occurred to him that the air-bag in his Saturn might deploy in time to save him, only to leave him paralyzed. The Hell with *that,* he thought. If if sucks *this* bad now, how much worse would *that* be? Now he couldn't even kill himself. Jesus!

He got back to Duluth, (fuck, what the fuck was he doing still living in Duluth? He was from across the bridge in Superior. She even ruined that!) and knew he had to contact Deena. He got on his computer and did a search for Mrs. Abbott online. He didn't know whether he was going to beg Deena to come back or use every rotten word in his mind to tear her to pieces, hitting all of her weak spots along the way. Weak spots he knew so well.

He found a listing for a D. Abbott on a Yahoo white pages site. D Abbott, Hollywood, Florida. Now or fucking never, he thought. Of course he had to think about that for thirty minutes. Pacing back and forth, smoking cigarette after cigarette. Finally, just before dawn, he grabbed the phone. He punched the numbers in before he had a chance to change his mind. The phone rang, (blink on, blink off, red, dark, red, dark flashed in his mind) and he hung it up. Cursing himself for being such a pussy he grabbed it up and dialed again. Three long rings, and he was about to hang up, when the phone company toned, in their uniquely abusive way, that "this number has been disconnected.

No further information about this number has been provided. Please hang up and try your number again." No need for that.

That was when John realized that it *could* suck worse. Much worse. It could last forever.

44

While John was drifting in the haze of his netherworld, so was Dusty, only Dusty's was a haze of morphine and Dilaudid.

Land mines are funny things. Funny weird, not funny ha ha. They just lay and wait. Doesn't matter who put them there, and it doesn't matter who finds them. They are the truly neutral parties in the theater of war. Quite non-sectarian. They are programmed to do one job, and one job only. To explode. Does it matter if they explode while being put in place by the very soldiers who plant them? No. Do they care if a small child riding a donkey down a narrow mountain pass is vaporized? Not at all. They could really care less. They just bide their time and wait, deadly little Switzerlands that they are.

One such relic was biding its time in a lonely plateau in Afghanistan. A plateau higher than the foothills that led up to it, and situated at the base of a much higher mountain range. Russian made, a relic of *that* war. Its nearby brothers long since found and neutralized by an organization dedicated to ridding the world of left-over ordinance. Left-over, potential death. It had been late in the day, and this last trip-mine had been missed. The team had been finishing up its final pass over this particular area. Hungry, tired, wanting to get out of

Afghanistan and back to warm showers and warmer embraces. Now it lay alone, misplaced actually, by the Russian who had originally planted it, off to the side of the high field in an area not lending itself to maximum killing efficiency. Its gun-metal gray and olive drab brothers-in-arms all found and deactivated. Waiting patiently since 1987. Through dust storms, snow fall, flash floods and goat herders. Not even knowing how close it came to taking out a family resting nearby with its bow-backed donkey carrying all their worldly possessions. That was five years ago. Now it just felt the embrace of the soil surrounding it, its sense of purpose, its sense of duty still as strong as the day it was manufactured.

So close. Waiting. Click on, click off. Red, black, red, black. Waiting for that click, shift.

Dusty came close to liking Afghanistan, on this his second tour of the country. He had made up his mind that as soon as he could get out of the Corps, he would. His involuntary extension couldn't last forever. In the meantime, if he had to be at war, this was how he liked it. Left alone by most of the brass. Forward observing for small squads and platoons far away from CP's and military procedure and from the Micky Mouse of base camp military life. And things had mellowed out, for the time being, in Afghanistan.

He also felt they were doing some good. Anyone in their right mind knew that after September 11th certain groups of terrorists had to be hunted down. Hunted down and *killed* was how it was put to them. Neutralized, equalized, exterminized. Fair enough, thought Dusty—nobody more *American* than an Indian. Shit, Indians had been providing Homeland Security since 1492, or so the T-shirt said.

But fuck if he was going back to Iraq! He had been in on the invasion, which had gone better than he expected, but he had a bad, bad feeling about that place. Plus he would be royally pissed if he got involuntarily extended a-fucking-gain! Oh no, this was it for old Dusta-reenoh. This was one Findian that was getting the fuck out! I was involuntarily extended for Afghanistan, not Iraq, he told himself.

Dusty had been in-country for three months. Snooping and pooping. Skirmishing and attacking. Wore out by it all (and war out by it all) but still quite effective. A legend among the troops he was attached to and the officers that commanded him. One look was all it took. He was given his space by the boots and the hardened vets alike. Dusty was a salt and everyone knew it. His rows of ribbons were worn in the look in his eye and the set of his face. And when the shit hit the fan he was immediately looked to for leadership.

The over-sized squad he was attached to had been waiting for a chopper evac. They had skirmished with a platoon sized enemy encampment and had knocked the living shit right out of them. Dusty was still coming down from the adrenaline buzz while the squad had waited for the choppers. They had taken three prisoners and the rest of the enemy had either been killed or had run off. And Dusty didn't think many of them had run off either. They had stayed and died. Dusty liked that. It made things so much easier. They had taken only light casualties themselves. Two minor purple hearts and one corporal with a bullet wound to his thigh that should be fine.

The prisoners were tied and made to squat in a circle. The encampment searched and neutralized. Not a cloud in the sky.

Some of the younger troops had found a Frisbee, of all fucking things, in one of the caves they had searched and were tossing it back and forth throughout the make-shift LZ they had set up. Still jazzed from the firefight. Hooting and grunting, letting off steam. Dusty sat off to the side, on the edge of the plateau, at the steep beginning of the mountains that seemed to grow right out of it. His eyes always scanning, from to prisoners, to the two marines guarding the prisoners, to the skyline, to the everywhere. His radio operator sat next to him. Lance Corporal Jenkins. A white kid from North Dakota that tried to hide the fact that he idolized Dusty. He spoke only when Dusty addressed him, and he watched everything Dusty did. Stayed out of the way, while never leaving his side.

Dusty was looking up into the late afternoon sky. Not a cloud in it. A vivid blue. So empty and distant looking here in Afghanistan. He was thinking about John and Deena and getting the heck out. Of the possibility of having a life, now that he had earned his pension. He actually smiled. He sensed the possibilities Franklin Rose had talked about. The good possibilities. He wondered why he hadn't Helped anybody in some time.

At that thought came the flash. The oncoming rush of a Helping. Everywhere at once. As if in a dream his eyes were drawn to the Frisbee tossers. One of the troops couldn't throw a Frisbee for shit and he had spun it way over the head of its intended target to a spot about fifteen yards away from Dusty and Jenkins.

"Never Helped in a war zone before," Dusty thought.

At that moment Jenkins started to get up saying, "gonna grab that Frisbee for those newbies, Top." The Light poured out of Dusty as he turned toward Jenkins, now on his feet next to Dusty.

With no idea where this was leading, Dusty smiled and said, "Stand down, Jenkins. I'll show those girls how to throw that motherfucker."

Jenkins did as he was told. He almost fell down, obeying Dusty's order. He'd never seen his recently promoted master-sergeant this playful. Dusty got a kick out of it. As he got up and started toward the errant Frisbee he turned back toward Jenkins, "Hell, Jenkins, I wasn't *born* this old!"

Dusty started double-timing it toward the Frisbee. The men had all stopped and were watching Dusty. A cheer rose up from the troops. This legend of a master-sergeant, a man who never allowed the troops to see any display of emotion was double-timing, in full battle gear toward the Frisbee. Rifle slung backwards over his back, holstered pistol on hip, hand grenades bouncing, a war cry emanating from his lips.

A beautiful moment. Not a cloud in the sky. Not a worry on the horizon. The thrill of surviving the firefight in everyone's hearts.

Dusty was almost to the Frisbee when he turned back again to Jenkins. "Watch this Jenkins, watch how an old cannon-cocker does it." He stopped, looked up at the sky, and smiled. Frozen in time, the troops below cheering, Jenkins looking on worshipfully, even the three prisoners watching now. Dusty turned, took a step, and started reaching down for the Frisbee.

"I wonder who I'm supposed to Help?" he thought. The first thought that flew into his mind was John. Poor, sad-assed, lovelorn John back in the big stateside. "No, " Dusty dismissed, "can't be him." As Dusty was reaching down for the Frisbee he turned his head again and looked at Jenkins. When he did this his helmet fell off. It hit a rock and started rolling, haphazardly down the last, little bit of foot-hill that Dusty was bent over on. "Maybe it's Jenkins," he thought. "Wonder what's wrong with him?"

Dusty felt the beauty of the moment, the beauty of the oncoming Helping. He looked at his helmet and saw it slowly coming to rest in the sandy, rocky crease of the foot-hill, which led directly up to the high mountain-tops above them, at the edge of the valleyed-plateau they were on. He caught sight of something shiny sticking just above the surface behind where his helmet was settling. Quickly blocked from view by the helmet itself. Dusty thought of John's answering machine for some reason. Blinking off and on in a darkened room.

The long forgotten mine thought of itself as Charlie. The Russian factory where it had been assembled included workers from all over eastern Europe. Many of whom had taken to wearing the contraband, but permitted, Sony Walkman which were quite new behind the iron curtain. The East German that had assembled Charlie had listened to radio free America on his Walkman headphones. Had the volume up so loud that it bled out from the little headphone speakers and down onto his work area. There the mine had started listening along with the hulking worker. Just before the mine had been completed it had heard a newscast, bleeding out from above, that had mentioned many names. One of which had been Charlie. The newly assembled mine liked that name. So much so that it had taken it as its own. It had thought of itself solely as Charlie for the twenty or so years it had lain submerged beneath the Afghan soil.

Charlie heard the commotion with the Frisbee. Had, in fact, heard the firefight. Charlie was suddenly happy, owing as much to the company of the surrounding humans as the thought that maybe finally it could finish its job. It was the first happiness Charlie had felt in years. Ever since a flash flood had rushed through the edge of the plateau where Charlie was buried and uprooted him and turned him sideways, before covering him back up again with loose dirt. Only three-quarters buried with his bottom tilted sideways and his arming mechanism sticking back toward the hill. Glinting silver in the reflection of the sun pouring unheeded through a cloudless sky. Then the sun was gone as Charlie was covered in shadow as the nearby Marine's helmet lazily spun its way to Charlie. "Come here," Charlie thought and smiled.

Dusty smiled again at that same instant, his mind, his Helping, picking up on Charlie's thoughts without knowing where they came from.

The helmet spun one last revolution and made contact with Charlie's triggering mechanism. Charlie beamed.

"Charlie?" Dusty thought. "Who's Charlie?"

Click, shift.

Boom.

45

At precisely the moment the land mine exploded Franklin Rose rocketed out of a hellish dream and wretched himself upright in bed. He had received a letter from Dusty and knew that he was in Afghanistan again, and now he sensed trouble there. From his bed Franklin looked up toward the one small window in the bedroom of his mobile home in Hollywood, Florida. He needed to know if it was sunny or cloudy. For some reason this was important. From his position in bed he couldn't tell. Sunny or cloudy, he *needed* to know. He wouldn't find out until much later.

Just a few short miles away from Franklin a drama was unfolding in the birthing unit of Hollywood Memorial Hospital. A woman with blonde hair and darker, reddish roots, sweat-drenched hair pasted against her face, was finishing a difficult labor. The woman's mother was the only other family member in the birthing area. The mother was grateful for the surgical mask she was required to wear. She hoped it hid the look of concern on her face from her daughter. A look put there by the looks of the surgical team surrounding her daughter. Their faces, only half covered by their masks, were a study in tension —foreheads of the doctors and nurses alike, lined with worry and underscored with squinting eyes. A football huddle of professionals that barely allowed her in to clutch her daughter's hand.

At exactly the same moment that Franklin Rose shot up in bed, the woman snorted one final push and gave birth. The woman's mother couldn't conceal her worry now. The baby's umbilical cord was wrapped tight around its neck.

"Mom, what is it," shrieked the birthing mother, "what's wrong with my baby?"

The woman only held her daughter's hand tighter while the surgical team went to work. They held the baby up and now both women saw the baby.

"Oh my God, mom, she's Blue!!! Please save my baby. Please save my baby. Johnnie, help me! Please help me, Johnnie. Oh Johnnie, our baby's blue."

Twenty-one hundred miles away John Sloan loaded the last of his furniture into the U-Haul and slid down the sliding back door on the orange and white moving van parked downhill on a steep Duluth street.

"Should just let the whole fucking mess roll down into the lake," he thought. He was moving back to Superior. Back across the bridge to where he belonged. Maybe that would help.

Seven-thousand miles away Dusty Hakulla was airborne. An old man was panicking in his bed in Florida. A mother got her first glimpse at her dying child and hopelessly looked into her own mother's eyes. In Duluth, John Sloan lit his tenth cigarette of the day and didn't feel a thing.

46

Dusty was being sucked down a large tunnel, into a long, depth-less, funnel-like darkness. He felt no *physical* pain but he was filled with terror. His fall seemed endless and happening within a split-second at the same time. He had no idea where he had come from or where he was going. As fast as he seemed to be plummeting, he felt motionless at the same time. Large and small seemed to change places in his mind. Black was white and white was black. His sanity fled protectively.

When it seemed as if this was to be his reality, his last reality, he glimpsed a dim brightening of the tunnel's wall. This slight contrast gave him vertigo, as it pointed out just how fast he seemed to be rocketing. There *was* a subtle graying, off toward the distance, which almost seemed to give way to a bright pinpoint of light at the far end of the funnel.

Thoughts began filling his mind and his spirit. He seemed formless as he hurtled along. It was as if he had to reacquaint himself with who he was. Until that point in time he hadn't realized that he didn't know *who* he was. He had no sense of self or memories. At that thought, they came rushing back into him. Childhood, Red Cliff, Duluth,

Superior, Parris Island, Kuwait. His family, his friends, it all spooled back up in his mind. The thoughts racing to catch up with his flight down the tunnel. He was powerless to control any of it, and he was filled with a sense of dread that he would run out of tunnel before he ran out of thoughts. That he would come to the end of the narrowing funnel before he caught up to what had brought him here. His mind reeled as his mind reeled back into him, and at the same time, separately, he watched himself being loaded back up.

A familiar voice whispered, "who says you can't hold more than one thought at the same time?" He had no idea who it came from. His mind filling with where he had been and who he had known, and what he had seemed to have done. Throughout the montage there were bright, luminescent spots of Light, rocketing in and out in periods much briefer than the smallest measurement of time. "What *were* those?" he wondered, chilled by the lack of meaning any of it had. Watching a movie that seemed to be about him, but was unbelievable.

Now he was motoring at speeds that defied his ability to comprehend, adding to his disorientation. Panic setting in deeper as the pinprick of light was getting closer and closer.

"Who am I," he shouted.

His mind and his trip rushing to outdo each other. Spooling in and spooling out at the same time until all there was was terror. A great anguish filled him as he raced outward and downward toward the prick of light. He still could not grasp who he had been or what he had done. He knew he was going to lose the race. A great scream began to fill his mind, building and building, thinly veiling the *permanent* insanity on the other side of it. A place he knew he would go to and stay in. Panic, terror, rage all mushrooming up as he spun out into destiny. All happening right now, a now that was his forever.

"Noooooooooooooooooooooooooooooooo," he screamed. A scream that echoed off the walls of darkness, bouncing down toward the point of light. A scream that went on forever. A scream that was to be his reality. Every song, every voice, every sound he had ever heard rewinding backwards, audibly in his head. His mind fighting against every possibility, pushing out at every image. Endlessly screaming and hopelessly lost. A scream, a mind, a spirit, totally without time. Forever.

Dusty had no idea how long it went on, when he noticed it was all gone. All was still and in hopeless darkness, until he found that he had eyes to open. Now he was filled with the terror of opening them. At that thought they flew open and he found himself bathed in a Light beyond belief. A Light that was beyond "seeing." It was in and around and through him. No pain, no fear, no nothing. Just Light.

"I'm a Helper," he thought. He hadn't remembered until that instant. He was suspended in this limitless pool of Light, bathed warm by it, floating.

"I'm a swami," he laughed, thinking of himself as on a magic carpet. With that thought all the Joy that he could *never* have imagined, *became* in him. Bliss. Time out of mind. Indescribable.

He saw his last moments on earth. He saw the Light of his oncoming Helping there. He saw the look of surprise in Jenkins eyes. How Jenkins was thinking, "that should've been me." He watched as the squad's corpsman, "Doc" Gangnon, sprinted over and attempted to treat his horrendous wounds, while simultaneously yelling at Jenkins to call in a medevac. There it stopped.

He saw Franklin Rose thrashing in his bed, dangerously close to a stroke. He saw a woman having a baby born without breath, stare into the eyes of her own mother. He saw John Sloan flick his tenth cigarette of the day into the gutter and pull himself up into the orange and white U-Haul, spent. No longer a Helper. He saw and felt and knew it all, stilled, bathed in the perfect *goodness* of the Light.

He wanted to stay where he was at. He could never have imagined anything like where he was. He wanted to *stay!* He looked down again onto Franklin Rose and saw the word "choices" floating cartoon-like over his head. Franklin's dark skin suddenly so pale. His thrashings dying down. The blue and strangled baby between the mother's legs. The "nothingness" to John Sloan. Time running out for them all.

"I want to stay," he shouted. "I want to stay, but I'll do what I can."
Dusty did what he could.

47

Days turn to weeks, turn to months, like sand through an hour glass, John thought. How long can this shit go on? Sand through an hourglass. Fuck! How did I come to this? Sitting on my ass, watching, *no shit,* Days of Our fucking Lives on TV, that's how. Muted, cold, resentful as hell, John stared from gray TV to grayer window. Clouds and fog choking the flat view from his room in Superior. The top floor, corner efficiency in the Androy Hotel, downtown fucking Superior, Wisconsin. Souptown. Staring out at the gray hills of Duluth from his eighth-story window.

John was calling in sick more and more. He had to. One day, not long ago, he had been staring, lost in thought, through the eyepiece of his surveying theodolite. John was mindlessly reciting numbers to the new guy, Craig, when he had almost started crying. He had actually whimpered out a choked little gasp. Tears not far behind. Craig was a little freaked. He'd heard about his new foreman. How he'd gone creepy on everyone. How he couldn't stand up to having his ass kicked by a woman. Craig thought it was pretty "pussy" of the guy, but he didn't dare say anything. Not after the first time he looked in John's eyes. Dead eyes. No way and no, sir! Craig had been in county lockup enough times to have seen that look. The look in the eyes of one or two of the guys who weren't staying. The guys who were only in holding, waiting to be sent downstate to a penitentiary. Not pretending to be bad, just bad and past the point of giving a shit.

John had seen how the new guy and the rest of his crew, had starting looking at him. How they had started acting around him. Especially after he had kicked the shit out of that garbageman. The guy was being a smart-ass. He had kept his truck idling in the alley they were surveying, blocking their surveying lines of sight. The man deciding to eat his lunch there and fuck with the survey crew. The crew had stood back when John had walked slowly to the tarnished, formerly white garbage truck. They were already giving John his distance by this time. They couldn't hear what he was saying as he started talking and pointing at the driver. Not loud, not even aggressively, but he must have been saying something because all of a sudden the driver whipped out of the truck and got right up into John's face. They watched as John leaned imperceptibly into the fleshy, but strong looking man, as if to make sure he had heard something right. The driver put his hand in John's face as if to say, "yes, you did fucking hear me right." Boom, that was it.

The crew argued for weeks afterward as to how many times John had actually hit the garbageman. Estimates ran from three to ten times. What they did agree on was that after the driver put his hand in John's face, in actuality had pinched John's cheek, John had hit him. Beaten him down until he was sitting slumped on the foot-board underneath the truck's door. Here is where thoughts differed. No one could agree on whether John had then continued to beat the man to the ground or if he had just fallen. They just watched. It was over quickly.

The spell was broken when Terry Bishop said to the other two crew members, "'Ja see that? He pinched his fuckin' cheek!"

Lisa Samuelson, a crew chief herself who was only there because this was a sticky, in-town job, ran over to John.

"Knock it off," she shouted. This seemed to register with John, who had been standing over the crumpled man, looking at him but not seeing him.

"What is *wrong* with you, John?" Lisa knelt down to help the man. John walked back toward the other members of his crew.

"Cocksucker," was all he said.

All they saw was the look of nothingness on his face and the blood running down his chin. It seemed to have come from his lip, which looked like it had been bitten through.

"I think he bit through his own fucking lip," Terry told the others after work that day.

Lisa said she'd *never* work with him again and after that there were a lot of new guys on John's crew.

So, when John almost started sobbing in front of the new guy, he knew he'd have to start taking more precautions. And more sick days.

"Fuckin' bumped my eye on the eyepiece," was all he told the new guy.

After that John started chewing his way through sick time and unused vacation days.

"Man, how far have I fallen?" he said to the empty window. "How far have I fallen?" he asked of the mumbling television soap opera. Almost two years now and I'm still fucked.

"When is this going to change?"

48

John was waiting. He didn't know what he was waiting for, just that he was waiting. And he had plenty of time for that, since he had been laid off by Keenan Engineering. Old man Keenan himself had sat John down and explained to him that they would just have to let him go. Winter was coming on so things were slowing down anyway and John didn't seem to be able to improve his attitude. The old man had had his son, Ralph, speak with John on three different occasions to no avail.

"John, I can't get anybody that wants to work with you," the senior Keenan had told him.

"You take the winter to figure out if you can remove your head from your ass. If you can, see me in the spring, I might have a slot for you. If not, that's your choice. Here's your slip, you've done good work for me in the past so I won't fight your unemployment claim."

Yea, as if I have any choice in this, John thought. Abe Lincoln might've freed the slaves but that shit he said about everybody being just about as happy as they set their minds out to be was just that; shit. John could no more change his attitude and feelings than he could fly to the moon.

John had headed out the door without saying a word. Just as he was leaving Keenan's office, Keenan gave him one last bit of advice.

"It just ain't worth it, John. No woman is worth ruining your life over."

Hey, thanks for the pearl of wisdom there, Keenan. John had heard them all, over and over again, from his friends and family and co-workers. Yea, that little nugget may just save my life, he thought.

So John had plenty of time to wait. Winter had come on early and hard, which was fine with John. He had his efficiency apartment on the top floor of the Androy. There was a bar and a twenty-four-hour restaurant downstairs off the lobby, and he had his overstuffed chair that he kept pulled close to the corner window of his apartment—the better to stare out of. Between his savings and his unemployment checks he could hold out for quite awhile.

John had no idea what he was waiting for. He certainly held out no hope for his future. That was the only moment of peace he had gotten throughout this entire mess. The day he realized that he had *no* hope. John knew that hope unfulfilled was a motherfucker. And now that it was gone he didn't have to worry about getting his expectations crushed yet again.

He had even tried the shrinks at the VA outpatient clinic. They had tried a variety of anti-depressants and anti-anxiety medications. All they did was take away his hard-on, not that he was using it, and make him sleepy. And one had made him feel even more like a zombie than he already did.

"Doc, I can't even get a hard-on anymore. How's that gonna improve my situation? That doesn't exactly restore my fucking hope," he had said to his therapist Joe Burg. "I mean, Christ, it's not as if I'm using it, but Jesus doc, that's all I got left and you're taking that away from me too? No way. These things ain't working." He had stopped going to his sessions after that, and had stopped taking the medications.

John, was smoking cigarettes and staring out the window when he heard a knock on his door. He had been thinking about heading down to the bar for a couple of early afternoon drinks. Sometimes that allowed him to fall asleep. It should've been too cold to snow, but snowing it was. Blowing and swirling around his window, all gray and howling.

Knock, knock, knock. He heard it again. Damn, I shouldn't have left my radio on, he thought. County music poured out of John's transistor. Of course country music. It had all gone pretty pop but there was still some old-time country sadness left in some of the tunes that new, pop Nashville had yet to wring out.

John heard a muffled voice between knocks.

"I can hear the music. I know you're fucking in there. Open the fuck up."

John didn't recognize the voice and he knew from past experience that the "born-agains" weren't above prowling the halls of the Androy attempting to convert the lost. Course, this didn't sound like any born-again he had met in the past.

"John, open the fuck up!"

"Go away," he finally said. "Nobody home."

Bam, Bam, Bam, now. John thought he recognized that cop knock.

"Columbo, open this fucking door before I knock it the fuck down."

This last had started his neighbor pounding on the wall too.

"Fucking great," John thought. "Now that wino starts in."

John walked to the door and cracked it open against the chain.

"The hell you want," he said, before seeing who it was.

"What I want is to come in and sit the hell down. Now open this fucking door!"

Dusty.

John kept the chain in place and looked through the crack at his old friend. Dusty was in civvies, blue jeans and a pressed, blue chambray work shirt. John scanned him from top to bottom. Dusty was hunched over, a little bulge over his middle, leaning on a cane. And is that an eye-patch, John thought and quickly scanned back up? Sure as shit, a damn eye-patch. Dusty didn't look so hot, but he did look mad. As if John could care. Yet he found he did care, if only a little.

"Alright matey, c'mon in," John said, and unlocked and opened the door.

"Fuck you," Dusty said. "I gotta put up with pirate jokes from you now too?"

Dusty limped into the room and sat in John's other chair.

"Beautiful place you got here, John. Just lovely."

John turned his chair away from the window so that he could face Dusty, sighed himself down into it, and stared dimly at his friend.

"Hey, I'm doin' fine, John, thanks for asking. How 'bout you?"

John didn't know what to say. He was just too tired for it all. He was sorry that Dusty was so obviously busted up but he was just too tired to get involved in any long conversations.

Which reminded him of something short-timers had used to say in the Corps. "Man, I got one day and a wake-up call. I'm too short to get involved in any long conversations." For whatever that was worth.

To his credit Dusty waited him out. He didn't say anything and the two friends just sat staring at one another. It should've been weird but it wasn't. In fact it *was* weird but neither seemed to care. They just sat there staring at each other.

Finally John said, "Want a smoke, Dusty?" and shook a generic Old Gold from his pack and offered it over to Dusty.

"Bout fucking time you offered. Want some coffee, Dusty, something to eat, need to use the bathroom?" Dusty said, eying his friend.

They both sat and smoked for a few minutes when John finally sighed and said, "Well I suppose we should go downstairs and get a drink."

They made their way to the dark downstairs bar and found a corner booth.

"Lets sit over here in the corner," John said, "keep away from those bar chicks and their damn kids."

Dusty noticed that there were in fact three bar-fly women sitting next to each other at the bar, bad dye-job blonde hair hanging over their drinks, while their five kids alternately tugged at their hems and pounded on the pinball machines.

John drank beer, Dusty drank a ginger-ale, and finally Dusty got John to open up a bit.

"How'd ya find me?" John asked.

Dusty told him how it wasn't all that hard at all. He had just asked around for a drunken asshole and been directed to the Androy. Everyone had known who he had meant. Piece by piece and bit by bit they started catching up.

Dusty told him about Afghanistan and the land mine. About his thirteen months of convalescence in various VA hospitals ending with the last seven months at Woods down in Milwaukee. How his leg was about as good as it was gonna get with his smashed heel, his left eye still being there but how he wore the patch because it was now a blind, "go funny" eye and it freaked him out a bit. Freaked his Indian friends out even more.

"I go into a bar and they think I'm lookin' at 'em funny, and want to fight like I'm some evil spirit or some fucking thing, so I just wear the patch. Easier that way."

And finally about his ileostomy.

"Yep, I shit out my stomach into a bag, John. How's that for instigating a love connection. Only been laid once, at least that's still workin', and that was with a prostitute while I was waiting at the Greyhound station in Milwaukee. Fuck, funny thing is, I knew some of her family. Her auntie was from Bad River."

Dusty didn't tell John about the trip down the tunnel or his white light experience. There were a few other things he didn't tell John as well. Things he knew would get told, but best to hold off on them for now.

"And I know you're not a Helper any more either, John." Dusty filled him in on how he had come to understand this after leaving John and Deena the last time.

"Man, don't even say her name, Dusty. It still hurts too much."

Dusty had never heard of a Helper losing his abilities. He had asked Franklin about it when Franklin had visited him in the hospital in Virginia. Franklin hadn't heard of it either, and he'd been around a lot longer than Dusty. Dusty and John talked about this and John started opening up. He told Dusty about his last two years, feeling twice as bad for the telling of it. First, because he was reliving the pain, and second because he knew Dusty had it far worse.

Dusty could still read John's thoughts to a certain extent. Not so much because of his Helping abilities, more because of their shared history. He got John to get over the pain of telling as best he could, and listened while John poured out his heart. They talked for hours. John nursing beer after beer, seemingly without effect, and Dusty smoking and drinking the occasional soft drink.

One of the things Dusty *didn't* tell John was that he had a Helping coming on. A big one. A Helping that felt like it was the biggest of Dusty's life. A huge, staggering, pregnant *beast* of a Helping. And it was scaring Dusty.

John's story finally ran its course and the two friends once again sat staring at each other. Smoking and drinking.

"You know when Franklin visited me in Virginia?" John nodded as Dusty started speaking again. "He talked to me again about choices. Choices we make and choices not taken. I've got some choices coming up that I'm gonna have to make and I'll need your help with them."

John noticed that this was the first time in he couldn't remember how long, that he was actually considering helping someone other than himself. Help with a small "h", he was quick to remind himself.

"It may be time for a little payback," Dusty said. "The good kind of payback."

John continued to nod, not knowing where this was going at all.

"I know where Deena is, John. I know where she is and we're gonna go see her."

49

John froze when he heard Dusty's last words. He didn't know how to react. He didn't know how he was *supposed* to react. "Please God don't let it get worse," was all he thought. He couldn't handle it if it got any worse. No way. His mind raced ahead, imagining various possibilities and scenarios, none of which seemed pleasant in the least. "Uh-uh, no freaking way, baby." His mind was starting to dig in its heels when Dusty's voice broke through again.

"I know where she is and we're gonna go see her. I know that and feel it stronger than anything I've ever felt, John. It's something we gotta do. No arguments, no bullshit. Now let's get us a roll-away so I can crash with you tonight and we'll head out tomorrow. It's not as if your dance card is so fucking full that you can't get away."

And Dusty *did* know this for certain. He was convinced that this was the path he must follow. He knew it as surely as he knew that he had a Helping coming of gigantic proportions.

John said nothing, and better still, all of a sudden he *felt* nothing. A great big nothingness. And that was something to like. It didn't feel good, but at least it didn't suck. As a matter of fact, it sucked a whole lot less. He had somehow gotten shifted into neutral. "I don't care if this is only a respite before the bad comes on again," he thought. "I'll take it. I just need a break."

That night John watched as Dusty prepared himself for bed. He watched as he slowly undressed, his damaged body preventing any quick movements. His trousers slid down and his socks came off revealing his hideously put back together foot and ankle. He pulled up his t-shirt and showed John his ileostomy bag. Dusty gave him a quick, and self-deprecatingly funny, explanation of how it worked and what was involved.

"They call it an appliance. Like it's a damn Maytag that I'm gonna have to call a repairman for if it ever breaks down."

He finally pulled off his eye-patch and set it on the floor next to the roll-away bed.

"Still can't sleep with that fucker on," he said. "It's like it wants to smother me and I wake up howling at the moon. So I sleep with it off."

John didn't think it looked too bad, although, having known Dusty before, it was unsettling all the same. That eye that seemed to be always looking at the corner, checking for danger. And John realized something else too. It was the first time in a long time that he had thought of anyone else. The first time in *two years* that he had thought of someone other than himself. He had found himself touched as Dusty had explained his wounds and how he had received them.

Dusty smiled to himself just before sleep. *He* had seen that too.

They left the next day, the two waking up automatically before sunrise. Two quick coffees to-go downstairs, and they were out the door and into John's rusty but trusty F-150. Each carrying one sea-bag. Once again John didn't feel good, but at least he still felt nothing. And nothing was *good* as far as John was concerned.

John hadn't asked Dusty how he knew where Deena was but the story started unraveling as soon as Dusty said, "Just take Highway 53 south and I'll tell you when to turn."

"OK," John said and they took off into the morning snow.

Dusty filled John in as soon as they were out of town. He told John how he had been transferred to Woods VA in Milwaukee seven months ago. Feeling sorry for himself and pissed at the world. He hadn't told John about his death experience yet. He thought that should wait. He had been shuffling down the ward one day, getting used to walking with a cane, when he had passed a room filled with wounded vets. He had seen a telltale glow spilling out of the door before he had even gotten to the door. The vets were seated at small school desks and were being given college prep courses by a red-headed woman in her fifties. Dusty had stopped, turned, and smiled as he saw Mrs. Abbott teaching the crippled-up, battle-hardened vets grammar. She had them eating out of the palm of her hand. After a minute or so Mrs. Abbott turned, saw Dusty, and smiled. She motioned for Dusty to wait and ended the class shortly after that.

The two of them went to the cafeteria where Mrs. Abbott told Dusty about her life, and Deena's. How after the terrible delivery room experience they had decided to make a new start and had moved back to southern Wisconsin, Watertown in fact, to begin anew. How a bright light, a Helping Light, had appeared in the delivery-theater just when it seemed that Deena would fall over the edge and truly go insane after seeing her blue, lifeless baby daughter being born. How the Light had directed Mrs. Abbott to pack up and move them back to Wisconsin after it was all over.

"Thank you for that, Dusty," Mrs. Abbott said. "That Light was from you. You saved Deena's sanity and *so* much more."

Dusty realized now that it *was* him as their minds linked together in a Helper's meeting, and he saw all that came to pass in the delivery room and after. This also allowed Mrs. Abbott to experience Dusty's dark tunnel and white light trip as well.

"I swear I didn't want to come back," Dusty told her. "Ever! I just wanted to stay there and not have to Help anyone or do anything ever again. Just to stay in the Light. Especially after that tunnel. It was horrible."

Mrs. Abbott held Dusty's hand and the two sat in silence, minds whirring back and forth, for quite some time. Mrs. Abbott pouring all that she had into his mind. Into his spirit.

At the end of the second hour, Dusty had known what he had to do. He wasn't sure if he should tell Mrs. Abbott about it, so he hid it from her. He was afraid that Deena would catch on and that might not be a good thing.

"I know what I have to do now," he told her. "I thank you for that. Give Deena my best."

Dusty and Mrs. Abbott spent a good deal of time together over the next weeks and Dusty's condition improved dramatically. Deena didn't visit. "She just can't," was all Mrs. Abbott would say. Which was fine with Dusty. He saw her life through Mrs. Abbott's mind anyway. And, he admitted to himself, he was still pissed at her for dumping John. Even if it was what she *had* to do, it still pissed him off.

"So I didn't get to see Deena," Dusty told John, "but I know where they are and tomorrow we're gonna pay them all a little visit."

John was silent most of the drive. Silent and empty. Which he was coming to appreciate, if not enjoy exactly.

The limping duo arrived to a dark, snowy winter afternoon in southern Wisconsin. The snow having followed them the entire eight-hour drive from Superior. They checked into the Welcome Inn, in downtown Watertown, and dragged themselves and their bags to their room.

"Call downstairs and order a pizza from JT's for nine-o-clock," Dusty told John. "I'm gonna go on a little recon and find out how we're gonna do this thing tomorrow. I'll be back in a couple of hours. You sit tight."

Fine with John. He still didn't know what he was supposed to do, so doing nothing was just fine with him. He'd had a lot of practice with it lately, and it was maybe the one thing he *could* do. Maybe the only thing.

Dusty came back to the room just after nine carrying the pizza.

"You didn't go anywhere or call anyone did you?"

"No," John said. "Just sat here and watched a little tube. NFL films had an old special on Vince Lombardi playing. It was pretty cool." This was about the most Dusty had gotten out of John since coming back, and he liked it. His Helping groove was expanding and, although he didn't have the slightest clue as to how or who he was supposed to Help, it made him feel better to see John a little less comatose.

"Screw Vince Lombardi," Dusty said, rehashing an old line of his. "Joe Kapp, man. Now that was one rugged motherfucker. Remember how he ran over that linebacker for Cleveland in the playoffs? Ran right the fuck over him, and the *linebacker* was the one that had to be carried off the field. That guy had balls the size of Lake Superior. He couldn't throw a spiral to save his life, but man he was tough." This got a small smile out of John. "Injun" Joe Kapp being the quarterback for the Minnesota Vikings in the late '60s, and the one hero outside of boxing, that Dusty had ever admitted to having. In that less enlightened time he had been given the nickname Injun Joe because he looked Native -American, even though he happened to be Mexican-American.

"Yea, he was tough," John admitted. John had liked him too. Liked him a lot, although he couldn't admit it to anyone without being scalped for liking anyone from the Packer's hated rivals.

They ate their pizza to CNN. Dusty talked a bit about the war, and the two wound down the evening. John not asking about Dusty's recon and Dusty not telling.

At eleven o'clock Dusty said, "Lights out, Marine. Get some sleep, we got us a day tomorrow."

John fell asleep immediately, something he hadn't done in a long time. Dusty stared up at darkened ceiling, listening to his friends' even breathing, and congratulating himself on the confidence he had shown but certainly not felt. Dusty was still holding back a few secrets and one of them was just what in the hell he was supposed to do about all of this. He hoped he would figure it out soon, because as of right now he didn't have a clue.

50

The Light intensified within Dusty and by midnight a plan had formed. It all made perfect sense now. He knew what he had to do and how he must present it. He felt like he was floating, the oncoming Helping washing through and over him. He almost felt like he was immersed again in the Great Light after his death. And man it felt good. He thought of Franklin Rose and of John. Of those choices Franklin spoke of so often and how they applied to John. He thought of Goldie and Luke and of all the Helpers he had met and of all the people he had Helped. He even thought of Uncle Lou, as he did almost every day of his life. Uncle Lou, who he had only *thought* he had gotten rid of that day. If he had known the rotten fucker was gonna stay in his thoughts forever he would've *Helped* him that day. But even thoughts of Uncle Lou didn't hurt. No, he was feeling good and feeling right. He was on his way. Now if the Light just played along, all might be OK.

"We keep waking up at dawn, we're gonna have to re-enlist." Dusty said to John after they both realized they had been laying in their beds awake for almost a half an hour the next morning.

John went for continental coffee and donuts and brought them back up to the room. Dusty had already dressed and taken care of his morning ileostomy chores.

"Man, Dusty, I don't know how you do it," John told him. "Losin' my hard-on when I was on those anti-depressants was bad, but man that must be tough having that bag and all."

Dusty smiled, he felt like he was on top of the world, "Small price to pay to be one of the world's finest." Another small smile from John.

"OK, sit down, John. This is how it's gonna go."

They sat down and Dusty began to explain the plan.

"You remember how Franklin was always talking to me about choices?" John nodded yes. "Well you're gonna have to make some choices yourself. I've got a Helping coming on like I've never felt before and I know it's got everything to do with you." John continued to nod, a feeling almost like hope peeking from behind a corner in his mind.

"Even though I seem to have more Power, more Helping, than anyone we've ever met, I still seem to be limited a bit here. So you've got to make a choice, John. Or else it will be made for you, but I'm not even sure about that. I can't seem to see that part clearly." The little bit of hope left John as quickly as it had appeared.

"A choice is going to be made, and you may or may not be the one to make it, but here it is. I know I can Help you get back with Deena. And I know I can make you a Helper again. But I can't do both. That pretty much seems like how it's gonna work. You getting all this?"

"Yea, I'm getting it," John said, his first words since they had started this conversation, more scared now than ever. Wanting the emptiness back that he had been feeling for the last day. Realizing how much he had missed Deena but at the same time aware of just how much he missed being a Helper. How maybe if he *was* still a Helper he could get over Deena. Get over her like everyone had told him to do, and get on with his life and with Helping other people. Oh, how he missed that. How he missed that feeling he got during a Helping. The Light, the Peace. The beautiful "in the middle of it all" feeling he got from it. But he also knew how much he missed Deena. How much he missed what they had shared and the glimpse of the future together they had had.

Dusty reached over and plucked John back from these thoughts.

"Whoa, Johnny boy. Fucking whoa. Don't go thinking too much. I know what you're thinking and stop it. You're not necessarily gonna have a choice in this matter anyway. You *may* have one when it happens but thinking about it isn't gonna help. That I *do* know."

John stopped his mind-melt and looked back at Dusty.

"Eat a fuckin' donut while I write her address down. You know exactly where it is, but I'll write it down anyways." Dusty's rough talk bucking John up a bit.

Dusty handed the address to John and said, " Now go see her. Whatever's gonna happen will happen and you'll know what to do when you know it."

John looked at the address. He did know it. It was right down the street from where his family had lived after their move south. It was just around the corner from his parents' former house. 1411 Neenah street. Shit, he even knew the family that used to live there. The Tylers. Just down the street from Clark Park and from the abandoned brickyard where they had fished and ice-skated as kids, after moving down from Superior. Just down the street from his past.

"Go, John. I'll be here when you get back."

51

John took the long way to the address. He drove through streets he had spent time growing up in. The snowstorm had stopped, the temperature had dropped to below zero, and a brilliant winter sun shown down on the white, snow- covered yards and trees. He even stopped at the old Brickyard and walked part-way around the frozen little pond. The fresh snow covering the plowed skating area and blanketing the warming house.

John was terrified. What if he made the wrong choice? What if he didn't even get to make the choice? What if it was made for him and it was the wrong one? Fuck, this was worse than before, he thought. Please God, don't let me get this close and jerk it away again. He had no inkling of what he was supposed to do. None.

He walked down on the skating ice and went over what Dusty had told him. He still had no clues as to which action he was to take. Dusty's voice finally came into his mind. "Of course you know what action to take, Columbo. I fucking *told* you what action to take. *Go to her house!*"

The emptiness suddenly came back and John welcomed it. He didn't feel good, he didn't feel sure, but he *was* back to feeling nothing and that was enough to get him going. He climbed the snowy bank and got back into his car. 1411 Neenah street was just two blocks away.

John slowly drove down the road, his window half-open, cigarette smoke billowing out, hearing the crunching of the snow on his tires. He crossed the last intersection, seeing the house on the other side of the street, still having no idea as to how this would work out. He parked across the street and sat in his truck. He was there a few minutes when he saw the front door open up and a little girl came tumbling out followed by an older woman. The girl was all of two years old or more, and bundled up in enough winter clothing as to make her as wide as she was tall. John didn't recognize Mrs. Abbott at first, but he soon came to remember the outline of her face and the spark of her smile. A few more lines now, more than a few really, but still that same old smile. The little girl ran out to the snowman standing in the front yard and started running in circles around it, singing and clapping her hands, her breath steaming out in little puffs. Mrs. Abbott watching and joining in from time to time.

John was sure Mrs. Abbott hadn't noticed him there yet. I guess that's one good thing about not being a Helper anymore, he thought. She can't *sense* me at least.

And then, as if with that thought, she did seem to sense him. She looked up, and snuck a quick glance at John's car and then she did something that struck John as funny. She just went back to the front porch and sat down. She sat down on the steps and watched as the little girl tumbled over and started to make snow angels.

A voice flashed in John's mind. "Now or never, Columbo!" It was Dusty. All of a sudden the sunshine was brilliant. The sun's reflection off the snow almost blinding John. A great Light seemed to rush in and a great weight seemed to ease a bit.

John got out and slowly started crossing the street. The little girl hadn't noticed him yet but Mrs. Abbott seemed to have. She just wasn't letting on that she knew. She continued to watch the little girl, but her posture had changed. John wasn't sure if it stiffened or brightened. He had no way of knowing.

He walked to the yard and stopped at the curb, unsure of what to do. He had no idea of who the little girl was but it seemed as if he was supposed to walk to her. The little girl looked up from where she was laying on her back and eyed him. She stopped flaying her arms and legs, stopped making her most recent snow angel, and sat up and looked right at John.

"Walk to her," Dusty's voice said. John didn't notice that now another person had entered the scene. A woman stood inside the house, looking at him through the window of the storm door. The inside door open and in her hand, just inside the home's entryway. Deena, standing and watching him from just inside.

John walked toward the little girl who by now had gotten to her feet, wobbling back and forth, dizzy from her bundled clothes and her snow angel escapades. John stopped six or seven feet away from her. The little girl alternately looking at John and back at Mrs. Abbott, who was still sitting on the front steps. Eventually her gaze stayed locked on Mrs. Abbott's. After some moments Mrs. Abbott nodded to the child, their eyes still connected, and a shimmer of Light and of Understanding passed between the woman and child. Then the little girl turned toward John and started walking toward him. After three steps she started running.

"Daddy!" she cried. "Daddy!" She was laughing and crying and stumbling, arms open, toward John. It was all happening too fast for John to comprehend, when suddenly everything went still inside of him.

"Welcome home, Marine", and "Welcome home, my fine young matriculating gentleman," echoed simultaneously inside his mind. Dusty's voice and Mrs. Abbott's. He reached down, scooped the child up and instantly knew the score. "I'm a Helper again. So this is how it's gonna be." He was instantly fine with that.

He also knew much more than that. Scales fell from his eyes and he knew that this was *his* daughter. His and Deena's. A daughter that

Dusty had saved while in the Light. How Dusty's Helping had shone into the delivery room and breathed life into that little, blue baby, while saving her mother's sanity at the same time. All while he was going through his own near-death experience. "Surprise," Dusty's voice sang softly in his mind.

The little girl was laughing and John was crying, as he hugged her and spun them both around in circles. He looked over his daughter's shoulder at Mrs. Abbott and saw her, hands clasped and eyes closed, staring at the sky. Glowing. It was then that he noticed the woman standing just inside the door. The woman, who at this very second was opening the storm door and walking out onto the porch. Deena. Her arms holding her flannel robe, oh how John had loved that flannel robe, tight against the chill.

John was suddenly afraid again. Very afraid. He hadn't fully realized his being a Helper again, but he now knew that it was nothing in comparison to Deena.

"No, God, don't let me fall back," his spirit screamed. "Let us work this out, please. Let me *at least* be a father."

Dusty's voice was back in his head now. Weaker than before, but there all the same. "Walk to her," it said. John did. With his newly found daughter perched on his hip he walked toward the porch and the two waiting women. He was halfway there when Deena came flying down the steps, feet covered only in slippers, oh God how he had loved those slippers, and started storming toward him.

Oh, please don't let it be bad, he thought. He was afraid that she was rushing to rip the little girl out of his arms. Then he saw the tears running down her face. He saw the look in her eyes. "Surprise again," Dusty's voice whispered, weaker than ever in John's mind. "I guess the choice wasn't yours to make after all," and with that Dusty's voice blinked out.

Deena grabbed John and tried to wrap her arms around both John and their daughter. Crying and laughing, their minds open and flowing back and forth washing over each other. Their spirits joining and singing, all wrapped around each other and their daughter. John caught a glimpse of Mrs. Abbott's face, which seemed to darken questioningly for a brief second, before filling with joy once again. She's thinking of Dusty, perhaps, was all John got. The remnants of Dusty's remarks in his head, added to Deena and Mrs. Abbott's presence there, being more than any of the Helpers could handle at one time. Especially a time as filled with Light as this one.

Nothing was said for minutes. Nothing more needed to be said. The family walked together into the house. There is a Light. There *can* be a One. Sometimes there is. Click, shift.

52

The newly joined family went inside the house. Not much was needed to be said. John was a Helper once again and his mind joined Deena's and Mrs. Abbott's and the three of them flew back and forth into each other's spirits, bathing in the reunion. Little Della kept climbing into John's lap, saying "Daddy, Daddy" over and over again.

John could not believe his good fortune, nor believe he had ever doubted the Power. He *was* a Helper again. He *was* with Deena again. *And* he was a father. He could also tell how good this was from everyone else's perspective too. *He* knew it was good but he also knew, from his travels inside Deena and Mrs. Abbott's minds, that they knew it was good as well.

The little group finally settled down and sat admiring each other's company and their circumstances. Counting their blessings. The three adults looked into each other's eyes, and minds, at the same time and each came up with, "Dusty."

"We have to go thank Dusty," Deena said. "He made this all possible." All three knew this to be true. They each silently thanked him for it in their own ways.

"Oh Dusty, you are something special," Mrs. Abbott thought.

"Dusty, thank you soooo much," from Deena, "I'm sorry that I was ever afraid of you or didn't trust you."

John just smiled and said, "Thanks, man. Boy, do I ever owe you one now."

Deena and John left little Della with Mrs. Abbott and drove into the blinding winter morning sunshine back to the motel. They held hands on the way and talked about their mistakes and about Dusty. About how Dusty had somehow used his greater Helping Power to solve all of their problems. To save them all. To bring them back from the holes they had been buried in.

"John, it's been so dark without you. Even with finding my mother, and having Della after almost losing her, it was still so dark without you. The smiles were only half as bright. There seemed to be something missing even in the laughter. I'm so sorry I had to leave you. Please, please forgive me."

John couldn't find the words to express what was in his heart, so he just opened it up to Deena and showed her. He also thought of how he would wrap Dusty in the biggest bear-hug of his life and dance up and down with joy when he saw him.

The couple parked behind the motel and, using the back entrance, climbed the three flights of stairs to John and Dusty's room. They heard the phone ringing through the closed door. They rushed through the door hoping to find Dusty's grinning face. The room was empty and John just missed answering the phone.

"Dusty, where in the Hell *are* you?" John yelled. "Man, you could've *told* me what was going on."

"He's not here," Deena said. Their eyes were drawn to a note on the table. Folded over with the name John written in pencil on the outside.

Dear John,

So, does this finally make us even?!! Ha, Ha. I guess the choices weren't yours to make after all. They were mine. I finally figured that out and, sorry, but I couldn't tell you about it. I don't know why I was given so much Power or really why I misused it like I did. I only know that I saw an opportunity to set things right, and I was also given the opportunity to do so. I knew there might be consequences but those only helped me make my decision. It was easy really.

As I write this I know that you and Deena are back together and that you are a Helper again. And also that you have a new little bundle of joy in your life. You lucky guy!!! And man, you wouldn't believe it, but I never had a Helping so Powerful in my life. It just about took everything out of me and yet I feel like I'm already back in that White Light I experienced when I blew up. Can you believe that?!!! I actually blew up and lived to tell about it! Un-fucking-believable, man.

I'm so glad I got to pay you back. Love them John. Love Deena, Love Della, love them all.

You will always be my friend.

Your brother,

Dusty.

John and Deena read the letter and before they could begin to talk about it, before they could figure out where in the hell Dusty had gotten off to, there was a pounding on the door.

Bam, bam, bam.

"Dusty!" John called. "I'd know that cop-knock anywhere. Get your ass in here, Dusty."

John raced to the door and opened it only to find a young woman standing breathless outside the door. The front-desk clerk had her fist raised, ready to pound again.

"Are you one of the guys checked into this room?" she asked. John nodded yes. "Then you better come downstairs with me right away. There's something wrong with your friend."

The three raced down the stairwell to the front lobby. They could see the flashing lights of the ambulance blinking through the front door. They saw the gurney wedged into the lobby and the paramedics working on a man lying on the floor. Dusty. They could also tell by the looks on the medic's faces that they had been working for sometime and with no results.

Janice, the desk clerk told John what she knew.

"Your friend came down a while ago and sat on that couch over there. He grabbed a pen and slip of paper off that desk and wrote something and then he started talking to me. I was a little scared at first. Sorry, but he's kinda scary, you know? That eye patch and all. And his color was really bad. He looked gray! Plus," she said, lowering her voice, "we don't get many Indians around here. But he was smiling and so happy. He was telling me that he was finally going home. Something about a reservation up north where a great white light lived. He wasn't drunk or anything," she quickly added, " but I couldn't understand it all either. He sure was happy though. And he kept talking about you too. Said how he finally got to pay John back." Janice looked right at John when she said this. "He said that over and over. I finally got a chance to pay John back. How he finally got a chance to pay everybody back. Does that make any sense to you?"

"Then he just stopped talking, you know? He was just sitting there with this great big smile on his face. I couldn't help it." Janice had tears in her eyes now. "I started smiling too and then before you know it, we were both sitting there laughing." Janice, quite shaken up, looked away from John. She seemed embarrassed that thinking of it almost made her smile again. "He must be quite a guy, huh? Gosh, he seemed so sweet."

John broke away now and knelt down beside Dusty. The paramedics looked at John and just shook their heads. "Cerebral hemorrhage, man. Look at his eyes."

John did. Dusty's patch was pulled up and that eye as well as the other was bright red.

"He went fast," the medic told John. "At least he went fast."

John knelt over his friend and cried.

Finally the paramedics told John that they would have to take the body to the hospital and did John know of the family's whereabouts. John told them that he would take care of everything.

As Dusty's body was being wheeled out the door the desk clerk came over to John. "I almost forgot. Your friend told me to give you this." She handed John a small leather pouch that hung on the end of a long leather loop.

"He said that this was special medicine that had worked for you guys in the past. He said I should give it to you. Oh, and he said to dance for him. Dance like you danced in the desert. Does that make any sense to you?"

John took the small pouch and Deena wrapped him in her arms.

"John, I'm so sorry. Oh baby, I'm so sorry."

Deena opened the pouch and saw the tobacco and other small, handmade charms inside.

"There's a note in here too, Johnnie." She pulled out the crumpled slip of paper, unfolded it, and read it to John.

Dear John,

Sorry for all the drama. But you know me, I do things in a big, big way! Ha, Ha. Don't be mad and don't be sad. It was the only way I could save you guys and I wanted to go back anyway. Man, once you taste that BIG LIGHT you don't want to come back. I just figure God gave me a chance to even things up. So it wasn't really even much of a choice. I'll miss you guys. Think of me when the wind blows and when you dance. That's my only regret right now...that I didn't dance more. Dance the old way. Love that new family of yours, John. Love them! I'll always be with you guys as you'll always be with me.

Love,

Dusty.

PS. I want bagpipes at my funeral. Amazing Grace and I want you to invite everybody you can find from both sides of my family. Tell 'em Dusty wanted a great big old wild funeral. Indians and Finlanders and everybody else too. I love you man. Semper Fi. Goodbye my friend.

Epilogue

Even I have to admit, I do have a certain flair for the dramatic, don't I? If you're gonna go out, why not go out with a big finish?! Can't help it, it's just my nature. I do think the bagpipes line was a nice touch too, don't you? And you should've seen the funeral they threw. Oh, it was a beauty. Not a dry eye in the church. And John and Deena giving my ashes to Franklin Rose to sprinkle on Wisconsin Point was something even I hadn't thought of. Wisconsin Point having been the ancestral home of at least part of my family. Not as long ago as you would think, either. Less than eighty years ago my people were still living in the woods on that small strip of land stretching out in the big lake. Man-oh-man, what a send-off.

I have to tell you that it has been all I could do to hold off letting the cat out of the bag. It really has. You don't know how many times during this journey we have just taken together that I have wanted to say, "Hey it's *me* telling you this!" I had to bite my tongue on several occasions to keep from doing it.

I had to force myself to tell you *exactly* how it happened as well. Not the story so much, but the lingo. I don't think I could cuss here if I *tried*. There just isn't any need for it here in the Light. There isn't any need for a lot of things back up here in the Light. I gotta tell ya, it's good to be back home too. Man is it good.

It really wasn't much of a choice that I had to make either. Let's see, Help your best friend in the world and die (but go back to a really cool place you've already been to), or stay and watch him disintegrate, maybe bringing others down around him. I must admit, I was a bit scared, however. I wasn't *positively* sure I would go back to the Light. And that tunnel shit, oh I guess I *can* still swear when I need to, really freaked me. Plus, once I knew that John was who I was to Help, I wanted to stay and enjoy the life he was going to live. Friends are like that, you just want to be around them to see how it all works out. To see them enjoy something that you've had a part in them getting. But I can still see John and Deena and the whole crew any time I want to. Plus, my time was done down there. And this Light stuff is a *trip!* It really is. Makes the whole deal worth it.

Ahhhh, the Light. I could go on and on and still not describe it. So I will only say this to you, Doubting Thomas. There is a Light. *The Light is*! Make no mistake about that, there is a Light, baby! I am in it right now, as sure as I am telling this tale. I am here and you are there and there is a Light. The next time you're saved by those eyes peering through the bushes remember that. Remember it for longer that a week or two. Don't get so caught up in the routine that you forget the clicks and the shifts that you've experienced. Especially the good ones. I see them, I know about them, but do you? Look for them right now. Take a moment and pause. We're almost done here anyway. I'll Help you.

See what I mean? Now just remember to reflect on them from time to time.

Wow, am I getting Buddha-ee or what? Ha! The Light'll do that to you. But I still enjoy a good trick from time to time. And I have a feeling that I haven't used up all my tricks either.

So I'll leave you with this. Instead of trying to figure out who the Helper of this story really was, me or John or Franklin or Deena or Mrs. Abbott, just realize that Helpers are there. And that you may be called on from time to time to be one yourself. I mean would you have really bought this book if you thought the Helper in the title was a mixed blood Findian from northern Wisconsin? Some tricks are necessary. Some cons are good. Some are *needed*. Just remember, there is a Light and you are in it too.

And, if you should ever feel those eyes upon you from behind the bushes, remember they just may be mine.

Dusty.

Somewhere in the Light.

The End

ACKNOWLEDGMENTS

Thanks to all who have listened and encouraged over the years, especially:
Randy Leys
Jim Gangnon (and the entire Gangnon family, who truly are my second family)
Cliff Rawnsley, Jr.
and Rocky Catman, who inspired me to finally get this done!

And, of course, my sister and brother:
Ellen Jean Conant and Donald "Mick" McLean Snow, Jr.
And their spouses Jim Conant and Gloria "Fuzzy" Snow, who are more brother and sister, than in-laws.

Thanks to my "readers" who contributed greatly over various rewrites:
Tom Powers
Tracey McBride
Joe Walpole
Jim Reinhard
Geoffrey Tomb
Pam Bartee
Andrea Diskin
Joanna Marie Rando
Betsy Langan
Smilin' Dave Lauer (may he Rest In Peace)

For the music and more, many thanks to:
Dave Rubinstein
Kathy Fleischmann
Greg McLaughlin
Luciano "Looch" Delgado

Finally, a great big thank you to Floyd Patterson, who has "pulled me through the knot-hole" time and time again.

Apologies to all I may have forgotten.

ABOUT THE AUTHOR

M. N. SNow's bio includes years as a public radio host and anchor, primarily in the south Florida market, but also for Wisconsin Public Radio. M. N. has had various short stories published and was a contributing writer for *Reader Weekly,* in Duluth, MN. M. N. is also a published cartoonist and a former Marine Corps NCO. After spending some years at home in the Twin Ports of Duluth, MN/Superior, WI, the author is currently back living in Key West, FL.

Made in the USA
Charleston, SC
30 December 2016